TERMINAL SURF

BRENDAN DUBOIS

SEVERN RIVER PUBLISHING

Severn River Publishing
www.SevernRiverBooks.com

ISBN: 978-1-64875-590-3 (Paperback)

ALSO BY BRENDAN DUBOIS

The Lewis Cole Series

Dead Sand

Black Tide

Shattered Shell

Killer Waves

Buried Dreams

Primary Storm

Deadly Cove

Fatal Harbor

Blood Foam

Storm Cell

Hard Aground

Terminal Surf

To find out more about Brendan DuBois and his books, visit
severnriverbooks.com

To Elsie Ekstrom of Perth, my most devoted and distant fan, and

To the memory of my brother, Michael J. DuBois
December 9, 1950—July 27, 2021
My big brother, first reader, and number one fan.

"There is no love like the love for a brother. There is no love like the love from a
brother."
Astrid Aluda

1

On that early October morning, the body started coming ashore from the surging surf of the Atlantic Ocean shortly after seven a.m. From my rear deck I had noticed the sodden form coming in on top of the cold waves at the small cove to the rear of my home, a converted U.S. Lifesaving Station from the mid-1800s, and I had grabbed a cellphone and put on a jacket and high-topped rubber boots before going out.

I went out the front door, across the dirt and scraggly tufts of grass that I maintain is a lawn—to the amusement of the few visitors who come this way—and I went down among the rocks and dirt to the rough shore. There was no sandy beach here like there was on North Beach a mile or so south from my home, just large rocks, smaller rocks, and bits of gravel and small stones.

The surf was still rough and foamy after yesterday's storm—which had ended during the night—and which had also started bringing in the bodies. Paula Quinn, the assistant editor of *The Tyler Chronicle*, had left about a half-hour ago after her cellphone had woken us both up just after sunrise. I had gotten a brief kiss and a news flash from her as she nearly tumbled downstairs, trying to get dressed while grabbing her car keys. "Tyler cops and Coast Guard are reporting three bodies have washed up on Tyler Beach. Call you later, bye," she'd said.

Well, I hadn't been able to get back to sleep after that grim wake-up call, though I did stay in bed and just relaxed in the warmth and the scent of her on the sheets until finally I got up, dressed, and grabbed my initial cup of coffee before stepping out on the rear deck—and spotting what I saw.

I waded in about a foot into the cold salt water and stood still. The body had on a sodden old-style life jacket, the kind you see in past photos of Boy Scout camps, rectangular and stiff across one's torso. The body was about a dozen yards away and I patiently waited. Something horrible had happened last night in these near waters from an overcrowded boat trying to make shore just as the storm was winding down, and I had a pretty good idea of what had gone on but didn't want to dwell on it.

The waves moved again, knocking the body towards me. I recognized the torso as a person, face down, arms splayed out, legs submerged, head face down. No movement, no shouts, no cries for help. Just a drowned victim, finally finding its way to shore.

I looked out to the horizon and to the south, where the main Tyler Beach was located just beyond the bulge of Weymouth's Point, and I saw watercraft at work, though I couldn't tell who they belonged to. Then a thrumming noise came my way, stirring up lots of bad memories, and a dark green helicopter flew towards the south. It probably belonged to the New Hampshire State Police. Pretty much everything they own, from cruisers to ATVs, was colored the same dark green.

The waves moved the body even closer. There was a sodden mess of long black hair at one end, and I guessed the body was a woman. Even with the life jacket, I saw she was wearing a floral quilted jacket.

Something queasy was forming within me, seeing this body come closer and closer. Years ago another body had washed up near my house, farther south, but that one had been the result of a criminal act focused on one male victim. This poor woman out there had also been the victim of a criminal act, one involving scores of people. That offense had occurred here a few hours ago, on my beloved seacoast and this part of the Atlantic Ocean, and now I couldn't look out at the nine Isles of Shoals, boats, lobster traps and sea birds, without thinking of the death that was now washing ashore.

Closer.

I decided not to wait anymore.

I started wading out, taking my time, because there was no smooth beach sand under my feet, just mud, rocks and gravel. I'd hate to fall on my butt in this water, but I'd also hate to have my boots fill up with cold salt water and have the indifferent waves drag me out. The waves broke closer and then in a matter of seconds, the body came in and knocked me down.

I fell back, caught myself with my hands, managed not to get too soaked, and then splashed myself erect and grabbed a strap from the soaked life jacket. I turned and slogged my way to shore, my boots filling with water that weighed me down. I got to shore and turned and, using both hands, slowly pulled the body ashore. The body seemed heavier than it should have been.

When I got her out of the water, I tried as gently as I could to drag her up beyond the high tide line, and by now, I was cold and exhausted. I sat down on a dry boulder and emptied one boot, and then the other. Then the boots came back on my feet, and I looked over at the body. It was a woman, dark skinned, with black hair. In addition to the life jacket and quilted jacket, she also had on a dark blue skirt. Her legs were swollen. One foot still had on a leather boot and sock. The other foot was bare. The shape of the body was odd, like it was hunched over for some reason.

I took out my cellphone, dialed a number from memory. It was answered on the second ring.

"Yes?"

"Paula, where are you?" I asked.

Paula Quinn said, "Right now I'm standing on the wrong side of a police barricade at the south end of the main beach. Cops around, a helicopter, and looks like a news van from Channel Nine is coming up the road."

"Look, I—"

"Lewis, I really don't have time to talk right now."

"Quick question: are you able to see what's going on?"

"No," she said. "I'm about a hundred yards away. All I can see are cops and firefighters. Any photos I take are going to be blurry and not show a damn thing. I've got to go."

"Come back to my place."

"Why in God's name should I do that?" she asked.

"Because I've just recovered a body in my back yard, that's why."

She swore. "Cops there yet?"

"Not yet."

"On my way," she said. "I'll be there in ten minutes."

She disconnected.

I checked the time on the cellphone. It was four minutes after eight in the morning.

I waited.

Another helicopter swirled around, headed back to Tyler Beach. This one seemed to be from one of the Boston television channels, coming up here to this stretch of the Atlantic Ocean to report on the second time a newsworthy event like this had happened—namely, a boat of desperate migrants sinking off the coast of New Hampshire, with scores of dead bodies washing ashore.

This had happened three weeks ago, right after the famed end of summer at Tyler Beach—Labor Day—and the bodies had floated in at North Tyler and its northern neighbor, Wallis.

The dead refugees last time around were Syrians.

At some point this woman and the others would be identified, for whatever good it would do.

I checked my cellphone's little display.

Nine minutes had passed since my call to Paula. That meant in another minute or so, Paula would come trotting down my dirt driveway to get to work.

But it was also time for someone else to come visit me.

I opened up the cover to my phone, dialed yet another number from memory, and yet another woman answered, this one older and more seasoned than Paula.

"Lewis," she started right off, "I'm so busy and pissed off now that I don't have time."

"Detective Sergeant Woods," I replied, "I'd like to report a drowning victim at my home."

A second passed. "I usually like your jokes, so this better not be one."

"I wouldn't joke about something like this. Where are you?"

"Getting my fat butt pulled away from a crime scene."

"The bodies at the beach?"

"Yeah," she said. "Homeland Security and ICE have rolled in, taking control. There was a jurisdictional dispute that we lost. But tell me again what you have."

"What I have is an apparently middle-aged woman, drowned, wearing an old-fashioned life jacket. She washed up about ten minutes ago."

"Damn it," she said. "Okay, I'm off. See you soon."

"You bet."

I signed off, turned and heard a car pull in up by the near parking lot of the Lafayette House, one of the few Victorian-age hotels still surviving in this part of New England. It's white with turrets and steep roofs and a wide front porch, and its parking area is across the street, and from there, you can gain access to my property.

I checked the cellphone clock once more.

Ten minutes had passed.

That had to be Paula arriving.

I looked at the drowning victim and saw I had misjudged the incoming tide. Water was washing off her feet and I couldn't stand the thought of having her tugged out again to the cold and unforgiving ocean.

I got up and went to the dead woman and grasping the straps of her life jacket and the shoulders of her sodden jacket, I got her up a few more feet, and as chance would have it, I rolled her over and found out why her shape had been canted and odd.

An infant was strapped to her chest.

2

From up beyond my house came a shout. "Lewis!"

"Down here, Paula!" I shouted back, and I turned and walked and sat down on a near rock. I shook for a moment and looked at the dead woman and her child, thankful that when I had let her down, she was still curved so the dead baby was hidden.

Paula came around the corner of my house, past the pilings holding up the deck, and she slowed as she saw the body. "Oh...Christ," she said. Her blonde hair was cut shorter this year, and even had a faint color of light auburn around the edges, but her ears still stuck out and she had a pug nose that I still thought was adorable after all these years.

She had on black slacks, flat shoes, a green turtleneck sweater, and a short waist-high tan jacket. Over her shoulder she had a soft leather bag, and she took out a digital camera that masqueraded as a 35 mm Nikon, and quickly started taking photos as she approached.

"Do me a favor?" I asked.

"Name it."

"Don't take a photo of the woman's front."

"Why?"

My chest was getting colder with each passing second. "There's a dead baby strapped to her chest."

That froze her in her tracks. "Oh, Lewis, for real?"

"Quite real."

Out on Atlantic Avenue, also known as Route 1-A, sirens were coming our way, and I said, "The cops will be here in a few minutes. Better get as many photos as you can."

"Did you call the cops?"

"I did...after I called you."

She moved around, getting closer, still taking photos but not getting close to the woman's curved-over front.

"Why did you do that?"

"Civic duty, what else?"

She turned to see if I was joking, I think, but not seeing any humor in my face, she said, "I get it. You wanted me to have a few minutes to get photos before the gendarmes showed up."

"That was it. How come you weren't allowed onto the beach? I thought your press pass got you through police lines."

"Police lines, yes. Homeland Security...not so much."

"Really? They must have been on the road quick when the first call came in."

Paula waded into the foam and water, even though she wasn't wearing the right footwear, trying to get additional photos. "Yeah, well since the last boat sank and drowned scores of refugees, Homeland Security has set up a regional office up in Porter. Means they can get anywhere they want on the seacoast in less than thirty minutes or so."

She climbed out of the water, not even bothering to check her wet feet, but instead she glanced at the little display on the rear of her digital camera, flipping through to make sure she got the photos she needed.

Then she shook her head and plodded over to me and sat down next to me on the rock. "Mornings like this, you feel like a damn vulture."

"Sorry."

"No apologies, please," she said. "Like it's been said, many times, this is the life I've chosen. But it sure as hell has changed a lot since I started. Never thought I'd be writing stories and taking photos of an international refugee crisis, right on our own pretty little shoreline."

I put my right arm around Paula, and she leaned into me. The sirens grew louder and then they shut off, right about when I guessed the police had rolled into the Lafayette House parking lot.

"Where do you think she came from?" she asked.

"No place good," I said.

She looked out at the gray moving waters. "Wonder where the mother ship went."

"After they were paid and dumped the refugees in rubber rafts or leaky lifeboats, probably as far away as possible."

I thought I could feel her shiver. "Imagine being locked in some leaky tramp freighter for weeks on end, then brought here and dumped overboard in an overcrowded raft, being told paradise is waiting for you...right in the middle of last night's storm."

"I don't want to," I said. "You get enough photos?"

She turned around. "Enough at the moment. I'll get some more once the police and EMTs show up."

"Aren't the EMTs down at the beach?"

"Nope," she said. "Homeland Security has their own ambulance service. Wouldn't let our local firefighters come in. Oh, speaking of which...here comes your girlfriend, Detective Woods."

Diane Woods came around the other side of my house, followed by a uniformed female officer named Trenton and two male EMTs from the Tyler Fire Department, carrying a metal Stokes litter between them.

"She's not my girlfriend."

Paula smiled. "Then you must have somebody else in mind."

"Very much so," I said. "And would you like some eyewitness comments for your story?"

"Did you notice anything unusual?"

"Besides a refugee from across the world washing ashore on my property? No, not a thing."

"Then I think I'm good," she said.

Diane looked angry as hell, a sign I could tell from a few feet away from a scar on her chin that she got from a long-ago brawl in the police station's booking room back when she was a patrol officer. She had on short black leather boots, blue jeans, and a dark blue Tyler Police Department windbreaker. Her thick brown hair was tousled by the wind, and the closer she came, I could see that her other facial scars from a brutal beating she had suffered some time ago were still fading.

"Lewis," she said to me, and to Paula, "Give me a few minutes to secure the scene, all right? Then I'll answer whatever I can."

"Fair enough, detective," Paula said, standing back. They had known each other for years—longer than even me—and had a polite and professional relationship, even though when Paula or Diane were alone with me, each would complain about the other. Diane would say that Paula was always getting in the way, asking impossible questions, and was generally a pain in the ass. Paula would say that Diane was always difficult to reach, never liked answering a direct question, and was generally a pain in the ass.

But after a glass of wine or two, each would also say the exact same thing: "Still, she's better than whoever would replace her if that ever happened."

Paula stepped back and took photos as Officer Trenton helped Diane with her photos, measurements, and general inspection, while the EMTs stood aside, patiently waiting. At one point, Diane bent over and gently rolled the dead woman over, exposing the dead baby strapped to her chest, and Officer Trenton had to take a deep series of breaths.

When she appeared to be done, Diane motioned to the two EMTs to step forward and start their work, and a male voice from back up at my house yelled down, "Stop that! Don't move that body!"

Things got real interesting right after that.

THREE MEN CAME DOWN to this increasingly crowded stretch of New Hampshire shoreline, all dressed the same, in dark gray jumpsuits and military-style black boots. Paula stepped back and they brushed right past her without a word, going straight up to Diane. Two of the younger men in jumpsuits were carrying some sort of collapsible stretcher between them, and they eyed the EMTs with suspicion and just a bit of mocking. The two EMTs shifted their feet and looked uncomfortable. They were typical small-town firefighters, maybe a bit lumpy and out-of-shape, but they were dedicated to this town and its visitors. The Homeland Security guys looked like they had just come from a parade ground where they had spent the last hour marching around and saluting each other, including the gent who was their leader.

He was an older guy who looked like he had his jumpsuit washed, starched and pressed every week. He put his fists on his hips and slowly nodded. His face was weathered but fleshy, like the tendons and muscles around his skull were finally tiring of working to hold the skin still in a permanent angry glance. His head bore a swatch of gray-white stubble up top and his gray eyes did not look happy.

"Detective...Woods, isn't it? Thanks for securing the scene. We'll take it from here."

"And you are?" she asked in a polite voice that I and maybe two others could tell was coming through barely repressed anger.

"Special Agent Mark Stockman, Homeland Security."

Diane said, "Sorry to disappoint you, Agent Stockman. You're not taking anything from here. This is my scene, not yours."

He said, "What makes you think this is a crime scene?"

"I didn't say it was a crime scene," she snapped back. "This is an unattended death. It belongs to me and, eventually, the state Medical Examiner."

He took a step forward, and if he thought he was going to intimidate Diane, he was definitely on the wrong track, like a racehorse at Belmont going in reverse. Diane took his step and raised him two more, going right up to him. Off to the right, being ignored by everybody except me, Paula took a couple of photos and then started scribbling in her reporter's notebook.

He tried to smile. It didn't work. "Be reasonable, Detective. This is obviously a migrant who drowned sometime last night, along with the others we've recovered on Tyler Beach. That's an immigration matter, and as such, it belongs to me."

"What you're seeing here might be obvious to you," she said. "That's probably why you work for the Federal government. But I prefer to have facts in hand before making any assumptions. I don't know and you don't know for sure if this deceased woman and child are migrants."

I looked to the dead woman for a moment, tried to think of what horrors she had witnessed at her home, horrors so bad that they brought her here, all the way to my beach, to die with her child next to her.

"It's obvious," he said. "She's dressed similarly to the other deceased migrants and is wearing the same style of life jacket."

"I wouldn't know," Diane said, crossing her arms, "since you didn't allow me or any other Tyler police to get to the scene."

"Because it was my scene, just like this one is. So why don't you and your officer and firefighters depart, and we'll take over. And, of course, we promise to pass on any pertinent information we discover."

"Sure," Diane said. "Under your definition of pertinent. Sorry, not going to happen."

"It happened two hours ago at Tyler Beach. Explain to me why it won't happen here."

Hoo-boy, I had an idea of where this was going, and Diane didn't disappoint.

She took another step forward, close enough for her to unfortunately smell whatever cologne he might be wearing. "Because you had authority, misbegotten as it was, to seal the crime scene at Tyler Beach. That part of the beach is a state park, belonging to the State of New Hampshire, and because you and your ilk have the governor's balls in your pretty gray jumpsuits, you could take control and evict the rest of us. But this stretch of land doesn't belong to you. It's private property, situated in the town of Tyler, and you have squat for jurisdiction. So get the hell out of my way."

The two EMTs who had been looking a bit embarrassed a few minutes ago seemed to stand taller, as one of their own took on this bully, and even the supposedly neutral observer Paula looked amused.

But Stockman wasn't amused at all. He said, "One minute, if you please." He stepped back, took out a cellphone, made a call, and turned so none of us could read his thin lips. Officer Trenton looked happy to be in Diane's presence, but the two other Homeland Security guys didn't look bothered at all.

Stockman turned back, extended the phone and a bony hand to Diane. "Here," he said. "It's for you."

Diane's face colored and I knew who had to be on the other end, and Diane took the phone and said, "Chief?"

She listened to him for a minute and said, "Chief, if I—"

The Tyler police chief cut her off. She bit at her lower lip and said, "Very well," and handed the phone back to Stockman. She dropped it—on purpose, I'm sure—but for his size and age, Stockman moved very quickly to pick it up.

She said, "Congratulations. You told him that a Homeland Security grant that we were going to get next month was about to get canceled."

"I just told him that was a possibility," Stockman said, returning his cellphone to his jumpsuit. "I told him the grant would probably end up going to a police department that was more cooperative."

"Cooperation through bribery, in other words."

"In other words," he said, "getting the job done. You and your officer and the firefighters may leave. And you, miss? A journalist?"

"Paula Quinn, *The Tyler Chronicle*," she said.

"You may leave as well," he said. "This is now a Federal crime scene, and if you want any more information, please contact our media affairs office. In Washington."

"You have the number?" Paula asked.

"Try the Internet," he said. "There's something called Google that might help you out."

Then he seemed to finally notice me.

"Who are you?" he demanded.

"Just a concerned citizen," I said.

"Well, concerned citizen, you should probably leave."

"Nah," I said. "I like it here."

"I don't care," Stockman said.

"To state the obvious, I don't care that you don't care."

"Move," he said. "This is a Federal crime scene."

"Can't do that."

He stepped up to me. "Why?"

I motioned up to my house. "This is my land. I own it. And you're standing on it."

That made him pause, just for a second.

"I could have you arrested."

"For what? Sitting on a rock?"

"For obstructing a Federal agent."

"Not obstructing a damn thing. And the question of what kind of arrest powers you folks have over American citizens is still up in the air, isn't it?"

By then I could tell he didn't like me much.

"That's true," he said. "But I could have you arrested by the locals."

I smiled. "Try it. I don't think they feel very cooperative today."

Well, he looked over at Diane and Officer Trenton, and the two EMTs, who then picked up their gurney and started back up to the parking lot. Diane and the uniformed cop turned their backs to this little scene unfolding before them. Paula was just a ways above Diane, and she was still taking photos and scribbling notes.

Stockman turned back and said, "Stay out of our way."

"Works for me."

He gestured to his two other agents, and they came forward at a pace and then went to the body. Stockman stood back and let his boys do the grim work. Their folding stretcher came with an attached zippered body bag. They zipped the bag open, spread the sides out like some enormous, winged insect, and then they picked up the woman's body.

A few seconds ago I was having a bit of fun with this pompous agent before me, but I didn't feel very funny now. The women's body was heavy, with her clothes sopped through, and one of the officers muttered, "Shit, do you see this?" when the infant was spotted.

Water dripped and dribbled from her clothes and hair as she was placed into the open bag, and then the two men had a hard time of it, pulling up the flaps, trying to get the whole damn thing zippered shut. It was a chore because they had left the life vest on, and because of the infant, and there was low swearing and muttered words back and forth, until they carefully undid the straps holding the drowned infant, and from where I sat, it looked like they put her or him in the crook of the mother's arm.

As much as I didn't like seeing what I was seeing, it was at least the right thing to do.

The bag was finally zippered shut, and then they grabbed the metal handles, and started back up to the parking lot. With the body secured, everyone had left up there except for Paula, who kept pace at a distance until the sad procession moved out of sight.

Leaving Agent Stockman and me alone by the moving water's edge.

"What's your name?" he asked.

"Lewis Cole."

He nodded. "I'll remember that."

I said, "I'm sure you'll give it a go."

3

Back up to the front of my house I was disappointed to see I was alone. I was hoping either Diane or Paula had stayed behind so I could offer them a cup of coffee in exchange for some information, but it was not meant to be.

I went through the front door, kicked off my rubber boots, and then sat on the couch in the living room to strip off my wet socks. My house used to belong to the Department of the Interior until it was deeded to me some years ago in exchange for keeping my mouth shut over a terrible accident I was involved in when I was a research analyst for the Department of Defense. Since moving here after being discharged from the DoD, I've grown to love the old girl.

Like me, she's gone through a lot, although the past several months had been particularly difficult for her, suffering through a fire caused by arson, a soaking from a passing hurricane, and most recently, a shooting and beating that had taken place in this very living room.

Yet we both persisted. I was sitting in front of a stone fireplace with a television set to one side, and behind me were other large comfortable chairs and crowded bookcases. To the left was a small dining area next to a sliding glass door that led out to my deck, and adjacent to that cozy scene, a small but satisfactory kitchen.

Off to the right was the main door, two smaller doors—one for a closet, the other leading to a dirt cellar—and the stairs going up to a bathroom, my book-cluttered office, and my bedroom, with a smaller deck overlooking the rocks and sand of North Beach.

I stretched my wet feet out. A warm fire right now would feel nice, but I felt jumpy, out of place.

I felt like I needed to do something.

So I did just that.

WITH DRY SOCKS on and a different pair of boots, a Navy watch cap for my head and the same red L.L. Bean jacket, I went back outside with a collapsible hiking stick, returning to my little cove. I went down to where the poor woman and child had been taken away by Homeland Security and wondered about something.

I looked up and down my little stretch, and then up to my house, with the stone foundation and tight old wood and the little deck, and I shivered. After being lowered into that overloaded inflatable raft last night, in the pouring rain and wind, with your crying child at your breast, was the hope starting to outweigh the fear? Were you thinking that the long trip from some smuggler's port in the Mediterranean was finally coming to an end, that after just a little while longer in this raft with all the other refugees, migrants, illegal immigrants, undocumented immigrants—whichever name was popular this month—you and your child were going to finally step on dry land?

I couldn't look at my safe house anymore. I looked out to the ocean, still gray, moving, unforgiving, not caring. Now, then, in the raft, heading to shore, hugging your child, whispering that it would all soon be safe. That while there were challenges and fears approaching, that at least you were going to a place where the cities weren't bombed, where civilians weren't machine-gunned, where you were starved and cut-off because of your last name and where you grew up...

Then it happened. Maybe a rogue wave swamped the raft. Or the engine quit. Or the old hull just tore apart from the movement and the waves.

And you're in the cold Atlantic. Trying to keep your child's head above water.

You turn. There are screams, sounds of people frantically splashing, shouts at the departing freighter that had dropped you off, the lights of the freighter slowly disappearing into a storm bank.

You're frightened. Your child is screaming. The old life jacket is barely keeping you afloat. You turn and, in the distance, at the shoreline of the promised land, you see a couple of lights.

Safety.

Warmth.

People.

Frantically you start paddling as best as you can toward the flickering lights, toward what must be a place of safety, and then you tire, and you tire, and you can't swim, but you try to keep your baby's head above water, and oh God, she's not crying any more, and you start weeping, for the lights over there are so close, oh so very close.

I kick at a large rock before me, toss it into the water.

Yeah.

I'm sure the poor drowning woman saw lights last night, just before she drowned.

The lights of my home.

And I was right there, comfortably safe and ignorant of what was going on, just scores of yards away in the Atlantic.

I started walking.

IT WAS ROUGH GOING, but that was partially due to Mother Nature and her brat child, Man. More than a century-and-a-half ago, my home was part of lifeboat station, set up here to rescue sailing ships and then steamers that got too close to the Isles of Shoals and other rocky outcroppings out there, patiently waiting to rip out the wooden and then steel hulls of unlucky ships. When the call came out, the brave and slightly crazed men here would go out at all hours and in all sorts of weather to save whomever they could.

Back then there had been a long stretch of sandy beach, allowing the lifeboats to go out and come back, sometimes bringing the nearly-drowned victims up the rise a ways to the Victorian splendor that was the Lafayette House, but after the station was abandoned and used for other purposes, new road construction came through and there had to be a place to dump some of the boulders and rocks that had been removed and shifted, so they had been dumped here.

I moved gingerly through the smaller rocks and larger boulders, using the walking stick to keep me upright. I wasn't sure what I was looking for and I wasn't sure if I was looking for anything, but I kept on moving. There were bits of plastic debris, a beer can turned light silver from its surface being washed away, stinky clumps of seaweed, and other bits and pieces of the flotsam that always makes its way to shore during the normal give and take of the tides. After a big storm, lobster traps usually were dragged ashore, and others and I left them there so lobstermen could retrieve them on their own. Sometimes old tires, boat fenders, tree trunks from who knows where have also come here, and once, many, many years ago, a boy nearby found a Viking coin.

My hands were cold and I should have brought a pair of gloves, but I kept on moving. Another helicopter thrummed overhead, heading down to where it seemed most of the bodies had washed ashore. It was October, post-tourist season, but it looked like the roads down there would be crowded after all, with reporters and sightseers.

I sloshed along, knowing how easy it would be to break an ankle or knee on these rocks, and after about twenty minutes, I gave up. Great slabs of wet dark granite the size of small cottages blocked my way, and I was satisfied that I could go no farther, and I was also pleased I had found no more bodies.

Then something bright yellow caught my eye, jammed into a rock fissure. I bent down with some difficulty, popped it out. It turned out to be a plastic drinking cup, but of a skinny design I've never seen before. It was cracked on one side, and I turned it over, saw the manufacturer's mark on the bottom.

RITZENHOFF

I managed to slip it into my coat pocket without breaking it any more, and it seemed fresh. Debris that's been in the water for a while gets battered around as it comes to shore, and like the beer can I had found earlier, it doesn't take long for the paint to wear off.

Back at my little cove I kept on walking, and there was nothing there to remind anyone that a dead mother and her child had washed up here not less than an hour go. I walked south until more boulders and slabs of stone, these draped with huge stinking strands of seaweed, prevented me from going any farther.

I went back to my cove, leaned on my walking stick. This little stretch of my property had seen a lot over the centuries, beginning with native tribes associated with the Abenaki, followed by Vikings—maybe an Irish monk or two—and then secretive Basque fishermen, who probably came here in the 1400's or 1500's, fishing the huge schools of cod that were plentiful back then. Disease and war nearly eliminated the Abenaki, and then the English, and then the Americans placed their hopes and banners here.

Lots of history. Hurricanes, shipwrecks, warships traveling up and down. Wooden warships being dispatched from Porter beginning during the Revolutionary War times, and up to today, when its famed shipyard now worked on overhauling and working on nuclear submarines. Lots of death out there as well, from plane crashes during training accidents in World War II, to the many, many ships that foundered over there at the rocky isles, or at other stone ledges up and down the seacoast. My home's first presence appeared here in the mid-1800s, and then it became officers' quarters for the coast artillery unit up the ways at Samson Point, defending these shores against Spain, Germany and then Germany once more.

For a while, Samson Point was then converted to a radar station, looking out there for Soviet Bison or Bear bombers, until being deactivated around the time I was born.

Samson Point was now a state park.

The guns were long gone.

My home—a staging area for rescues and then a home for the military —was now in civilian hands.

Pretty damn peaceful.

I scraped my foot against the wet soil and gravel.

But death kept on coming here, washing up, and this time, it was a woman and her child.

I thought of Detective Sgt. Diane Woods, and of Agent Mark Stockman from Homeland Security.

Diane had started through the forensic and investigative process of beginning the long task of finding out who this woman and her child were, and how they died, and how they ended up here.

Stockman?

No measurements, no photographs, no search for evidence.

Her body and that of her child were just tossed into a large, heavy plastic bag and then hauled away, like some embarrassing piece of drifting debris that had ended up somewhere where it didn't belong.

I moved my stick around some, drawing a circle, and then I looked out to the wide empty sea.

"I'm going to find out who you were, lady, and your name, and the name of your baby," I said aloud. "And then I'm going to find out who abandoned you both here and make it right."

Then I started back up to my house.

4

Among the other things I learned later was that *RITZENHOFF* was a German manufacturer of plastic drinking ware, among other products, and based on its relative newness and the fact about 99 percent of all such plasticware was now sold at Walmart and supplied by China, I thought there might be a good chance that this was given to the refugees on their long North Atlantic trip.

When it came time for lunch, I broke bread and meat with Paula Quinn at the offices of *The Tyler Chronicle*, the local daily paper that is hanging on by its very fingernails in this age of tweets and news feeds that pump out lots of content and information without bothering to actually send out real news.

The offices were in the center of Tyler proper, just over two miles from its famed beaches, and since I've known Paula, the poor *Chronicle* has fought a losing battle in both circulation and real estate. Its offices, for example, have shrunk considerably and a good chunk of its former self has been taken over by a dance studio. I once innocently asked Paula if she planned on taking lessons in the studio during her off hours, and she in return innocently dumped a diet Coke in my lap.

She was the paper's assistant editor, and in her small private office, I had a hot steak-and-cheese sub while she worked through a chicken Caesar salad. She looked up at her monitor and said, "Well, that's that, the paper's running and should be on the streets in an hour."

I said, "Funny, I don't hear the printing presses running."

"Unless you have super hearing, you won't," she said. "The printing plant is about fifty miles away."

"I have many superpowers, but hearing isn't one of them," I said.

In her small office she looked good, in charge. The real editor was an old timer named Roland Grandmaison, who seemed to be burning through as many sick days as possible before retirement came knocking at his door. Paula's office didn't have much in the way of decoration, just a calendar from the New Hampshire Emergency Management Agency, giving future dates and future possibilities of what to do if the Falconer nuclear power plant down the coast had an accident, and several framed awards from the New England Press Association.

"So say you," she said. "I've got two nice front-page stories about the events this morning. Thanks for giving me a heads up."

"You successfully seduced me last night," I said. "What else was I going to do?"

Paula smiled, ate a bite of her salad, and then gave me a knowing glance. I tore off a chunk of my steak and cheese and passed it over to her, and my fingers managed not to get nibbled on.

"Remind me again," I said. "Calories from begging don't count, right?"

"Not begging," she said. "Sharing."

"Then share me this," I said. "Two stories? I think the drowning victims would be story number one. What's story number two?"

She washed down her stolen food with a swallow of her Diet Coke. "The creepy Homeland Security response, that's what."

"Tell me about it."

"You can read it in the paper later."

"I'm an impatient fellow."

"Yeah, you are," she said, wiping her sweet fingers on a paper napkin. "Look, it's like this. They have a new office up at the McIntosh Air Force Base, they're quick to respond, and they don't like answering questions."

"Typical Federal government. You're surprised?"

"No, but there's a different level. They come in, secure the scene, scoop up the bodies, and that's it. There's no…"

"Investigation."

Paula nodded. "That's right. No investigation. They don't interview any witnesses, they don't take any crime scene photos, they act like they can't be bothered. They do what they have to do, and then they leave."

"Like they're hiding something."

She rolled her eyes. "Of course they're hiding something. The government's always hiding something. Like I had to remind you."

Paula looked to me again and I tore off one more piece of my fast-disappearing lunch. I said, "Any idea where the bodies are brought to?"

As she chewed, she shook her head. "No, not really. They hire out a private ambulance firm to transport the bodies up to McIntosh, and that's that. They should end up at the state medical examiner's office, legally speaking, but they're not. But the truth is, the state M.E. is so buried by all the dead bodies piling up from our on-going opioid crisis, they're probably grateful they're not getting the extra work and responsibility."

I finished off my steak-and-cheese before Paula gave me any more sharing gestures. "Your last story said it was thought that the refugees were coming in from a freighter from the Mediterranean, and then being dropped off somewhere near the Isles of Shoals. Still true?"

She mournfully looked at my empty hands and went back to work on her salad.

"Of course it's still true," she said. "No fake news here, thank God, as long as my name's on the masthead." She stirred around in her salad and triumphantly came up with a piece of chicken. "I got that information from the Congressman representing this district. More often than not, he's as batty as a church belfry, but he got some intelligence information that he was willing to share with the news media, on background."

Paula popped the chicken into her mouth, chewed, swallowed. "The Med is getting more attention from various nations' coast guards and navies. Too much pressure. Overland routes are being blocked. But boats can still slip out of the Med and head here. Pricier, of course, but if you're a dad wondering if your three teen daughters are either going to get raped or drafted to become suicide bombers, what price is too high? They get stuck in some rust bucket, spend two miserable weeks in the hold, crowded together, and when they get to the shores of the land of the free and the brave, they get dumped overboard in old lifeboats or leaky life rafts."

I picked up a few napkins, passed them over to her. There was a drop of salad dressing on her chin, and I saved one napkin to wipe her clean. That was rewarded with a smile that still made me tingle.

I said, "Two freighters in the past few weeks have dropped off migrants that eventually drowned and washed ashore."

"True."

"That probably means one or two freighters and their passengers probably made it in, with no drownings. Also means another is probably on its way now, stuck out beyond the Azores."

She nodded. "Strange place to send refugees, don't you think? Our coastline is only eighteen miles long. Can get crowded."

"Not very crowded now, post-Labor Day," I said. "And you have the interstate plopped right next door. You get thirty, fifty, sixty people ashore, in a few hours, they're in Boston, on their way to New York or Montreal."

Paula said, "But why are you so confident another one's heading this way? When so many have drowned?"

I wish I didn't have to say what I said next. "Paula, the smugglers get paid to bring them to the coast and put them in the boats. They don't care what happens next."

"Cruel," she said.

Thinking about that dead woman with her infant strapped to her chest, dead in view of my house, I could only nod.

A LITTLE WHILE later there was a knock at her door, and a young man with distended earlobes with some sort of dark round jewelry in them passed over a newspaper to Paula, and seeing me in there, stepped back and came back with another edition.

It was a good-looking front page, with the lead story being the drowned migrants at Tyler Beach—including, as Paula noted, one being found at the property of a local magazine columnist—and noting it was the second mass drowning in less than a month. There were three photos, all by Paula: a long shot showing Homeland Security working at Tyler Beach, a close-up shot of the poor woman and hidden child in my rear yard, and a dramatic photo of Detective Diane Woods and Special Agent Stockman nearly coming to blows, or as diplomats say when two parties go at each other, "having a frank and open exchange of views."

"Nice photos," I said. "If this reporting gig doesn't work out, you should look at photography."

Paula suggested that I perform an unnatural act upon myself, and I laughed and went back to the front page. The next story was a write-up about the confrontation between the locals and the feds, and there were two other stories in the paper rounding off the front page: a report on a planning board meeting in nearby Falconer that nearly came to blows over a proposed development, and a feature story about a young Tyler couple just finishing a hike across the famed Appalachian Trail.

"Nice front page," I said. "You should be proud."

She turned a page. "I'm always proud, but what are you pointing out?"

"That all your stories are written by you or others, and it's all local stuff. You're not relying on wire services to fill out your pages."

"Leave that to our competition," she said. "*The Porter Herald* does that... hell, last month, they rewrote a press release from Fish and Game and put that on the front page. The day I'm told to do that, Lewis, I quit the paper business and move in with you, and in my spare time when I'm not lounging around and being treated like the princess I am, I'll start writing the Somewhat More Than Adequate American Novel."

I smiled but I noted what she had just said, a suggestion of moving in with me. So far in this part of our relationship, we each had our own place —hers being a condo unit up on High Street, a couple of miles from my house—but there hadn't been a mention yet of changing that arrangement.

Until now.

"Go ahead," I said. "But only if you promise to live in sin during your off hours."

She smiled. "Only if there's no squalor."

Then she turned another page and that was that.

I was ready to head out and said, "Who's head of the Tyler Fishermen Cooperative nowadays? Is it still Harry Bragg?"

"Well done," she said. "Yeah, it's Harry Bragg, and, luckily, not his older brother Billy."

"What's up with his older brother? He's a fisherman as well, right?"

"Broad definition there, Lewis," she said. "Let's just say he's a constant person of interest from the Coast Guard, Fish & Game, and the National Marine Fisheries service for overfishing, stealing, and underreporting what he's up to out there at night."

"Thanks."

I got up and kissed her, and got a nice mixed taste of Paula and salad dressing, and she said, "You're off to see Harry Bragg? He probably won't be back to the harbor until four this afternoon. That's when the fish brokers show up."

"Eventually," I said. "But I think I'm going to take a run up to McIntosh Air Force Base, see if I can have a chat with Agent Stockman."

"Lewis...good luck with that. He's a Fed, through and through, and hates the news media. It doesn't matter that you're just a magazine colum-nist, he won't tell you it's raining if your hair is plastered to your skull. Every time I try to pry a word or comment from him, he just shoves me off to their media relations folks in D.C., who are very talented at reading from mush press releases."

"I think he'll make an exception for me."

"Why? The man's a true believer. Probably an ex-spook."

I smiled at her. "You forget, so am I."

5

McIntosh Air Force Base was in Lewington, at the northern end of Wentworth County, bordering Great Bay, where four rivers rush in and cause incredible tidal surges and currents four times a day. Many years back, when I was still an infant in New Hampshire and before my parents moved us to Indiana, it had been a large, sprawling base, part of the Strategic Air Command ("Peace is Our Profession") and home to B-47 bombers, then B-52 bombers and KC-135 refueling aircraft, and then for a number of years, the weird swept-back bomber mutant called the FB-111.

Now, the Strategic Air Command is no longer, the Cold War is an old nightmare with fresh flashbacks, and the only aircraft with military markings are old KC-135 refueling tankers assigned to the New Hampshire Air National Guard. How old are the KC-135s? They were built on the Boeing 707 airframe, and the last American civilian Boeing 707 landed in 1983, never to take off again.

Yeah, that old.

It used to be that to gain access to SAC bases like McIntosh, you had to present identification and be closely inspected by uniformed Air Police, but on this day, I just drove through and went to the part of the base still controlled by the Department of Defense. In the distance there were barbed wire fences, small brick buildings, and two KC-135s at ease, but before the gate to this restricted part of the base, there were two low-slung concrete and brick buildings that looked fairly innocent, connected by a walkway.

I pulled into the parking lot and noted that the buildings and their surroundings weren't that innocent. The windows were narrow slits, built in the old medieval style of European castles. Concrete planters were set in a long row in front of the entrance, to prevent any truck bomb or car bomb from coming too close, and there were surveillance cameras set up on near utility poles.

I got out of my Honda Pilot, resisted an urge to wave at the cameras, and then walked past the gaps through the planters, went to the front door, and immediately went back in time, back when I was paid by the same folks who paid these people.

The waiting area was small, with two couches, a coffee table, a locked access door and a thick bulletproof window showing an office area. There was a grim-looking young woman sitting there, wearing a severe two-piece gray outfit with an ivory blouse, frowning at me. She wore a government issued ID around her neck. Around her were cubicle walls, desk, a computer terminal, and filing cabinets.

"Yes?" she asked as I stepped forward, her voice distorted through a round speaker. There was a shallow opening in part of the thick glass, and I slid through my New Hampshire driver's license and my official press identification badge, issued by the N.H. Department of Safety, identifying me as a reporter for *Shoreline* magazine.

"Lewis Cole," I said. "I'd like to speak to Agent Mark Stockman."

She fished out my two IDs and stared at them like I was an underage college frat boy, trying to sneak in where I didn't belong. She then glanced down at some paperwork on her desk and said, "You don't have an appointment."

"I never do," I said. "Is he in?"

"You don't have an appointment."

"Yes, I realize that."

Her frown deepened and she said, "Take a seat."

Which I did.

She picked up a telephone, and I didn't hear what she was saying. I looked at the coffee table and its collection of year-old magazines with the address labels torn off, and before I picked up a *Sports Illustrated* that had a humorous article about the Chicago Cubs, the woman leaned over and to her surprise and mine, she said, "Agent Stockman will see you now."

I dropped the magazine, went to the door, and she buzzed it open for me.

SPECIAL AGENT MARK STOCKMAN was waiting for me just past the doorway, wearing dark gray slacks, black shoes, a crisp white dress shirt with a blue necktie, and a holstered pistol at his right side.

He held out a hand, I gave him a shake, and I said, "Thanks for seeing me on such short notice."

"Not a problem," he said, and gestured me to walk in front of him. My first instinct was to ask him if he had a secret twin brother with a rotten attitude, for this Agent Stockman was nothing like the grumpy guy in the gray jumpsuit that had been on my property that morning. If this was the real Agent Stockman, he certainly had cleaned up well.

"This way," he said, and I went into his office. No windows. No decorations. No framed photos. The desk was clean and tidy with computer monitor and keyboard on one side. I took one of the two chairs across from the desk and he sat down.

"*Shoreline* magazine," he said. "What's it about?"

"It's a magazine that covers the New England coastline, from the upper reaches of Maine down to Connecticut. I write a column called 'Granite Shores.'"

"Hunh," he said, folding his hands over his belly. "Is that all?"

"Excuse me?"

A sly smile, almost like he was saying, *I know something you're keeping secret*, and he said, "You worked at the Department of Defense for a number of years before coming to New Hampshire and working at *Shoreline*, a magazine owned and edited by a retired Navy admiral with interesting connections."

"Next time I see him, I'll ask him if he likes being called interesting."

"I'm sure," he said. "And that's why you're here today. I'm always willing to assist someone who's worked at the Puzzle Palace."

"Thanks," I said, taking a notebook out of my coat pocket. "A few questions, if you don't mind at all."

"Not a problem," he said. "But can I begin by asking you a couple of questions?"

"That's pretty unusual," I said.

"These are unusual times."

"True," I said. "Go right ahead."

He slowly nodded. "I imagine you have a fair number of contacts in the local community."

"I know where to get the best fresh lobster, if that's what you mean. And you'll quickly find out that all the pizza shops in New Hampshire are owned by Greek families. Don't know why, but that's how it is."

"You got a fine sense of humor," he said, and it felt like he really meant it.

"It keeps me going."

"You know what I mean," he said. "Contacts in journalism, law enforcement, political activists of all kinds, fishermen and sailors who go out on the ocean every day. Folks who pass along rumors and stories. Rumors and stories that we'd love to hear."

"Excuse me," I said, "are you asking me to be an informant? Really?"

He sighed, removed his hands and gently tapped on his clean desk. "I'm sure you realize this, Mister Cole, but we're in a war. A different war."

I wrote that down in my notebook. "That for attribution?"

His face readjusted some, like he was trying to keep his temper under control. "You're retired, with a fine home and great private view of the ocean. Not much in the way of responsibilities. But we are in a war, as much as you'd like to ignore it."

"The war against refugees?"

A pronounced shake of his head. "No. That's too simple, too clichéd. You're smart enough, Mister Cole. Those poor folks drowning in front of your house are just a symptom, that's all. We're in a war between order and disorder. Those folks...they represent a collapse of order a half-world away. And with a collapse like that, all sorts of nasty things come along for the ride. Drugs, fanatics, terrorists...and it's up to us to try to control what's coming our way."

"Not doing a particularly stellar job of it, are you."

"You're a hundred percent right." He made a wave to one side of his office. "Out there is the big wide Atlantic, and we should have the Coast Guard on patrol, tracking and intercepting those tramp steamers coming in to toss those refugees over the side. But there's another conflict going on, against the opioid epidemic New Hampshire knows so much about, so most of the Coast Guard is down in the Caribbean, trying to slow down that particular scourge."

I was about to say something, but he was on a roll. "And the Navy should be there, at least, tracking the steamers, but since the sequel to the Cold War has taken shape, they're back at their old job, following Russian subs, and a new job, reacquainting the Chinese with the laws of free navigation. You see where that leaves us?"

"I think I do," I said.

"So don't get so offended and uppity when I ask for your help. You worked a number of years helping this country, at a time when the threat was very real and very much at our borders. Would it be too much to ask for your help again?"

"That was some time ago," I said. "In a different place and time."

"Sure," Stockman said, leaning forward in his chair, smiling. "Back when you were at the Pentagon. Working for the Department of Defense. Your official organization was called the Room 119 Subgroup, but you and your co-workers called it the Marginal Issues Section."

Hearing those words spoken aloud felt like a cold chunk of ice had suddenly appeared behind my eyes.

"Like I said," I replied. "A long time ago."

"Sounded like an interesting group. Interesting times. Care to say more?"

Coming into this building earlier, I had the sensation of coming back to my old way of life, with its military people, code words and phrases.

How right I had been.

"Sorry," I said. "I signed a number of non-disclosure forms before departing my employment."

He nodded. "From a medical facility in Nevada. True?"

I kept my mouth shut.

Outside there was the slow whine of jet engines as a KC-135 started to prepare for a mission.

He said, "I pushed you too hard. My apologies. All right. Your turn. Ask away."

There had been a number of questions arranged in my mind before coming in here, and now they were all tumbled together, like the letters from a Scrabble game.

"The bodies," I said. "Why haven't they been turned over to the state Medical Examiner?"

"Because they're in our possession."

"Where?"

"At a secure facility."

"For how long?"

"Until our investigations are concluded. Then, at some point, perhaps they'll be turned over to state authorities."

"What kind of investigations?" I asked. "Isn't it apparent that they've all died of drowning? Why are you working to determine the cause of death in these cases?"

He chose his words carefully. "Who said anything about the cause of death?"

That got my attention.

"Sorry," I said. "That just seemed to be a fair assumption."

He ran a finger under his chin. "Were you known for your assumptions back when you worked in the Marginal Issues Section?"

I suppose I should have felt insulted, but I couldn't have fairly complained about his comment, for however rude it was, it was true.

One of the first rules I had learned, Back There.

Don't assume.

I said, "You don't care about their cause of death."

"Well...that seems a bit harsh, but pretty much, yes, in all of the cases, the cause of death is drowning. We don't have the time or resources to conduct a full exam and autopsy on each of the victims. There is an examination, but unless we find a knife wound or a bullet hole, we just go onto the next."

"Then..."

It came to me.

"You're not looking at them," I said. "You're examining the bodies to see what they're carrying."

A slight smile, an even slighter nod, like he was pleased that someone had finally come into his office that had met his high standards.

"Very good," Stockman said.

The sound of the KC-135 out there grew louder. I said, "You're looking for passports, documents, thumb drives, portable phones, anything that could provide intelligence."

"Very good again," he said. "We need the best and most actionable intelligence every day, every week. If we were to give up those bodies to state authorities, there'd be a jurisdictional pissing match and a delay in learning what those poor people possessed. There's always a chance that some terrorist from whatever faction out there wants to slip into the States by being among a large group of refugees, and if he drowns in the process, that's good news. The better news is that we might have a chance to find out more about his group and comrades by examining the body."

I tossed the question out, even though I knew the answer I'd get.

"Find anything of interest yet, Agent Stockman?"

Now he looked a bit disappointed, like the genius son in front of him who could multiply three-digit numbers in his head and come up with the correct answer, had suddenly lost the capacity to tie his shoes.

"No comment," he said.

"The bodies...where are they being examined, and stored?"

"As I mentioned, a secure, confidential location," he said. "Where else?"

"And do the bodies get identified?"

"Usually pretty quickly," he said. "They usually have their passports or papers close to them...sometimes even pinning it to their clothes."

"And the woman who washed up ashore at my place and her child. Any identification on her?"

"Not yet," he said. "Too soon."

"I want to find out," I said.

"Why?"

"Because it's the right thing to do," I said.

"There are lot of right things to do," he said. "She's on the list."

I got the sense from the brevity of his answers that he was looking to wrap things up, and so I took out my wallet and removed my *Shoreline* business card, which I handed over.

"When you do identify her, would you let me know?"

He looked at the card, gently placed it down on the desk.

"Why?" he asked.

"She and her child ended up dead on my property. I don't want her to be forgotten."

I got up and so did he, and after a brief handshake, he said, "Would you at least consider my earlier request? About passing along information to us?"

"I've already considered it," I said. "It took less than a minute. The answer is no."

His jaw set some, and then he said, "You seem to be a guy who likes to poke around and ask questions."

"That's what I get paid for," I said.

"Good for you," Stockman said. "But don't poke around or ask any more questions about my work and my business, Mister Cole."

I made to leave.

"That I'll consider," I said, and then I left his office.

6

About thirty minutes later I was at Tyler Harbor, walking past the fishermen's co-op building and to the set of docks that were built along the edges of the harbor that spanned both the towns of Tyler and Falconer. For years the fishermen here in Tyler and its neighbor Falconer were independent and ruthless, and fish brokers from Porter and Boston took advantage of that by cutting deals and doing their best to squeeze prices down from as many fishermen as they could.

A while ago, soon after I came back to New Hampshire and in a stunning and unexpected development of citizen cooperation, the fishermen banded together and founded the co-op, meaning they could buy and sell in bulk and stave off the inevitable collapse of New England's fishing industry by a few years.

The building was built like a large, wide barn, painted a dull gray, and there was a paved section facing the harbor that was reserved for fishermen and their pickup trucks. There was a long floating dock that rose and fell with the tides, where the fishermen would come in at about four p.m. every day to offload their haul. There was room for four boats and power winches to bring up their catch.

When I got there, vans were pulled up from area restaurants and fish brokers, and there was a brisk business going on as the boats grumbled in.

Most were stern trawlers, about eighty to ninety feet in length and with a cabin up forward. At the rear was a big rolled-up net on a wide winch, flanked by wooden boards. When the net was deployed, the boards fell to the side and "flew" in the water, keeping the net wide open while it was submerged.

After a few hours of dragging, the bulging net would be hauled up, opened on the wide and open stern, and then the catch would be checked, with different fish tossed into different containers, and lobsters and small fish and other catch not worthy being tossed back into the Atlantic.

As the boats grumbled in, a flock of seagulls were diving in and out overhead, looking to grab any scraps they could. The harbor stretched out to the west and south, and there were other boats out there as well, including lobster boats, moored sailboats, and three larger boats that brought out sport fishermen for a day of fishing, drinking, and sometimes vomiting and fighting.

Nearly hidden in the sailboats was one called *Miranda*, owned by my friend Detective Sergeant Diane Woods, and which she hadn't taken out for a good sail since her injuries last year.

That was a melancholy thought. I went back to looking at the stern trawlers coming in, and one named *ELAYNE D* came up.

Harry Bragg leaned over and tossed out two lines, and co-op workers tied her off. Harry was a few years younger than me, short but wide, built like an NFL defensive lineman. He had a closely trimmed brown beard and wore black fishermen waders up to his chest, a khaki T-shirt, and a stained Patriots baseball cap. After the load was pulled out in large plastic bins, he talked to a younger man and a much older man, and there were handshakes all around, and when Harry was by himself, I walked over and said, "Harry?"

"Yeah?" he asked, face open and friendly.

"I was wondering if I could talk to you for a few minutes."

His eyes narrowed in the relaxed style of a man used to working outdoors, and he said, "Hey, you're that magazine writer. Lewis..."

"Cole."

"That's right."

He gestured to the stern. "Jump aboard. I'm going to moor the old girl and have a post-day adult beverage. Care to join me?"

"Sounds great."

He nodded. "Undo the stern line, will you? And then we'll shove off."

I untied the stern rope from the rear cleat, curled it up in my hands, and then jumped aboard just as Harry went to the open wheelhouse and manipulated the throttle. We growled out at a slow speed to the middle of the harbor, and he aimed the boat toward a round, orange plastic buoy that had a small white dinghy attached to it. As we came closer, he slipped the engine into neutral, went forward with a pike pole, grabbed the buoy and hauled it aboard, then tied off a line to a bow cleat. Less than a minute later he was back in the wheelhouse, the engine off, and the instant silence was sudden and nice.

"Hold on," he said, "one more task to do."

Near the stern he turned a valve attached to a pipe and took out a garden hose and started washing down the stern. Fish blood, scales, bits of skin and other remnants were washed out through scuppers in the stern and side, and as he ran the hose back and forth, he said, "One thing my Dad always told me, was that when you're busted-ass tired and want to go home, don't skip one thing. 'Cause you skip one thing, you'll skip another, and another, and before you know it, your boat smells like month-old fish scraps and it's starting to rust."

He flipped the valve shut, rolled the hose back in, and then with a wide, thin-bladed mop, slid the rest of the soiled water back into the harbor.

"That was my Dad you saw there," he said. "Retired fifteen years and still wants to come out, even though some weeks I can't pay him."

"The other fellow? Your son?"

"Not old enough," Harry said, picking up the mop and slapping it on the near gunwale. "That's Tim, from UNH, studying oceanography."

"Nice hands-on way of studying."

"Beats textbooks and lectures," he said, and then added, "Okay, one more minute," and he went back into the wheelhouse and down below through a narrow set of stairs. In the wheelhouse was a padded chair to the right, an instrument panel, switches and toggles, and a few photos of what looked to be his wife and a little girl and boy. There were also framed certificates that looked to be from the Coast Guard and other government agencies.

Harry came back up with two Sam Adams beers, and he popped one top off, and then the other, and passed one over to me, and we sat in the open stern on padded benches. There was the smell of diesel oil, fish and salt water. We clinked the bottle necks together and he said, "Long life."

"Ditto," I said.

I'm not one for afternoon drinking, but I made an exception this afternoon. There was something relaxing and very New Hampshire-like in floating in a harbor, the sun working its way down to the west, past the flat salt marshes and the concrete structures of the Falconer nuclear power plant, and the thin stretch of Route One.

"The thing about living here and working so close to shore, you don't make as much money as those sword fishermen or crab fishermen you see on TV," Harry said. "But then again, I'm home every night so I get to see my family, and sometimes even make it to school plays or dance recitals, even if I do doze off in the audience."

I took a nice cold swig and said, "How was the day?"

"Long. Up before dawn with about a dozen of my other fellow idiots, and as you can see, just got back."

He took a nice long swallow himself and I said, "Why idiots?"

He laughed. "What else would you call us?" He pointed out to the Atlantic, out beyond the harbor drawbridge and the breakwaters. "Out there are trawlers bigger and more powerful than us, slurping up every bit of living material in the ocean, leaving us the scraps and leftovers. Owned by foreign corporations who'd have a hard time finding New England on a map, never mind New Hampshire. Me and my fellow idiots, we're part of a dying family business, passed on from generation to generation. Time was there were thirty or forty boats just like mine out here. Now...maybe a dozen, fourteen."

We sat silent for a couple of minutes. I said, "Then why keep on doing it?"

His face shifted some, and he quietly said, "My family came here about 1640, a couple of years after the Reverend Bonus Tyler and his congregation landed. We've been here ever since, decade after decade, fishing the waters.

I'm not going to be the last one to work these waters, and I won't be the first to give up."

"Good for you."

Then he looked at me like he was just realizing that I was there. "So. Mister Lewis Cole. Magazine writer. What kind of questions you looking to ask?"

"The bodies," I said.

He grimaced. "Yeah. Bad stuff all around. The *Poppy Marie*, out of Falconer, that crew snagged up a drowned teenage boy a few days back. From the Middle East, I guess. Awful. We're used to weathering storms, high waves, sinking boats. That's our business, that's our livelihood. But it'd be a hell of a thing to get off a freighter into something small in the middle of the night and try to make it to shore, scared, hungry and dehydrated, not used to being out on the ocean."

"You see anything these past few weeks?" I asked.

"Like what?"

"A freighter," I said.

"Hah," Harry said. "So that's what you're looking for, wondering if we've seen mysterious freighters, hugging the coast, blinking out code messages at night. Stand in line, Lewis. Me and the other fishermen here have been asked the same questions from Homeland Security, the Coast Guard, N.H. State Police, Massachusetts State Police, FBI, and everybody else in between. Seen anything strange out there? Crap, all we ever see out there is strange."

I kept my mouth shut. When people liked to talk, as an interviewer, you just let them talk.

He said, "But we're out there to do a job. I know there's all that romance about the bold, lonely fishermen, out there hauling a life and food from the angry ocean, all that crap. Hell, I'm even college-educated, though a lot of the tourists who float by think that can't be."

"What did you study in college?"

"Law," he said. "For two semesters until I gave up and came back to the water." A slight smile. "Supposedly most of our blood is made of salt water. I guess mine is just a bit more salty than others." He turned and looked out at the light changing over the water, as the sun made its way to the western horizon. "But we do wrestle a lot out there. It's a way of life. But it's a job. And Lewis, when we're out on a job, we're focused on our job. Not on freighters going around in circles."

"I see."

He said, "Hell, if somebody's in trouble, we'll go over to help in a second. That's the way of life out on the water. But we mind our own business. All of us. Besides, the timing is all wrong."

"In what way?"

Harry said, "We usually head out about four or five a.m. out to the best fishing grounds. We leave in the dark but at about the time we get to where we drop our nets, the sun's come up. But we don't go blundering around in the dark. Too many chances of bad things happening. You know what they call the wives of fishermen who go out in the middle of the night?"

"Widows," I said.

He grinned. "Very good. That's exactly right. Widows. Besides the shoals, driftwood and other stuff floating out there, there's lots of stuff on the bottom that can snag a net and damn near pull you over. Wrecks, rock shoals, JATO equipment dropped from B-47s years ago when they took off over the ocean from McIntosh Air Force Base. Nope, sorry, we can't help those looking for mysterious freighters."

I nodded, went back to my Sam Adams.

"Sorry I wasn't much help," he said.

"That's all right," I said. "Lots of times, absence of information is still information anyway."

"You doing a story about the bodies?"

"I write a magazine column," I said. "That will probably be the topic of my next one."

"Nice to have a story like this drop in your lap," he said.

"It didn't drop," I replied. "It washed up near my house."

"Ugh," he said. "A body, then?"

"Two," I said, surprising myself at how strong my voice was sounding. "Mom and infant child, strapped to her chest. I want to find out who they were, and how they ended up dying near my house. And who was at fault."

"Sounds pretty personal."

"As personal as it gets," I said.

"And where do you go from here?"

I shrugged. "Ask some more questions. Poke around. That's most of what journalists and magazine writers do."

He stretched out his legs, clothed in dirty patched jeans, and said, "My turn."

"Go ahead."

"You like being a magazine writer?"

"Most days," I said. "What I like is being my own boss."

"Yeah, me too," he said, "that's what I like to say in public, but that's a lie. Who are you responsible for, besides your readers?"

"My editor."

"Where is she or he?"

"In Boston."

"And that's it?"

"Pretty much."

He said, "That's pretty good. I'd like to think the same, but it just isn't the same. I'm responsible to the bank, to the suppliers I owe money to, my family, my two girls, and the rest of the fishermen here, since in a moment of madness—or weakness!—I decided to become head of the fishermen's cooperative. And there's things I'm not responsible for, all the way from an unexpected storm to some stupid feud involving our local congressman and some congressman from Georgia."

"I'm sorry," I said. "Could you repeat that last one? What the heck does Georgia have to do with you?"

"Not just me, but everybody who uses Tyler Harbor," Harry sighed. "The harbor's in trouble. It's starting to silt up. There are sandbars and such that will cause some boats to bottom out if they're not careful in how they maneuver in and out of the harbor. So we desperately need the harbor to be dredged."

"Held up in Congress?"

"Yeah, like a goddamn train robbery from the old West. The Georgia congressman is some senior bull on some committee that controls the purse strings, and our other local rep somehow pissed him off about something. So until that congressman apologizes to the guy from Georgia, the bill authorizing the dredging is held up in committee."

"I guess no apology is forthcoming?"

"Yeah, I guess that's a polite way of saying it," Harry said. "Both are standing on principles, both are in a dick measuring contest, and if something doesn't happen quick, this deep-water harbor isn't going to be anything else except for a wading pool. Hey, you done?"

I took one last swallow and handed the empty to him, and he went back deep into the boat and checked his watch. "Time to get rolling, if you don't mind. My sweet Connie, she likes to have dinner on the table at about 5:30, so we can eat as a family. 'Course, it makes it sound like we're collecting Social Security and getting ready to go to the Early Bird Special, right?"

I just smiled and followed his lead. He sat on the gunwale and lowered himself with practiced ease into the dinghy, which had a small outboard motor in the rear. He pumped a little black rubber gas ball, flicked a switch, and pulled the rope. It started up after three tries and he kept it in neutral.

"Your turn, Lewis."

I lowered myself down on the gunwale and dangled my legs over the edge, and something just froze in me, like the time I went on a training mission with paratroopers from the 101st back in my day. I wasn't going to jump that day—thank God—but just observe. And when the side doors were opened and you could see the land and meadows and trees rushing by you, it just made you realize how incredibly vulnerable you had become.

Same feeling here.

I suddenly realized I had no life jacket, that it was October, I was slightly woozy from the beer I had quickly consumed, and both the *Elayne D* and the dinghy were bumping and rolling, and now the dinghy seemed awfully damn small, and Harry had made it look oh so easy.

If I fell in…

Harry said, "You okay?"

"Yeah," I said. "Give me a second."

I now wish I had set up the interview back on the dock, not aboard his fishing trawler.

"Lewis…"

I pushed myself off and in the brief seconds it took for me to fall into the dinghy and collapse like a weightlifter who's been training all day, I had another realization, of what it must have been like for that poor drowned woman and her child, trying to get off that freighter at night and in the rain.

One leg went into the dinghy, the other was about to go into the harbor, but Harry's strong grasp pulled me back in and sat down.

"Pretty damn clumsy there, Lewis," he said.

"Yeah."

"Think you could undo the bow line without falling in?"

I leaned to the front, felt a flush of embarrassment, the kind of feeling you get when something is wrong with your car and you bring it into the shop, and suddenly, you don't know anything at all, and those mechanics who do aren't shy about showing off their aptitude to someone who's challenged by a leaky water faucet.

I got the line free, let it drop into the water, and sat back. Harry slipped the motor into drive, and we started back to shore.

"Word of advice?" he said.

"Stay on land from now on?"

He twisted the throttle handle, as we sped to the docks. "No, that'd be my second word of advice. First one is, be careful of poking around, asking questions."

"That's what I do."

"Without a doubt," he said. "But remember the people running those freighters, they're probably not from around here. They have agents here up and down the seacoast, taking in the refugees, get them someplace else. There's a lot of money, a lot of money involved in something like this, and someone from away who doesn't know much about American journalism and the First Amendment might want to keep you from poking around. With no hesitation."

"Thanks for the advice," I said. "But it sounded more like a warning."

"If you heard it, that's all that counts."

A FEW MINUTES later we were at the north end of the long floating dock, where about a dozen other dinghies like the one we were in were tied off. Harry gently bumped us into the collection of small boats, switched off the engine, tied us off. He helped me up and out of the dinghy, and I was ashamed at how shaky I felt. He noticed that and said, "It takes a while to get your sea legs. Don't fret."

"Thanks," I said. I pulled out my wallet, slipped out my *Shoreline* business card, passed it over. "If you hear something, or think of something, call me, will you?"

He held the card in his callused fingers and said, "What, like a good price on scallops?"

"That'd be fine, but I think you know what I mean."

He slipped my business card into his coat. "I do know, and I wish I could do more for you, but the chances are, I'll be calling just for a discount price on shellfish or fresh cod. See you later."

"Thanks for the beer."

This section of the docks was a floating pier, and we took a gangway up to the paved area. I went left and he went to the line of pickup trucks belonging to the other fishermen, and that's when it started.

A guy emerged from between two of the trucks and yelled out, "Hey, Harry! Over here!"

Harry swiveled his head and his shoulders slumped, like he was a Depression-era farmer, being ambushed by his banker. Harry started walking to the guy and as he got closer, I saw he was about the same size and shape as Harry, but was dressed much worse. Battered and stained dark yellow barn jacket, duct-taped repaired rubber boots that came up to his knees, and a scraggly beard that came down mid-chest and was streaked through with white.

His eyes were sunken in some, but they sure looked angry, and he started pointing his finger at Harry, jabbing, and then it came to me.

Billy Bragg, Harry's older brother.

The one that Paula reminded me was constantly a "person of interest" among various law enforcement and fishery agents.

Harry's voice was softer, but he was sure giving it back as much as Billy was giving it out, and a couple of other fishermen came up the gangway behind me and walked by them, giving both a wide berth.

I stayed for just a few seconds longer. I was born an only child and with my parents long gone, I occasionally had that empty feeling that comes from wishing one had an older or younger brother to hang out with, or spend holidays with, or at least share some family memories.

But seeing this vicious fight unfold in front of me a few yards away, I didn't feel unlucky at all.

I walked past the co-op fishermen's building, got to my dark green Honda Pilot, and started back home, going up a side street past summer cottages with about a yard's distance between each one, all boarded up for the approaching winter, and I made a U-turn and started north along Atlantic Avenue, the beaches of Tyler and the ocean on my right.

It was about a fifteen-minute drive home, and I got there just in time to see the riot.

7

But it didn't look like a riot when I made the right-hand turn into the parking lot of the Lafayette House, which allowed me access to the bumpy dirt driveway that led down to my pretty much hidden home.

Since the near lot for the Lafayette House has only enough room to pick up and drop off passengers, along with a half-dozen spots reserved for those vehicles with handicapped placards, this parking lot was a pretty good size, and with it being off season, not many cars or SUVs were parked there for paying guests.

Which left lots of room for about sixty or so people, moving in two groups, holding signs, yelling at each other, giving each other obscene gestures. I braked hard and then pulled over farther to the right, trying to figure out how to pass them when a Tyler police cruiser roared in, lights flashing, followed by another one.

Three cops—two women and a man—emerged from the cruisers and tried their best to keep the angry people separated, but I saw from their whitened faces and nervous looks that they knew just what kind of danger they were putting themselves into. Ninety-nine times out of a hundred, your average person will do the right thing and not harm another person, or cause any damage, or do anything even remotely against the law. But during that one time out of a hundred, when a person is part of a mob, then anything could happen. There was a humming feeling in the air, an electrical feeling like a hidden thunderstorm was about to strike, and a sense that all the rules were suspended, that anything could happen.

I was wondering just what in hell was going on just a number of yards away from my home when the signs were turned to and fro from the opposite sides, and I got a good read on what was happening.

Signs from the left:

SEND THEM BACK!

SAY NO TO TERRORISTS!

DROWNING = A GOOD START!

And from the other side:

OPEN BORDERS!

LAND OF LIBERTY, NOT DEPORTATIONS!

WE'RE ALL HUMANS HERE!

Maybe we were all humans, but what were these angry humans doing here?

The crowds jostled, moved back and forth. A cup of coffee was thrown from left to right, and from right to left, a juice bottle came flying over. The cops were yelling, batons in their hands, trying to keep the two groups separated. It looked like a losing proposition, because some of the braver or angrier of each group would quickly race past the cops—like young students trying to run past playground monitors—and push and shove the opposition.

Other cars and pickup trucks pulled up, people tumbling out. I looked around, trying to see what had caused this, why these people were here in this parking lot, near my home, and then another disturbance started across the street at the Lafayette House, and there were two camera crews, bright lights illuminating their way. As they tagged along, a tall woman was in the center of a scrum of journalists who were keeping up with her as she came across Atlantic Avenue and into the parking lot.

I recognized her.

I didn't know her name, but I recognized her all right. In the few times I've chosen to watch the low-brow entertainment that passes as cable news channels, this particular woman with long neck, bleached blonde shoulder-length hair and a prominent nose, was also a prominent spokesman for those who thought the immigration laws went to hell back when the Know Nothing Party was stomping around the rural lands of a young America.

I got out of my Pilot to see what was going to happen next.

She made her way to the parking lot, and somebody put a loudspeaker in her hand and she started talking, her amplified voice echoing across the parking lot.

"My name is Alice Hackett...as some of you know and as some others of you hate—"

Cheers, boos, and a loud voice, "We love you, Alice!"

She smiled at the attention, both positive and negative, and then looked around and continued. She had on a red wool coat and very short black skirt with black high-heeled shoes.

"I've come here today to join up with some real Americans—"

Boos, applause, some obscenities tossed out.

"We need more than to protect our borders, we need to protect our shores as well—"

The roars of approval outweighed the jeers and boos. She smiled wider. The crackling energy from the crowd that was worrying me seemed to have the opposite effect on Alice.

"Not really P.C. to say, but these people are not our problem, and to suggest otherwise is wrong," Alice said.

The mood in the crowd seemed to increase, to darken. A brawl broke out on the far side of the lot, and two Tyler cops tried to break it up. More sirens sounded in the distance. I started to back away, bumped into someone.

"Oh, sorry," I said, turning, not wanting to start my own scuffle, but I instantly relaxed, seeing it was Paula. She had her notebook in one hand, her camera in the other, and she just nodded, looked at the shifting, moving crowds, and said, "What a mess."

"You got it."

I gave her a squeeze and she smiled, "Back to work."

"Dinner?"

"Of course," she said, "and breakfast, too, if that's okay."

"You bet."

She moved to where the brawl had calmed down, more photos being taken, and I lost sight of her when it was like the crowd had pushed me forward, only yards away from the red-coated Alice Hackett, and the gunfire broke out.

A hard series of *pop-pop-pops* and, like most in-tune Americans nowadays, unfortunately, the people sprawled to the ground, and there were screams, and I was trampled. I got up and I saw Paula ducking to one side of a light blue Volvo, frantically scribbling away. That was the only bright spot. Near the parking lot entrance Alice Hackett was pushed down, folded over by two burly men, and a black Yukon SUV roared up. She was tossed in, and then it roared away, as two more Tyler police cruisers and then a dark green State Police cruiser came blasting in, halting and doors flying open.

I tried to move, and another series of *pop-pop-pops* rang out, and I ducked to the ground again, and two men, breathing hard, charged into me as I got up. I fell again, my face scraping on the pavement, feeling raw and burning.

Then I got up and sat up against the tire of an F-150 pickup truck, suddenly tired.

Was this where we had ended up?

FUNNY ENOUGH, it didn't take that long for the parking lot to clear. When the gunfire opened up, the differing and fighting crowds had reacted as one, running across the lot and along the sidewalks of Atlantic Avenue, north and south, and I'm sure a few of the more desperate ones trespassed onto my property, and I didn't care.

I just felt tired, not wanting to move.

Another police cruiser came up, lights flashing in its grill and above the windshield. It came to a slow stop, and Detective Sergeant Diane Woods came out, frowning, running a hand through her hair, her other hand holding a clipboard. She talked to a uniformed officer and then a State Police trooper, and she went to the trunk of the unmarked cruiser and came out carrying a black duffel bag in her hand.

I still sat there.

I glanced around at the parking lot, didn't see anybody on the ground.

A good sight.

More sirens.

Two Tyler Fire Department ambulances came up, and I was happy to see that it appeared that they weren't going to get any business.

Diane saw me sitting there and came over, looked down and said, "You okay?"

"A couple of former football players ran me down in their rush to get the hell out. How are you doing?"

She shook her head. "Looks pretty straightforward, for now. Shooting breaks out at a protest."

"Why here?" I asked.

"Two reasons, I guess," she said. "One was that you had two bodies come ashore this morning."

"But still...that only happened this morning."

"Alice Hackett was in town because of the other drownings. And you think she's going to stay at your local Motel 6? Nope. She's staying over there at the Lafayette House, and to get to this latest newsworthy site, well, it's just a short stroll across the street."

She frowned, squatted down next to me.

"What happened to your face?" she asked.

"When those two football players ran me down, they scraped my face."

She took out some folded tissue from her coat pocket, gently patted the right side of my face, right at my temple.

Diane took it back and showed it to me.

It was sopping wet with my blood.

"Lewis, you've been shot."

8

The drive to Exonia Hospital went fairly quick, even though I really didn't want to stretch out on the folded stretcher in the rear of the bright red ambulance from the Tyler Fire Department. But the childish part of me still thrilled at the sound of the siren, so there was that. The quiet and professional Tyler firefighter/EMTs—one male and one female—took my blood pressure, temperature, and put a temporary bandage on my right temple.

By then we were backing up to the Emergency Room entrance at Exonia Hospital, and I shook both of their hands.

"Glad to see my tax dollars going to such great service," I said.

The woman smiled. "Be a lamb and go to next year's Town Meeting when our budget comes up."

"That's a deal," I said.

The other EMT opened the door and got out, took the far edge of my stretcher. "Trust us, Mister Cole, Amy and I were fearing the worst when we heard there was shooting at that demo. We were expecting a half-dozen bodies on the ground, at least."

"Glad to see you disappointed."

Amy said, "Me, too."

Getting in and admitted was also pretty straightforward, and I was taken off the Tyler Fire Department gurney and placed on a bed in the emergency room. After two male nurses again took my body's readings and—more importantly, I'm sure—the status of my health insurance, the curtain was swept open and an out-of-breath Tyler police sergeant was there, his nameplate saying GOLUMB.

"I need to ask you a few questions," he said, pulling up a chair.

"Where's Detective Sergeant Woods?"

"Busy processing the scene. You doing all right?" He was mid-thirties, bit stout around the middle, with a smooth, unlined face and light brown eyes that suggested he hadn't yet seen too much blood and chaos over the years.

"As well as could be expected," I said.

Another *swish-swish* of the curtain and an ER doctor came in, face covered with stubble, blond hair and light blue eyes, and he looked at me, and I looked right back at him.

"I know you," he said, his voice accented by Dutch, "You're...that magazine writer, correct?"

"Right, and you're the doctor from Holland."

"*Ja,*" he smiled, extending his hand. "At your service. Did I treat you?"

"No," I said. "You treated a friend of mine, a couple of years back. A newspaper reporter, caught up in a shooting connected with a demonstration at the Falconer nuclear power plant."

"Ah," he said, and then he seemed to notice Sergeant Golumb. "And what has happened, then? Are you under arrest?"

"No," Sergeant Golumb said, standing up. "Mister Cole is a shooting victim, from Tyler. I'm here as part of the investigation."

The ER doctor with a good memory nodded, smiling, but his voice was now steel. "How worthy of you. You will excuse us, then, and you can come back when we're finished."

But Sergeant Golumb held his own. "Please, doctor. I understand. But I really need to take some photos of his wound before it gets dressed."

He pondered that for a moment, and said, "Agreed. But when you have your photos, you will leave us, correct?"

"Correct."

"Then let's get to it."

The doctor got to work, and I winced when he tugged away the tape and the temporary bandage came off, and he said, "Looks good, all things considered. The wound isn't that deep, and it's starting to clot. Sergeant, do your work."

Sergeant Golumb used his iPhone to take a number of photos at all sorts of different angles, and the doctor was not only more relaxed now that he saw my wound status, he even held a small ruler so the wound's measurements could be recorded.

Then the sergeant looked down at his iPhone and said, "Came out great. Thanks, doc. And Mister Cole, I'll see you later."

"Don't think I'm going anywhere soon."

A nurse came in as the doctor got to work, and he swabbed, washed, and said, "Is this wound from a gunshot, then?"

"Sure was."

"You were quite fortunate," he said. "Another few centimeters, not a good outcome. Perhaps you should purchase a lottery ticket on the way home."

"No thanks," I said. "I think I've used up my luck for the day."

A smiling Hispanic nurse said, "Try a week."

A bit more work and the doctor said, "Lucky you, no stitches required, but definitely two butterfly bandages. Shouldn't take too long to apply, and then you'll be on your way."

"Thanks," I said, and sure enough, within fifteen minutes, I was relaxing in the room, ready for discharge, and then Sergeant Golumb came in, and I wasn't so relaxed any more.

He was polite but persistent as he started.

"You feeling all right, Mister Cole?"

"Please, it's Lewis," I said.

"Okay," he replied, scribbling in a small notebook. "What time did you get to the Lafayette Hotel parking lot today?"

"At about five."

"And why were you there?"

"I was going home."

"Were you part of the demonstration?"

"No," I said. "I didn't even know there was going to be a demonstration there today."

"I see."

He kept on scribbling, chewing a bit on a lower lip. "So it came to you as a surprise."

"Completely."

"Even though two bodies were recovered from your property this morning," he said.

Funny how that plain sentence still struck me. Two bodies. No, I thought, a desperate mom and frightened baby, both drowning within eyesight of my safe home.

"Still a surprise."

A bit more scribbling. The side of my head was throbbing, and it was like I could feel the two butterfly strips doing their adhesive work, keeping my severed skin in place.

"There were two groups there at the parking lot, correct? Holding competing demonstrations?"

"That's right."

"And which group were you with when the shooting started?"

My head kept on throbbing. "Neither."

"Then why were you there?"

"Like I said before, I wanted to go home."

"And where's home?"

"Just beyond the parking lot, to the north. There's a dirt driveway that leads down to my home. It used to be a lifeboat station back in the mid-1800s."

He looked up at me. "Oh. I know that place. When I was a kid, our high school history teacher took us on a field trip down there. It looked like a dump."

"I've made improvements," I said, wanting this interview to wrap up, but it seemed like Sergeant Golumb was either in love with his own voice or his notepad.

"So," he said, flipping a page. "Where were you when the shooting started?"

"Minding my own business, at the south end of the parking lot."

"How many shots were fired?"

I closed my eyes, tried to recall and re-hear what had happened an hour or so earlier.

I opened my eyes. "Six. There were six."

"Are you sure?"

"No," I said. "I'm positive. There were six."

"And did you see where the shots were coming from?"

"The north," I said. "I didn't see a damn thing, but from the sounds, it seemed like somewhere in front of me."

"Did you see anybody with a weapon before the shooting commenced?"

I was feeling pissy and I said, "I certainly did."

That sure got his attention. His eyes snapped to me and he said, "Where? And how? And could you recognize them again?"

"I sure hope so," I said. "They were three officers from your department."

THE INTERVIEW DRIBBLED off after that, and after he gave me his business card and left, he slipped through the curtain just as my cellphone rang, and it was Paula.

"Holy Christ, are you all right?" she said, voice loud, filled with concern. "I ran and hid in the Lafayette House, thinking maybe you managed to get home. Never thought you'd be hurt, Lewis."

"I'm okay, honest," I said. "Just a graze to my right temple." I was going to say it was just a flesh wound, but I couldn't bear the thought of uttering that cliché, as true as it might be.

"Any arrests?"

"Not that I know of," I said. "How are you? Are you okay?"

"I'm fine," she said. "I'm back at the Lafayette House, trying to get a hold of Alice Hackett, but if she's there, she's not coming out. Are you sure you're okay?"

"Very sure," I said. "No stitches. Just a couple of butterfly bandages to hold things together."

"Are you staying overnight?"

"Nope," I said. "I'm just waiting to be discharged, after all the paper-work is signed and blessed."

"Okay," she said. "Give me a call and I'll come pick you up."

"But what about Alice Hackett?"

Paula said something extraordinarily rude about Alice, and then signed off.

Which was pretty ironic, considering a woman's voice came through the curtain, saying, "Mister Cole, do you have a moment?"

And without me saying a word, the curtain slid open and there was Alice Hackett.

9

Considering she had just come from a violent demonstration that had involved fighting, shoving and shooting, she looked pretty serene and composed. She still had on a red wool coat, which was now unbuttoned, revealing a plain starched white blouse and a short black skirt.

"Sure," I said. "I guess I have a moment."

She chuckled with the sincerity of a banker explaining how a bounced check for fifty cents had resulted in overdraft fees of fifty dollars. Taking a chair next to me, she extended a hand and I gave it a brief shake. Along with Alice were two men, one who was tall, wide, and unsmiling, and who had a curled wire ending up his right ear. The muscle. I think I had seen him tossing her into the black Yukon earlier when the shooting had broken out. The other guy was shorter, narrower, and was wearing a tan topcoat and gray two-piece suit underneath, and behind horn-rimmed glasses, his eyes blinked a lot.

"This is Brady, my assistant," she said.

Brady stepped forward, gave me a quick handshake as well, although his hand felt moist and oily compared to his boss' grip.

"Alice," he said, stepping back. "We're running behind. You know you've got that call-in to the Boston radio show in fifteen minutes. We don't want to be late."

She waved a hand in a dismissive motion, said hand bearing ten bright red fingernails. "Brady, it'll be okay. Howie and I go way back. It won't be a problem."

"But we need to get to a place where—"

"Brady," she said, her voice an octave higher, "take Walter with you and fetch me a cup of coffee, will you?"

He shifted a leather briefcase from one hand to another. "All right," he said.

"And see if Mister Cole needs anything," she added, and I shook my head, and then the two men left, the curtain slid back into place, and she folded her long legs and clasped her hands together over her right knee.

Her brittle persona seemed to fade away right then, and her voice softened. "Honest, how are you doing?"

"Doing all right," I said. "Quite lucky that a bullet just grazed me."

"Stitches?"

"Not a one."

"That's good news."

"I think so. Tell me, how did you get in here? Usually the ER is pretty strict when admitting non-relatives to see patients."

She smiled, flicked an unfortunate piece of dirt from her skirt. "Being a public person has its advantages, especially when it comes to breaking the rules."

Having a TV and book personality in my ER cubicle was odd, but not the oddest celebrity sighting or get-together I've ever experienced. I live in the state of the country's first presidential primary, so seeing politicians and their various supporters was a given, and over the years in New Hampshire I've talked to and shared warm punch with two future presidents, a Secretary of State, and another, more famous cable television personality.

So I think my reaction to Alice was unnerving her.

It was something to see.

She pulled out a cellphone from her large purse, started flicking through the screen, and said, "What do you have going on at ten?"

"Tomorrow? Not sure."

"No, no, no," she said. "I meant ten o'clock. Tonight."

"Probably in bed with a painkiller and my significant other, trying to go to sleep."

With her head bowed over, her blonde hair didn't move an inch, as her red-fingernail fingers worked the keyboard. "Oh, no, you've got to come on my show."

"Why?"

Her face came up and she looked at me as if I wasn't a fully competent *homo sapiens*. Perhaps a Neanderthal throwback.

"I want you there to tell the world what happened," she said. "That while at a political demonstration, trying to lend your voice to those of my many supporters, that you were shot and nearly killed."

"But—"

"Don't worry, you won't have to go to a studio," she said. "My suite at the Lafayette House will have the necessary set-up. With that bandage, you'll be perfect. All we have to do is—"

"No," I said.

"Then we could—"

"No."

I think I finally got her attention.

"What's the matter?" she asked.

"No, I'm not going on television tonight."

"But you were shot at my demonstration," she said.

"I think some folks would disagree that it was your demonstration," I pointed out. "And I was there because I wanted to go home. Nothing else."

Her tone and voice instantly sharpened, like she was on some cable show on-air debate concerning veganism, and she had just found a photo of me eating a cheeseburger.

"You mean you're in favor of open borders, of allowing anyone in without a background check or any sort of law enforcement at all?" she said.

"I'm in favor of wanting to go home, that's all. And that's what I'm going to do in just a few minutes, and being with you on television isn't on my schedule. Why don't you talk to some other locals who have opinions they want to share."

"The only local I want to talk to is you, Mister Cole."

"This local isn't available," I said. "Why not look up the local Homeland Security rep, the one who seems to be running the show."

Her face pursed into a scowl. It looked normal on her.

"Mark Stockman? Typical government bureaucrat, expert in not saying anything, following rules and regulations, and carrying a weapon. It's bureaucrats like him that shows the Founding Fathers were correct in putting the Second Amendment into the Constitution."

"I'm a big fan of the Nineteenth Amendment myself," I said.

She was about to say something sharp and cutting, I'm sure, when the room's curtain swept aside and her assistant Brady stepped in without looking at me.

"Alice, we have a situation here," he said. "There's a state senator in the lobby who really wants to see you."

"Why should I care?" she asked.

"Because his uncle is on the board of directors at Commonsense Publishing," he said. "Your publisher."

"Oh," she said, standing up. "Okay, I'll give him five minutes, and then I need to get this mess with Mister Cole straightened out."

They both left without closing the curtain behind themselves.

I was a mess.

Who knew?

A FEW MINUTES later I was officially discharged with the proper paperwork and instructions and warnings about what to do if the wound at the side of my head were to suddenly split open and start oozing out brains, when an old friend strode in like he owned the place, smiling at me and at the female medical assistant in her thirties who was just leaving, my signed paperwork in hand.

The medical assistant smiled back up at my visitor and then she walked out, bumping into a chair, and then went on her way.

"What is it with you?" I asked, and Felix Tinios just shrugged and sat down.

"I don't know," he said. "Guess I'm just having a good day." He gave me a thorough look. "Better than you. What the hell happened?"

I gave him a rundown while he sat there, taking it all in. Felix was taller than me, better muscled, with olive skin and thick dark hair. He has a keen and sharp face, like he's always been on top of things over the years, but I've seen him sunning himself in the backyard, and he has an interesting collection of puckered scars on his skin.

He had on dark gray slacks and a black wool coat that in other times and places would be called a Navy pea jacket, but I'm sure his coat probably cost five times as much as anything Navy-issued.

For a number of years Felix had lived and worked in the rough-and-tumble organized crime field out of Boston's famed North End, but he had left that job at about the time I moved into Tyler Beach. "I couldn't stand the hours or my co-workers," he had once told me, and now he listed his profession each year on his tax return as a security consultant.

After I was finished with my tale, he came over and gently touched and slid his fingers over the bandage and whistled. "You want to pick up a Megabucks ticket on the way home? You sure as hell got a streak of good luck going on. Another inch you'd be dead, or eventually stuck in a rehab center somewhere with a feeding tube going down your nose for the next ten years or so."

"No thanks," I said. "The doc who fixed me up suggested the same thing. From where I'm sitting, I think my luck's been used for at least a few weeks. Hey, no offense, but what are you doing here?"

He sat back in the chair, shrugged. "I heard there was a shooting in the Lafayette House parking lot. Made a call or two. Found out you were here. Decided to come over and see how you're doing."

"I'm doing fine," I said. "You know, it's against the rules for hospitals to give out patient information unless you're a relative."

"Yeah, I've heard about that. You doing okay?"

"Ready to go home," I said.

"Want a ride?"

Paula had offered but I knew she was having a busy day, and if I were to phone her right now, it would take about fifteen or so minutes for her to get here. Right now, the thought of being with Felix as he gave me a ride home was a cheerful thing indeed.

"Sounds great," I said.

He stood up. "I need a coffee fix for the ride home. Let me grab something from the cafeteria and I'll be back in about five minutes. You want one, too?"

"Please, Uncle Felix," I said, and then he left, and like I was in some rollicking Broadway farce, he was replaced just a minute later by Brady, Alice Hackett's assistant.

But Brady didn't take a seat. He just stood there, glaring at me.

"You really need to change your mind," he said.

"I have," I said. "I was thinking about grilled cheeseburgers for dinner, but now I'm leaning towards take-out seafood. Maybe a nice lobster pie. It's been a long day, and I don't feel like cooking tonight."

He shook his head. "No, you don't get it. You need to be on Alice's show tonight."

"No, I don't," I said.

"Yes, you do."

"You're not paying attention, are you," I said.

He stepped closer, like he was trying to prove how tough he was by invading my space. It came off like Rhode Island threatening to invade California.

"Listen, people regret going against Alice Hackett. She's a powerhouse. She has influential friends in the news media, academia and government, all across the country. Lots of people want to be on her show, lots of people want to be her friend. Play along tonight, be her guest, and it'll pay off down the road."

Felix came back, holding a cardboard caddy with two coffee cups secured. He gave Brady a good glance.

Brady didn't take it so well.

"Brady, this is my friend and chauffeur Felix," I said. "Felix, this is…oh, I don't mean to be rude. What's your last name, Brady?"

"Hill," he said. "Brady Hill."

"Thanks," I said. "Brady, my friend Felix is now taking me home, from whence I'm not departing for the foreseeable future. You got a problem with that?"

It seemed Brady did have a problem with that, but he didn't say a word. He just turned and walked out.

I got out of the bed, took my coffee from the cardboard tray. Felix said, "Who was that?"

"Some guy who thought he was my better," I said.

Felix said, "I don't know him, and I already don't like him."

10

I've never been one to be in love with a special car or SUV—as far as I was concerned, one mode of transportation was pretty much the same as the other, doing its job, getting you from Point A to Point B—but being in Felix's Mercedes-Benz made a good attempt at changing my mind.

He used to drive a Mercedes convertible, but he got tired of it a couple of years back, explaining, "My summer passengers are getting smarter. I used to be able to rub some sunscreen on them before going on a long trip, but that doesn't work anymore. They goop their skin before I pick them up."

"A pity," I had said. "I'm sure helping put on sunscreen made the drive more pleasant."

"You have no idea."

So this Mercedes was a hardtop sedan, one of the models denoted by a mix of numbers and letters, but the interior was soft, comfortable, with not a speck of dirt or dust. We got onto Route 101, heading east to the Atlantic Ocean and my home, and I made a quick phone call to Paula, saying I was heading home with Felix, and she said a brief "Unh-hunh" and told me she'd be coming by in about an hour.

I clicked the call off and I said, "Paula says hi."

"No she doesn't."

"Well...I just don't understand it."

"What's that?"

"She's about the only woman I know that...well, you know."

He said, "It happens."

"You don't sound too upset."

Felix said, "It doesn't happen that often. That's why I'm not upset."

Traffic was light and Felix maneuvered his car expertly as he traveled east. It was dusk and I hated knowing that in a couple of weeks, this dark moment would be occurring an hour earlier.

We missed the exit to downtown Tyler that would have led us on a shorter route, and we took the state highway all the way to the beach. Soon the flat marshland was stretching out to our left and right, and along the thin strip of the beach, lights were on for the few cottages, hotels and restaurants still open following the Labor Day weekend and the short time that was foliage season.

Felix took a left when the road ended, and we started going north, and he said, "So what was the demonstration about?"

"There were two of them," I said.

"Representing what?"

I thought of a quick answer, and then said what seemed to be a better answer.

"Anarchy," I said. "They were both in favor of anarchy."

Atlantic Avenue was now bordered by a heavy concrete seawall, blocking off the view of the water and the beaches, and to our left was row upon row of condo units, built over the razed remains of one-story cottages and simple homes that used to house folks who spent an affordable week at the beach.

The phrase "affordable week at the beach" was no longer spoken in any company on the New Hampshire coastline, polite or otherwise.

"Tell me more," Felix said. "I don't like anarchy. I like rules."

"The better to break them, eh?"

"Tsk, tsk. Do go on."

"Anarchy," I repeated. "One side wants open borders, letting anybody and everybody come in. The other side wants a Fortress America, high walls and heavily armed Border Police."

"Sounds like a fun mix."

"It's all fun and games until the shooting starts," I said.

Felix slowed down when we got to the Lafayette House, and I was surprised to see that there weren't any cops around. A piece of fluttering yellow and black police tape was caught up in the boulders marking the end of the lot that overlooked the ocean.

"Hold up for a moment, will you?"

"Sure.

He pulled into an empty spot, killed the headlights, and we sat there for a couple of minutes, just listening to the slight whisper of the Mercedes' engine running in neutral.

"What do you know?" I asked.

Good for Felix, he didn't try to push back, or deny, or argue with me. We both knew each other well enough not to let stuff like that slide.

"There's new faces, movements," he quietly said. "Nobody I know, nobody I want to know. I've done my best to stay away from drug traffickers over the years, and human trafficking...damn. Selling and trading a banned substance is one thing. Selling and trafficking with desperate people...I don't want to even go there. It's a whole different depth of evil."

"But these new faces are out there."

"Yeah."

"Anybody approach you? Try to hire you to serve as a local guide?"

"Whoever they are, they know better. So no is your answer. Nobody's reached out to me."

I kept quiet, seeing some lights out there on the water, wondering if it was fishermen coming home, or boats used by the traffickers, checking the waves and the other marine traffic.

"My grandparents and great-grandparents, they came across the same ocean, and it was rough, but nothing like what those poor folks are facing," Felix said, his huge forearms draped over the steering wheel. "The crossing was rough, the sleeping arrangements and food wasn't the best, but at least they entered a port. It was regulated. It was legal for the time. These folks..."

"Dumped over the side at night in banged up old lifeboats or leaky life rafts, just paddling desperately for the shore," I said. "Not sure if you heard or not, but I found a drowned woman and her infant in my little cove this morning."

Felix's face tightened. "I heard some bodies had washed up here on the beach. Didn't know it had gotten so close and personal for you."

"It did," I said.

"How personal?"

I said, "I want to find out who she was, and her child, and make sure the two of them get a proper burial. Here, in the place where they wanted to live."

"That sounds pretty personal," Felix said. "Any luck so far?"

"I've talked to the Homeland Security officer who's responsible for this stretch of the Atlantic, and who's been retrieving the drowned bodies these past few weeks."

"He tell you anything?"

"Yeah, to shut up and mind my own business."

Felix reflected on that for a moment. "Hell of a thing, when you feel sympathy for a Federal employee going against you."

I opened the Mercedes' door and said, "Humor me for a moment, will you?"

"Why not?"

Outside the October air was crisp and the wind was coming strong off the ocean. The discarded yellow police tape was still flapping around. I went to the near rocks, tore it free, and started rolling it up in my hand. Felix kept pace with me, and then I walked to the part of the parking lot where all of the excitement had taken place a few hours earlier.

I just looked around, up at the Lafayette House, the northbound section of Atlantic Avenue, the sidewalk and the rocks and tufts of grass.

To the south was a stretch of some condos, more rocks, and not too far away, the lights of the northern section of Tyler Beach.

Traffic was slow and Felix came up next to me.

"Well?" he asked.

I said, "Alice Hackett was over there, about twenty or so feet away. Over there," and I pointed, "were the mass of the demonstrators. There was a group here to cheer Alice, and another group to do the opposite."

Felix looked up at where I was pointing.

"Where were you?" he said.

I went over to a parked F-150 Ford pickup truck, about three steps from where I was standing.

"Here. Somehow, I got pushed out in front of the crowd. It was me and Alice."

"How many shots?" Felix asked.

"Three at first, and then three more. Series of six."

"Rifle or pistol?"

I closed my eyes, tried to recall everything, and I opened my eyes and said, "Pistol. Almost certain it was a pistol."

"Okay."

Felix stood next to me, hands in his Navy peacoat, huddled up against the heavier breeze. I touched the side of my face.

Felix said, "Anybody else get shot?"

"Nope."

"Vehicles struck?"

"I don't think so."

"I see."

The lights of the Lafayette House looked so warm and inviting, but knowing Alice Hackett was holed up there with her sidekick Brady, the place didn't look that inviting any more.

"Felix?"

"That's me."

"The shots weren't aimed at Alice, or the first group of demonstrators, or the second group of demonstrators."

I paused.

"They were aimed at me. Somebody was trying to kill me."

Felix said, "Yeah, I figured that out, too."

"When?"

"When I saw you in the ER."

"And you didn't think of telling me?"

He looked hurt. "And take away your fun?"

11

Paula came to my home ten minutes after I got a meal delivery from the Lafayette House. With lasagna and a side of garlic bread for her, I made do with a baked stuffed scallop dish, and we sat at the counter in my kitchen, sitting on bar stools.

I had offered her wine and she had reluctantly said no. "I've got a planning board meeting tonight. I have a glass of wine, I'll be snoozing after one hour, instead of the usual two."

We ate and she kept on looking at my bandage, touching it at least twice, and said, "Are you sure it doesn't hurt?"

"It's aching a bit, but not too bad," I said.

"Show me again."

So I turned my head and she went *tsk-tsk* again. "I filed a report about the demonstration and said that a local man was slightly injured during the shooting, without mentioning your name. You okay with being a local man?"

"It seems to be my new secret identity," I said.

"You okay with me not doing a follow-up on you?"

"I'm very okay with that," I said.

We both went back to eating and she changed the subject, but I sensed something was off, and when there was a pause in her telling me about the new mileage reimbursement rules from the *Chronicle*'s publishers, I said, "Anything new about the bodies from this morning?"

"Not a thing," she said.

"And where the bodies went after they were recovered?"

"Still don't know that."

"And no word if any empty freighters have been spotted, heading back to Libya or Syria?"

Paula paused while wiping the last of the pasta sauce with a slice of garlic bread, and she said, "What, I wasn't making sense earlier?"

"Excuse me?"

"You asked me if there was anything new about the bodies from this morning," she pointed out. "I said not a thing. And yet you keep on asking me questions. You think I'm doing a lousy job?"

I felt like a paratrooper who was set to land in a nice safe clearing, and somehow ended up in the middle of a minefield.

"No, you're not doing a lousy job," I said. "And sorry I pressed you. That was inconsiderate."

She nodded. "Yeah, and you with that bandage on your head, I wasn't very considerate either. Sorry."

Paula picked up her plate and headed to the sink, and I followed her.

We did the washing in silence, and the drying of the dishes, and then she went out to the living room and picked up her coat and large leather satchel—containing the usual purse belongings of a young woman along with her notebook, pens and laptop—and she said, "Off to the planning board meeting."

"You coming back here?"

She shrugged on her coat, gave me a quick smile that made everything right for that moment, and said, "You feeling lucky?"

"I'll let you know that if you come back."

"Okay, you lucky boy, you."

Paula headed to the door, and I said, "I'll leave the lights on. And the door unlocked."

She didn't say anything.

Maybe she didn't hear me.

It didn't make any difference.

I switched on the outdoor lights and left the door unlocked.

LATER I WAS JUST POKING around the house, and I kept on looking and looking at my unlocked door. I didn't like it. A few hours ago someone had taken a shot at me, and by leaving the door unlocked, I felt like I was giving them permission to waltz right in and have another go, close up and personal.

If I had been smart, I would have killed the lights and locked the door, but Paula could come back to my place early, and I had made a promise.

But I still didn't like that unlocked door.

In a pantry drawer near the telephone with the local phone book—yes, I know I'm a dinosaur, what of it—and spare keys and other debris that manages to find its way into one's home, was my .32 Browning pistol. I gave it a quick examination and put it back into the drawer, and slid it closed, but not all the way.

I then went upstairs and went to my nightstand where my trusty 9 mm Beretta was kept, along with two spare magazines. I closed that drawer as well, but like the other drawer, not all the way.

I knelt down, looked under my bed. A piece of foam and resting on top of it, my loaded Remington 12-gauge shotgun. And then to my bedroom closet, where an 8 mm FN-FAL semi-automatic rifle was leaning up against the wall.

I touched my temple once more.

Even paranoids have enemies.

So why had I made an enemy so quickly this day?

Or was it something from my turbulent past?

I closed the closet door, but not all the way.

Speaking of the past, I still had a .357 Ruger of mine that was in the possession of the Secret Service, from events a couple of years back. One of these days, I really needed to take care of it.

But not tonight.

. . .

AT TEN P.M. I caught the New England Cable News Channel hourly update, and not surprisingly, the shooting at the parking lot just a hundred or so yards away from where I was sitting was the lead story. Their camera crew hadn't been there when the shooting had broken out, but someone had supplied them with a blurry cellphone video, and that was good enough.

I didn't see me in the confusing clash of falling and running bodies, but son of a gun, I was noted in passing at one point in the story, as "a local man was slightly wounded in the shooting and was later treated and released from Exonia Hospital." There you go. I was a local man once again. Not as much fun as a Florida man, but I would take it.

With the shooting story wrapped up, next up was an interview with the ever sharp and telegenic Alice Hackett, who despite the lack of my presence, was still making do with her conspiracy theory.

"Look what happens when the supposed good-hearted and warm-hearted come out to share their blessed voices against my popular positions and myself," she said, standing by the familiar rocks at the edge of the parking lot. "They love free speech, but only if you agree with them. They love speaking truth to power, but only if their truth is being spoken. And they love peaceful demonstrations, until gunfire breaks out."

The off-camera reporter—which meant that the poor journalist was acting both as reporter and camera operator—said to her, "Are you accusing the pro-refugee demonstrators of being the ones responsible for the shooting? Of using violence?"

Her sharp, white-toothed smile expanded. "I'm accusing you and others of using violence against the English language. Those on the other side aren't pro-refugee, they're pro open-borders. They don't want any enforcement of our border laws. They leave in a dream world where everyone is the same as everyone else, that if we just brush aside those pesky borders, then we can all sit down and sing 'Kumbaya' until our throats get slit."

Well, after that bracing interview, next up was a young woman with eyeglasses, short blonde hair, and rosy cheeks, wearing a simple dungaree jacket, who was being interviewed somewhere else on the coast. The graphic identified her as Mo Walsh, a representative of a group called Open Arms of the Seacoast. The off-screen reporter condensed Alice Hackett's words into a statement, seeking a response, and Mo laughed. I liked her laugh.

"For heaven's sake, no, we'd never stoop to violence," she said. "That's against everything we stand for. Look, certain groups and media-hungry personalities want to make this into a battle over illegal immigration. We won't join the fight because we're not interested. The only thing we're interested in is to provide open arms and shelter for those who get tossed up on our shores. These poor folks aren't illegal anything. They're just scared, desperate, and trying to find a bit of peace."

With that second interview wrapped up, there was another story from the very early part of this morning, about the second wave of drowned bodies washing ashore on a stretch of New Hampshire coastline, and the only government spokesman was a graphic of a printed news release from Homeland Security, saying all was in hand and that the investigation into these unfortunate events was continuing.

I got up and turned the television off, and then made sure the front door was unlocked, and the lights were on. I went through the house and left most of the lights on for Paula, and then I went to the sliding glass door that led out to the rear deck. Through the glass I could barely make out the waves of the cold Atlantic out there, the terminal surf that would catch you and drown you.

I switched on my outer deck lights as well, something I've never done before.

Then I went up and found my bedroom.

It had been a very long day.

12

It took some time to fall asleep, with the bandage on my temple rubbing up against the pillow, and when I did drift off, it seemed like about ninety seconds passed before the phone rang. I instantly reacted, reaching over with two hands, picking up the phone with my right hand.

"Lewis?" came Paula's voice, and I took my other hand from the night-stand, where the partially opened drawer was located, along with my Beretta.

"Yep," I said, checking the time. Just a shade past eleven p.m.

"Sorry to wake you up, but I didn't want you to worry," she said. "The damn meeting got over late, and I'm exhausted. I'm going to my condo to bed down. Sorry."

I rubbed at my face, tried to get myself more awake with each passing second.

"Okay. I see."

"It's just that you know me, I duck out around ten-thirty or so, no matter what's going on, and find out the rest later. But there's one big housing development project that's under review, and I had to stick around for that."

"Sure."

"It's not that there's much open land left in Tyler after three centuries, so it's going to be a nice story of the conflict between the greedy out-of-state developers and—"

"Paula."

"Yes?"

I sat up in bed. I always talk better when I'm sitting up.

"What's going on?"

She paused, and I paused. I was wondering if I should repeat myself, when she sighed and said, "Please don't get mad at me."

"I promise."

"You don't even know what it's about."

"I can think of one or two things."

"All right, smartie, give me just one."

I said, "Seeing me get wounded is doing more than concerning you. It's frightening you."

I could hear faint voices in the background, and I figured she was still at the Tyler Town Hall. Paula said, "As long as I've known you, there's been a slight hint of violence about you. Not that you're a violent man, or that you seek out men and circumstances that can lead to gunplay, or punches, or things on the edge. It's just that proverbial hint of danger. I've always found that attractive in you, my friend. It puts a sharpness on the history-loving, book-loving Lewis that I've come to know. Most men I know are soft...and I don't mean in the physical sense."

A very naughty part of me was going to ask her if that was the case, why wasn't she chasing after Felix, but the bigger, smarter part of me shut up.

"Okay," I said.

"Not too long ago there was gunplay in your living room. I was there. There were no lights. Someone was trying to kill us with a shotgun. It was... well, it took a while for me to lock that up and put it behind me. For the most part. Now that you've been involved again with gunplay..."

I waited, not wanting to interrupt her, and when she paused, I said, "Bad memories are coming back. Stuff that was packed up is getting unpacked."

"Yeah. It doesn't mean I don't want to be with you Lewis, but until this... situation straightens itself out, I want to dial it back a little. Temporarily."

"Temporarily," I said.

"And when it does get resolved, well, I'll take a couple of vacation days and make it up to you. And us."

"Deal," I said. "How about lunch tomorrow?"

"I'd love that," she said, and that was about it.

And when we were done, I went back downstairs, locked the front door, turned off the front outside lights, most of the downstairs lights, but after a brief moment of hesitation, I left the rear deck lights on, leaving them lit for the night.

Then I went back to bed.

THE NEXT MORNING AFTER SHOWERING, shaving and having a quick breakfast of a cup of coffee and some toast, I went back upstairs and retrieved my 9 mm Beretta, and then ducked into my closet and took out a Bianchi leather shoulder holster. I shrugged it on, slid my loaded Beretta inside, and then put on a jacket, and went out to face the day, practicing my Second Amendment rights.

What felt odd was that it didn't feel odd, walking around armed.

But the small bandage on the side of my head probably had something to do with it.

I backed up my Pilot out of the freshly rebuilt shed that worked as a garage and drove up to the Lafayette House to fetch my morning newspapers from its gift shop. After I paid for my four daily papers, I then tried to avoid someone standing in the luxurious lobby, Brady Hill. But he must have had a sixth or seventh sense, working for Alice Hackett, for he turned right into my path, just as I was heading for the door. Brady glared at me, holding a large carry-out cup of coffee from the Lafayette House's dining room, something lumpy dragging down his left suit coat pocket.

"Coming over to tell Alice you've changed your mind?" he asked.

"Nope," I said. "You still running coffee errands for the fair lady?"

He said, "You seemed very sure of yourself yesterday, with that large man helping you."

"Oh, don't worry," I said. "I'm feeling pretty sure of myself right now."

People were milling about, including a camera crew, and I said, "Is Alice sticking around? For real?"

"Like it or not," Brady said, "this place is the current front line against illegal immigration. This is the story."

"If you say so," I said.

"You should cooperate," he said. "There's still time. We could go up to Alice's suite and get you on the air later today. You were a victim of the borderless activists. You should let the country know your story."

"No, thanks," I said. "I've got better things to do."

He made a point of looking at the four newspapers under my arm. "Like catching up on fake news?" he asked in a sneering tone.

"The thing is," I said, walking out, "I'm a real reader, not a fake one."

He tossed out one more thing as I left.

"People who go against Alice Hackett live to regret it!" he said, and I didn't have time for a snappy response.

As I was walking to the Pilot, my cellphone chimed, startling me. I'm happily about a generation behind when it comes to technological advances, and I use my cellphone for—get this—sending and receiving phone calls. I've had this particular iPhone model for nearly a year and have yet to use the text feature.

I fumbled with the phone, getting it out of my coat, and Diane Woods was on the other end.

"How are you doing?"

"Fine," I said. "Head's still on my shoulders, it's a beautiful day, and I'm talking to you."

"How about coming down to the station and talking to me in person? I want to ask you a couple of more questions about yesterday and tell you what I know."

"You got it," I said, signing off. I got back into my Pilot, headed out of the lot, checked the northbound and southbound traffic on Atlantic Avenue, and someone across the street caught my eye.

It was a dented, light yellow Toyota pickup truck, the bed cluttered with lumber and pieces of metal, four dented and used lobster traps, and the driver inside was staring at me.

I had the brief feeling of recognition, of knowing that I knew this scowling man with the thick beard, but not able to place how and where.

There was an opening in the traffic.

Neither of us moved.

He kept on staring.

Now I knew who it was.

It was Billy Bragg, the older brother of Harry Bragg, the head of the Tyler Fishermen Cooperative. I had seen him yesterday, vigorously arguing with his brother Harry on the dock, just after I had come back from the *Elayne D.*

So why was he here?

Late for the morning breakfast buffet at The Lafayette House?

I doubted it.

The traffic moved again, and, in a few seconds, he had joined the southbound traffic, and a minute later, so did I.

We split up about a hundred yards south, when he turned into a half-filled parking lot near the empty beach.

I kept on driving.

13

The Tyler Police Department was in the middle of a transition, upgrading its old concrete bunker-style building to something a number of taxpayers called "the Mansion on the Marshes," and when the light was right over the marshes stretching to Falconer and the horizon, I could see their point. Instead of the concrete cube that looked like it belonged on a Nevada test site for A-bomb testing back in the 1950s, the new place was going to be two-story, with lots of windows and exposed brick and faux turrets. At the moment it was enclosed by scaffolding, but it still looked large and out of place.

Usually small-town taxpayers like those in Tyler would never approve such a behemoth, but through a bit of judicious schedule-juggling and delayed voting, the funds for the project came up during the end of a long, drawn-out town meeting, when the bulk of voters had left in exhaustion and gone home. Earlier in the day, having spent nearly forty minutes debating the necessity of donating $500 to an area animal shelter that took in dogs picked up by the Tyler Animal Control Officer, the thinned-out voters at the end of the day spent two minutes debating the multi-million-dollar budget for a new police station.

Word on the street was Tyler's fire chief was prepping to do something identical next year, though some doubted the Tyler voters could be fooled twice in less than three years.

I found a parking spot among the police cruisers, parked construction vehicles and the pick-up trucks that nearly all New Hampshire police offi-cers drive in their off hours, and as I walked across the muddy parking area, I went up to the glass set of doors leading in and saw a new sign:

NO CONCEALED WEAPONS ALLOWED EXCEPT FOR L.E.

Well, I wasn't law enforcement, and I did have a concealed carry permit for the state of New Hampshire, and I knew almost all of the cops and personnel in the department but still...

Some days I tried to be a good citizen.

I went back to the Pilot, ditched the Beretta and shoulder holster under the front seat, and then went back to the police station, and in about a minute, I was meeting with Detective Sergeant Diane Woods.

Her office was in the rear, and the grimy window, which once offered a view of the marsh and the Falconer Nuclear Power Plant, now offered a view of some scaffolding. There was hammering, drilling and banging going on when I sat down across from Diane, and said, "Doesn't the noise drive you nuts?"

"What noise," she replied, and I was going to joke in return, but I don't think she was joking. I saw a fine dust over every space and folder on her desk, and I was glad I kept my mouth shut.

She picked up a pen. "Hey, how are you feeling?"

"Fine," I said, automatically touching the bandage. "It's getting itchy, which I take as a good sign."

"Sorry, I should have checked in with you earlier. But it's been busy around here."

"Nice understatement," I said. "What's going on?"

She twirled the pen in her hand. "Pretty broad question there, but I'll see what I can do. With regards to your little circus yesterday, I've been working it with the State Police, and we don't have witnesses, or bullet casings, or anything much else. Just one round, recovered from a fender. Plastic fender, so it's in good shape for an eventual match."

"The Lafayette House has a surveillance system on the parking lot, right?"

"True, my friend," she said. "But it's a narrow focus on the lot and Atlantic Avenue. Lots of people milling around, standing, and then you can see people break and run when the gunfire starts. I could even see a black-and-white Lewis Cole diving to the ground and getting trampled."

"I think that hurt more than the bullet grazing me," I said. "And it sounded like pistol fire or revolver fire. Not from a rifle."

"That's what we hear as well."

"Which is odd. If there was going to be sniper fire, why use a pistol? Unless you're very, very good, a rifle is the preferred weapon. One or two shots and you're done. Six shots from a pistol or revolver...sloppy."

"Unh-hunh," she said.

"But I have another thought," I said.

"Go ahead," Diane said. "Nothing we professionals like better than having over-eager amateurs suggesting clues or solutions."

"I'm not that over-eager," I said, "but thanks for listening. Borrow that pen and a slip of paper?"

"Here," she said, passing over a pen and a photocopied sheet announcing the agenda for the upcoming Tyler Selectmen's meeting. I turned the paper over and started sketching, and then showed my results to Diane. She peered down at what I had done and said, "Thank God you learned to type, friend, because you stink at drawing."

"This isn't drawing," I said. "It's sketching. Look. Here's the Lafayette House, its near parking lot, Atlantic Avenue, and the main parking lot. Alice Hackett was standing here, the mob was in one group over here...and look, this is where the second group was milling around. A couple of your uniformed were standing here..."

"Okay," Diane said. "And where's Waldo?"

"Getting a new set of specs...and this is where I was standing, over here."

Diane didn't move her head, looking down.

I went on. "There were six shots. Coming from...over here." I pointed to the north end of the lot, which had a large broken collection of rocks and boulders. "Now. Nobody else was shot or wounded, right?"

"Right."

"Any other rounds go into any of the parked vehicles?"

"Just the one," she said. "Which is in the hands of the State Police."

"So the only thing hit was...me." Diane kept quiet. I tapped the pen at part of my drawing. "Some of her folks are saying that this was an assassination attempt against Alice Hackett. But I was almost twenty feet or so away from her."

Diane finally looked up. "I was thinking that, but it was just one investigative line. But now that you've drawn—"

"Sketched."

"Sketched it out, it does make a certain sense." Diane paused. "You piss off any people lately?"

"I might have pissed off people who didn't like the fact that I reported the drowned bodies from my cove. Including our local Homeland Security friend. And there's the usual suspects from my interesting past, but nothing comes right to mind."

Diane rubbed at the scar on her chin.

"Anything odd happening lately? Hang-up phone calls? Threats? Odd people hanging around?"

I thought, well, there was Billy Bragg, he sure looked odd, but I didn't want to raise a fuss with him and his family. I still wanted to re-check with his younger brother Harry, to see if anything new was going on out there in the Atlantic since yesterday's visit.

"The usual oddball Tyler people and autumn tourists," I said. "But nothing beyond that."

She gave me a caring glance. "You be careful, all right?"

"I'm trying," I said. "Just so you know, I'm carrying for the current situation, though I didn't want to break any rules earlier. So my Beretta is back in my Pilot."

"All right," she said. "You just make sure you get it in your holster or on the passenger's seat when you get out there."

"Why the sign out in the lobby?"

She picked up her pen, twirled it again in her fingers. "If you haven't noticed, there's a disease out there, where we law enforcement members are in the crosshairs, being shot at traffic stops, restaurants, or even in stations. A sign like that won't do anything against a determined shooter, but it might deter someone who's carrying and who's having a bad day."

I nodded. "Makes sense. Anything else going on with the bodies from yesterday?"

"You mean the larger circus? Officially and according to various news organizations, the local Homeland Security office is cooperatively working with local and state police to determine why in hell we've had two incidents where illegals were dumped overboard at night near our fair coastline, with a fair number ending up drowned."

"That's a nice official story," I said. "Care to tell me what's really going on?"

"Sure," she said. "The usual cliché, that we're being treated like mushrooms. Kept in the dark and fed shit. We don't know where these folks might have come from, we don't have evidence of how and where they died, and we don't have evidence how they were shipped here."

Diane tossed the pen on her desk, and the sudden move startled me. She said, "A hell of a thing, with nearly a dozen dead victims in my territory, and I'm prevented from doing a damn thing."

"Have you talked to Mark Stockman from Homeland Security? He's got an office up at McIntosh Air Force Base."

"I know, and yes, I've tried talking to him. He has three messages from me, for all the good that's done."

I kept quiet, and Diane sensed that I was keeping something from her, and she said, "You've talked to him? Really?"

"Uh…"

"Lewis…"

"I visited him yesterday afternoon."

"Oh, really," she said, stretching out the syllables. "It never seemed to me that Agent Stockman was an enthusiast for reporters or magazine writers. How did you get in so quickly?"

"I showed up."

"Did you have an appointment?"

"No."

A smile barely registered on her face. "Supposedly that's ninety-five percent of life, just showing up. How in hell did you convince him to talk to you?"

"It wasn't me that did that," I said. "It was the me from a fair number of years ago, when I was working at the DoD. He was curious about me, my past and situation, and he invited me in for a chit-chat."

"What did you find out?" she asked.

Any other reporter or journalist would have probably said nothing to Diane, her being a government official and The Adversary when it came to press relations, but I'm not much of a journalist and she's much more than a government official.

"Not much," I said. "I tried to get information about why it wasn't easy to track ships at night, and he told me the same old same old. Lack of money, lack of resources, and most of the Coast Guard presence in this part of New England is down in the Caribbean."

She nodded. "Drug interdiction. Our little slice of a Hundred Years' War. Anything else?"

"I asked him where the bodies were being stored. He wouldn't say much, beyond the usual secure government location."

"Probably Area Fifty-One-And-A-Half," Diane said. "Go on."

"He also told me something I should have puzzled out myself," I said. "The bodies are being examined for evidence, like receipts, journals, cell-phones or notes, anything that can possibly track down who the traffickers are and where they come from."

"Plus to see if anybody coming in is on the watch list."

"Very good," I said. "That's the other point."

"Did he say if anything's been found?"

"No."

"Did you ask?"

"Yes," I said. "Even said pretty please and all that."

"Good for you," she said. "You two now best buds? Going out later tonight to have a beer and share secrets about the Deep State?"

A burst of hammering and electric saw humming overhead made us both take a pause, and then some more sawdust sprinkled down on Diane's desk. In the quick silence that followed, I said, "Definitely not best buds. He asked me if I wanted to do some snoop work for him and Homeland Security, and I told him no."

"Really?"

"Yeah, we couldn't agree on what kind of dental plan I'd get," and that made Diane laugh, which was good, and there was another burst of hammering, and then someone up overhead shouted, his voice muffled, "Shit! Hit my goddamn thumb again!"

Diane shook her head, swept the sawdust off her desk again, and I said, "When does this little home improvement project get finished?"

"Sometime next year," she said. "Though if some of those workers make it without being threatened with bodily harm by then, it'll be a miracle."

"It sure looks like one big project."

"Yeah," she said. "The chief worked his way up from being a patrolman, up through the detective bureau and the officer ranks. He always said once he became chief, he'd turn this station into something he could call his own. Bless his little heart, it looks like it's going to happen."

"And what's going to be left to do when you become chief," I asked, and if her eyes had been equipped with laser beams, I'm sure I would have quickly turned into a pile of smoldering ash.

"Hah," she said. "Hah. Hah." There was no humor in those words, and then she said, "Things okay with you and Paula? She start nesting yet?"

"So far so good," I said. "And what's nesting?"

"Poor boy," she said. "First she starts with a toothbrush. Then some spare undies. Maybe some slacks and a top. And before you know it, half your bathroom is filled up with her makeup and doodads."

"No nesting yet," I said. "But there is a toothbrush."

Another smile. "So it begins. Anything else you can give me, either about your unfortunate incident or your meeting with Agent Stockman?"

"No, but I'll let you know if something comes up," and I started getting up from my chair, recognizing her politeness in not telling me to get the hell out of her office so she could get back to work.

"Thanks," she said, and I added, "Oh, can I ask you a question?"

"Since you've been the model of a cooperative citizen, sure," she said. "What do you need?"

"Billy Bragg," I said. "Local fisherman, brother of Harry Bragg, who's—"

"Oh, we know the Bragg brothers pretty well around here," she said.

"In what way?"

"Harry's the good brother, runs the co-op, volunteers on the Conservation Commission, stuff like that," she said. "Rumor is that he might run for selectmen next year. Poor bastard."

"And what about Billy?"

"I don't have enough time to go into our run-ins with Billy," she said. "Let's just say we know him quite well, as do the State Police, the Wentworth County Sheriff's Department, and various state and federal fishing agencies. Anything else you need to know?"

"Where he lives."

"For real?" she said. "What for?"

"Just trying to cover all the bases," I said. "I want to see if he knows anything about what's going on out in the near waters."

"Good luck with that," she said. "Make sure you're on your best behavior."

"Detective Sergeant, I'm always on my best behavior."

"Yeah, well, you better be, or you'll be visiting the Exonia Emergency Room two days in a row," she said. "If you really need to see him, go check out the Tyler River Campground. That's where he's staying."

"Thanks," I said, moving toward the door, and then thinking of something. "Wait a sec. I thought the campground closed after Labor Day?"

"What, you like to hang out at the campground on your off hours, playing horseshoes or tether ball?"

"No," I said. "I just remember seeing the sign outside the front gate, saying open from Memorial Day to Labor Day."

"Well," she said, raising her voice as the hammering grew louder. "Sometimes signs lie."

"What about town ordinances? Don't they restrict the campground's operating hours?"

"Go away," she said, but smiling at me. "I'm a police detective, not the code enforcement officer. You'll find out soon enough."

14

The Tyler River Campground was a ten-minute drive from the police station, going west on Route 101 bordered on each side by marshlands, and then getting onto Route One, heading south. If I drove another ten minutes, that would take me into Massachusetts, but our neighboring fair commonwealth wasn't on today's agenda, so I stayed on the road until I got close to the town line with Tyler Falls and saw the sign for Tyler River Campground. Sure enough, it said OPEN FROM MEMORIAL DAY TO LABOR DAY, and other, smaller sign said, CLOSED FOR THE SEASON, SEE YOU NEXT YEAR! but the gate was open, and I took a right onto a narrow dirt road.

The road was bumpy and led into a pine forest with widely spaced trees, and past a small wooden cottage with a small wooden sign that said OFFICE. But the door and the windows to the cottage were boarded up.

Then the campground proper came into view, and I slowed down.

There were trailers scattered throughout the thin woods, each with their own site, but this wasn't the type of campground that you saw in glossy brochures or on the website of the Greater Tyler Chamber of Commerce. Most of the trailers were small campers with hitches and wheels, but all were disconnected from cars or trucks, the hitches kept straight and in place by wood beams or cement blocks.

About half of the campers had blue tarps stretched over their roofs for additional protection from rain and snow, and there were also clotheslines stretched between trees, some campfires or outside gas stoves slowly burning, and some kids running around. There were also some tents out in the woods.

I got out of my Pilot. Some adults stared at me, and then went back to what they were doing: mending clothes, cutting firewood, working on the open side of a trailer, or smoking and drinking.

This wasn't a campground.

This was a village.

Dogs raced around, barking and chasing each other.

A woman stepped out from a near tent, spotted me, frowned, and came over. She had on dirty blue jeans, black rubber boots, gray sweatshirt and a dull red down vest, zippered open. Her hair was black streaked with gray, pulled back in a ponytail, and her face was worn, eyes suspicious, like in her life every other person she had met had done her harm.

She came up to me as dogs barked in the woods. "You a cop?"

"No."

"You from the town?"

"No."

She slowly nodded. "The county? The state? Some welfare group?"

"No on all three counts," I said.

"Hunh," she said. "Then who the hell are you?"

"Lewis Cole," I said. "I live down at the beach. I'm looking for Billy Bragg."

"Don't know Billy Bragg," she said.

I looked once more at the collection of trailers and the few tents. "I'm sorry, may I ask who you are?"

She shrugged. "Guess that's all right. I'm Fran Dependhal."

"Are you the owner here?"

She spat on the ground. "Do I look like I own anything as grand as this dump?"

I said, "I'm not sure what you look like."

Fran gave me what some folks called a stink eye, and then slowly smiled. "This place is owned by my cousin Bonnie and her idiot husband

Paul. When the end of season came, I convinced them to keep the place open."

"But I thought it was against town ordinances to keep campsites opened year-round."

"Yeah," Fran said. "Look, you got a smoke?"

"Sorry, I don't."

A woman from one of the trailers yelled out, "Fran! My honey pot is near full. You sure the truck is coming today?"

Fran yelled back, "That's what they told me! If it don't come, then go to a neighbor to do your business. Don't need you stinking up the place none."

I said, "Who are these folks?"

Her eyes hardened, and she said, "Whaddya think? They're the ones around Tyler and North Tyler and Tyler Falls who pump the gas, clean out the motel rooms, and serve pricey dinner specials that could feed their family for a week. Rents and real estate around here for scores of miles are out of reach for folks like that. Here, they could live near their jobs and do what has to be done."

"But the town..."

"So far, so good," she said. "Nobody's made an official complaint, no neighbors have raised a ruckus, and so far, the town of Tyler is looking the other way. Sure, we're breaking about a half dozen rules and ordinances keeping this place open for the winter, but these folks have no other place to go. We also don't want the state or welfare folks poking in. They do that, lot of these kids will be stripped away and put in foster care."

"But the liability...how did you convince your cousin and her husband to keep the place open?"

Fran squinted and smiled wearily. "Two ways. One was with Bonnie. She's active in her church and I convinced her that it'd be her Christian duty to support local folks, instead of raising money for overseas missions. So she worked on her idiot husband Paul...which took a bit of effort, but it all worked out."

"How?"

The weary smile widened. "Because I called Paul and told him that unless he kept the campground open for the fall and winter, I'd tell my cousin that he tried to squeeze my boobs three Christmases ago, under the mistletoe. That worked."

I wasn't sure how to respond to that, and she said, "You from a bank?"

"No."

"Loan company?"

"No," I said. "I'm a magazine writer."

"Which magazine?"

"*Shoreline*," I said. "I write a column for it called Granite Shores."

"I see," she said. "Never heard of it. Can you prove it?"

Her questioning seemed off, but it also seemed like I was making progress. I took out my wallet, passed over my business card and also my New Hampshire press identification.

She kept the business card, gave me the press identification back.

"Why do you want to see Billy Bragg?"

"Working on a column about the bodies washing up the past several weeks," I said. "I wanted to see if he had seen anything odd or unusual."

Fran said, "Well, let's go over and see if he's home."

"Thanks," I said, being too polite to point out that a few minutes ago, she denied even knowing him.

She led me along a dirt path that wound its way among various camp-sites, and she returned a few shouts and "hellos," and I still could not believe what I was seeing, here in my Tyler, and here in a very rich part of the state.

I said, "This campground. It looks like something out of the Dust Bowl."

"The Dust Bowl?" she asked.

"Yes," I said. "The Dust Bowl, back in—"

Fran interrupted me. "I wasn't inquiring. I wanted to make sure I had heard you correctly. The Dust Bowl. Came in three waves, 1934, 1936 and 1939. A lengthy drought and poor farming techniques caused it, and it was mostly centered in Oklahoma and Texas. About a half million families were left homeless."

She stopped talking, and so did I.

We resumed our walking, and after three paces I said, "My apologies. I sometimes get into lecturing mode. I didn't mean anything by it."

Two paces later she said, "I used to teach American history and geography in Manchester. Left teaching, went into administration. Ended up as an assistant principal over in Hooksett."

"Oh," I said.

"You want to know how I ended up here?"

"If you want to tell me," I said.

"Hold on," she said. "This is Billy Bragg's place."

The place was a small camper, its hitch held up by concrete blocks. A blue tarp was hanging off the roof, held down by ropes and twine. The side door had a NO TRESPASSING sign hanging crookedly off to the side. A heap of wire and metal lobster traps were piled to the right, along with piles of rope, buoys, chains, scraps of plastic and canvas. There were two rusting 55-gallon drums where it looked like trash had been burned in the past.

"Charming," I said.

"It works," she said. "As you can see, he's not home."

"Any idea when he might be back?"

"Billy keeps his own hours."

"That's what I hear, among other things."

She shoved her hands into her down vest pockets. "Like what?"

"Like...he gets around."

"Oh, yeah, I know," she said. "Drunk driving arrests, getting into trouble with the Tyler Police, Coast Guard, Fish and Game, Marine Fisheries. That's what folks hear. But there's more to him than that. You see those traps?"

"I do."

"Maybe he keeps a few of the lobster shorts he pulls up, instead of tossing them over the side like he should. Maybe he catches cod when he shouldn't be catching cod. And maybe that lobster and fish comes back here, for free, to help these families eat something fresh and healthy for a change."

I just looked at the sad-looking trailer and the equally sad trailers and tents around us. She said, "This place is rough. It's not perfect. It's cold and gonna get colder, and the town doesn't provide any services. But we make do. And I run a tight ship. No heavy drinking, no fighting, no late night hell-raising, and the only drugs I let in here is some pot. That's it. And if I need muscle, if some hard case is giving me lip and doesn't back down, I call on Billy Bragg to help things out."

"I see."

"Good," she says. "When he comes back, I'll pass on your business card to him. He might call you tonight. Or tomorrow. Or in a month. That's how he works."

"Thanks," I said. "I appreciate it."

"He's been busy lately," Fran said. "He says something big is going on. Something he hopes will change his life around. Said he'd spread the wealth around here, to his neighbors."

I remember him arguing with his brother, down at the Tyler Fishermen's Cooperative.

Something big is going on.

Fran sighed. "I hope he's right. But sometimes...you know, sometimes you chase after something, and it might turn around and bite you in the ass." She turned and I turned with her, and she said, "Once I thought I had it all, the world by the proverbial tail, all that happy horseshit. Started off being a teacher, slipped over to administration, thought my future was bright... then I couldn't sleep at night, started drinking, and started doing more when things got worse."

She was talking, so I kept my mouth shut. A couple more dogs barked, some kids were laughing, and there was another shout of, "Fran! When you get a moment, can you come over here?"

"Lost my job, made bad decisions when it come to my partners, both male and female...and here I am."

"Here for the duration?" I asked.

"Oh, Christ, yes," she said. "I...I've changed. Things have changed. I can't keep a job, I can't take orders, and I can't live under a roof. I need to be someplace where I can step outside and have room to breathe, look up at the sky, look up at the stars."

"Fran!" came another call, from an older man this time, and she said, "Looks like I gotta go. Hey, tell me this. You think Billy Bragg might be involved in smuggling those poor people ashore? I mean, that's what I thought when I heard him talk about something big happening soon."

"I don't know," I said. "And from what I know so far, I don't think he'd tell me if I asked him."

"Yeah, that's about right," Fran said. "But I do know this. If I found out that he was helping these illegals come ashore, I'd kick his ass out of here so fast he'd have to crap through his nose. Even though he is one tough son of a bitch."

"Excuse me?" I asked, surprised at the change in her tone of voice.

Fran said, "These people out there, they can't make a good living on what they get paid. And when illegals come in, they get paid under the table, they don't pay taxes, their employers sure as hell don't pay for their health care or any other taxes. So the grunt jobs get taken...meaning the locals who only went to high school and couldn't do any better, they get screwed."

"But you can't just blame these people, can you?" I asked. "There's the government and the businesses who take advantage—"

"You heard me," she said. "I gotta go. And I'm going to see Isabelle, who's got three kids after two failed marriages, and all she knows is how to clean motel rooms, and she lost her job 'cause she was replaced by a woman who worked for half the salary and couldn't speak a lick of English."

Fran moved off to the woods, and I went back to my Honda Pilot.

15

I made a brief stop at the Tyler Post Office to get my mail, which was just advertising circulars, fliers, and a bill from my electric utility. I couldn't remember the last time I had even gotten a letter. Or even a postcard. When I got home and headed into the parking lot of the Lafayette House, the lot was about two-thirds full, with most of the cars and SUVs parked near Atlantic Avenue, so the paying guests wouldn't have to walk too far to get to their luxurious surroundings.

A dark blue Volvo, though, was parked near the dirt path that led down to my little home, and as I started that way, the driver's side door of the Volvo opened up and a woman stepped out, gave me a hesitant wave.

I stopped the Pilot and lowered the window. On the passenger's seat my 9 mm Beretta was still holstered, and I slid an advertising flyer from the local Hannaford's supermarket over the pistol. The woman from the Volvo had the look of someone who had never seen a pistol in her life, and I didn't want to frighten her.

"Yes?" I asked, as she came up to me. She seemed about five feet tall, wearing gray slacks and a black wool coat, and her light blonde hair was expertly cut and styled.

"Are you Lewis Cole?" she asked in a pleasant voice. "The magazine writer who lives in the old Coast Guard artillery building?"

"That's me," I said.

"And you're the one that discovered that poor drowned woman and baby?"

"I am," I said, wondering why she was here, and then she explained it all in her next sentence.

"My name's Mo Walsh," she said. "I'm from the Open Arms Coalition, and I was wondering if I could talk to you for a few moments."

Not that I didn't want to be polite and neighborly, but I really wasn't in the mood, and she seemed to sense that and said, "Please? Just for a few minutes. We could meet up at the Lafayette House for some chai. Or coffee."

A cup of coffee would be a nice break from the morning, so I decided to change my mind and be polite and neighborly. I said, "All right, Mo, I'll meet you up there."

"Grand," she said, and she went back to her Volvo, and I backed up my Pilot to drive across the street.

IN THE LAFAYETTE House we went to the restaurant and shared a table with a white tablecloth and fine clean silverware and very pricey breakfast items, and I had a queasy feeling that we were both a lifetime and a fat bank account away from the Tyler River Campground.

The waiter was a young man with two black stud earrings and moussed hair, and I ordered a plain cup of coffee, while Mo spent a few minutes interrogating the waiter about which teas might be free trade and organic —necessitating him going back into the kitchen twice to seek answers— and when he finally left with our complete orders, Mo gave me a satisfied smile and said, "Even one person can change the world, if he or she sets his or her mind to it."

I was going to say that the only thing she changed in the last several minutes was the previous happy mood of our young waiter, but I kept my mouth shut. "What would you like to talk about?"

She laughed. Her teeth were perfectly shaped and white, and with her coat off, she had on a light tan sweater with a string of pearls around her neck.

"Do you have a day? A week? A month?"

"Not at the moment," I said.

"Sorry," she said, clasping her hands together. Her fingernails were a fresh red. "My dear departed husband Troy, he said I could spend a week debating the finer points of international trade policy without taking a breath. I guess that's just who I am."

Our waiter returned with our respective cups of coffee and tea, and she said, "I just wanted to know what it was like yesterday, when you found that poor woman."

"Did you read *The Tyler Chronicle*?"

"Yes."

"That's pretty much it," I said. "Got up, saw something floating in my little cove, pulled in the body, called the police."

She nodded, blew over her teacup. "Did you know she was coming?"

"Say what?"

"Did you know she was coming."

"The drowned woman? How would I know she was coming?"

"Maybe I phrased it wrong," she said, taking a sip. Mo put her teacup down, leaned over like we were some part of a conspiracy. "I meant...were you expecting her? Was there an accident? Did the boat overturn?"

"I'm sure there was an accident somewhere, but I wasn't expecting her. Why do you think that?"

"Because your home is in a prime spot, that's why," she said. "Isolated cove. Ready access to Atlantic Avenue. From there, fifteen minutes later, you're on the Interstate. Your home would be a perfect place for a way station."

"Maybe so, but it wasn't."

Another prim sip of tea from her. "You can tell me. It'll be confidential, I promise."

"There's nothing to tell," I said. "Why would you think that?"

"Because of your background."

"A magazine writer?"

Her voice lowered some. "No...before that. With your work with the Department of Defense. As a spy."

While my previous employment prior to coming to New Hampshire wasn't a secret on par with that day's nuclear launch codes, I was surprised that it was so widely recognized that this random woman would know about it.

The curse of living in a small New England town. Pretty soon everybody knows your business.

"I wasn't a spy," I said. "I was a research analyst, working in a cubicle."

"Just words," Mo said. "It'd just make sense that perhaps you were feeling guilty for working at the Pentagon, and you would want to make amends by secretly helping out the refugees who try to make it to our shores."

As challenging as it was, I kept my voice low and even when I said, "I have absolute zero guilt about my service at the Department of Defense, so whatever you're thinking is one hundred percent wrong."

Mo didn't seem taken aback by that. She just went on and said, "However that might be, Mister Cole, we're still looking for people to help."

"Who's we?"

"The Open Arms Coalition," she said. "We think these poor unfortunates, they should be welcomed here, and not be made into criminals. Homeland Security and the other immigration agencies...they should be defunded and their resources diverted to refugee relief."

"Well...that's something," I said, still trying to be polite. "So, you're talking open borders, then?"

A crisp nod. "We're all humans in this world. All of us. Borders are just artificial boundaries, that's all. Look at the borders in Africa and the Middle East. They were drawn by the imperialists for their own needs and desires. Why should we honor the work of those privileged white men?"

"Because most countries and people have gotten used to them?"

She gave me the look of a first-grade teacher, looking at her dullest student, coming to the first day of school wearing nothing but pajamas.

"That's not progress," she said. "That's a hidebound mentality, and we intend to change it. And we'd like your help."

"My help? How?"

"We're having a get-together at the North Tyler Grange Hall tomorrow night," she said. "We'd love to have you as a public speaker."

"To speak about what?"

"About what it was like to recover that poor drowned woman. And her poor child."

"It wasn't much fun," I said. "How about that?"

"But you could say much, much more," she said. "Raise awareness. Put yourself on our side. Wouldn't you do that for us?"

Some time ago I was asked to join the side of Alice Hackett and her acolytes, to speak on her behalf, and now I was being asked to join Mo Walsh and her acolytes, to speak on the opposite behalf. North and South, Alpha and Omega.

The young male waiter came back and said, "Anything else?" and there was a hesitation in his voice, like he was hoping beyond hope that the woman sitting across from me wasn't going to ask for anything that would require a sociology lesson or a lecture.

I took pity on the young man and said, "Check, please," and he produced it so quickly that I had the feeling he had it prepared, just in case something good would happen, like our departure.

I put my hand out for the check and Mo beat me to it. "What's your answer, Mister Cole?"

"I'll pick up the check," I said.

"No, you won't," she said. "It was my invite, my responsibility. I will take care of it. And I meant the other question. Will you join us?"

I finished my coffee, used my white cloth napkin. "No."

"Why?"

"I like being independent, not joining any causes."

Even though she was paying for the check, she still looked disappointed. "Even when it's doing good?"

I got up.

"Especially when it's claiming to do good."

Mo lowered her head and started digging through her purse, and I went out, checked the time. I'd had a busy morning, and I was hoping to see if Paula was free for lunch, but I wanted to go home first, go through the mail, and do a couple of other odds and ends.

I got into my Pilot, turned around in the parking lot, and as I went up against Atlantic Avenue, it was déjà vu all over again.

Billy Bragg was waiting for me in his truck, across the way.

16

But this time, he didn't move. He just glared at me, face screwed up, angry.

So I decided to take the challenge.

When the traffic cleared, I pulled across Atlantic Avenue and stopped right next to his battered pickup truck, me facing the ocean, him facing the road.

He lowered the window of his pickup truck.

I did the same in my Pilot.

He said, "You've been asking questions about me?"

"No," I said.

His eyes were narrow with hate, and he said, "That's bullshit. You were at the campground just a while ago, poking around."

"I was at the campground, and I was poking around, but I wasn't asking questions about you. I just wanted to know where you were so I could talk to you."

"Why the hell should I talk to you?"

I know it's not fair but with both of our windows open, there was the scent of fish, stale beer, old tobacco and sweat wafting over to my direction. "Because of your friendly nature?"

"What?"

His hands were tight around the steering wheel, and I had the feeling he'd be happy to have them around my throat. I said, "Billy, I don't mean to cause you any trouble. I'm just a magazine writer, doing a story about the refugees drowning off our beaches."

"Why the fuck should you care?"

"Because two of them drifted ashore, right in back of my house. A mother and her baby."

"You think I got something to do with that?"

I thought about Fran, back at the campground, saying Billy was preparing for a big score.

I said, "You've got a lot of time out on the water. I just wanted to talk to you, see if you've seen anything out there newsworthy. That's it."

Billy wasn't having any of it. He swore at me a few more times and said, "Stay away from me, stay away from my business."

"I'll do my best, but I'm still a curious fellow. Sorry about that."

He grinned. Surprisingly enough, his teeth were shiny and white. "Yeah, there's a story about curious cats and what happens to them. Am I right? Like what happened to you at Alice Hackett's rally the other day. Somebody took a potshot at you, right?"

I was now glad my 9 mm pistol was within easy reach. "That's right."

"Well, you stop being curious around me, or my friends and I will see how much of a cat you are."

With that, he put his truck into drive and quickly pulled out into Atlantic Avenue, nearly T-boning a light blue Honda CRV that honked its horn long and loud in protest. I turned to see him disappear south, and then I closed up the Pilot's window and made my way home.

AT HOME I flipped through and trashed the mail, except for the electric bill from my utility, charmingly called Unitil. When I had first moved back to New Hampshire, the local utility had been called the Exonia and Tyler Electric Company, which just seemed so quaint and right. Now, with quaintness being stamped out and ground down whenever possible, I still missed that cute little logo on the billing envelope that suggested my power came from a couple of guys named Tom and Frank.

With my mail examination completed, I went to my phone, called the

Tyler Chronicle to see if Paula was available for lunch, but her extension went straight to voicemail. Back in the day, the *Chronicle* could afford to have a receptionist and telephone operator who would take a message and tell you where someone had gone—"oh, she's across the street getting a cup of coffee"—and that bit of quaintness had also been stamped out a long time ago.

I went to my sliding glass doors, looked out over the rear deck, at the churning Atlantic Ocean. Decades ago, somewhere out there, my Irish descendants had climbed into ships to bring them here. But they had come here legally, following whatever simple laws and rules were in place more than a century ago.

But suppose their quiet and peaceful hamlets were being shelled, strafed and dusted with mustard gas? Could I have blamed them for trying everything and anything to get out of there?

I felt like a walk.

I put my coat on and went back outside.

THE TIDE WAS RECEDING, and I made my way down to the small cove, sand, gravel and small rocks. I put my hands in my pockets and started north, looking and gazing, just trying to let random thoughts pass through, about what I've seen, who I've talked to, and just remembering how cold that dead woman had been, bringing her into what was thought of a promised land.

Some promise.

When I couldn't get much farther without climbing gear, I turned around and headed south, back to my house, and I came upon a man walking in my direction, dressed in knee-high boots, camo pants and jacket, and with what looked to be an AR-15 rifle hanging off his shoulder.

Not that I much mind folks exercising their Second Amendment rights, but my pistol was back up in my kitchen, and seeing heavily armed men in my vicinity wasn't a typical occurrence.

We both got closer, and he nodded at me, and I nodded at him. Typical cheery New Hampshire greeting. He seemed to be in his late twenties, with unkempt brown hair and beard.

"Hey," he said.

"How's it going," I said.

He stopped and I did the same, and I said, "I didn't think deer hunting season started this soon."

"It doesn't," he said.

"Mind if I ask why you're carrying, then?"

"Don't mind," he said, looking behind himself, and then past me. "I'm on patrol, that's all."

"Okay," I said, deciding I'd been remiss in making introductions. "My name's Lewis Cole. I live here on Tyler Beach."

He held out a hand and I gave it a quick, firm shake. "Josh Eaton. I'm from Falconer."

Falconer was two towns south of Tyler, and I said, "That's one mighty long patrol you're making."

He smiled. "Not that much. I started out down there, by Weymouth Point, and I'm working my way north."

I said, "Pretty soon you're going to run out of beach."

"That's all right," Josh said. "We got folks covering the rest of the shoreline, up and down, from Kittery to Salisbury."

I've been in New Hampshire long enough to know that seeing a man armed like this wasn't necessarily a matter of concern, though if he had been miraculously transported to parts of New York, Massachusetts and California, for instance, the police response would have been quick and severe.

But not necessarily in a state whose official motto was "Live free or die."

I said, "So who's we, if you don't mind me asking."

"Wentworth County Free Militia," he said.

"Sorry, that's new to me."

Again, the look behind him and beyond me. "That's all right, we haven't been around that long. We only started up since the bodies started coming ashore, and the government wouldn't do anything about the problem."

"The problem being..."

"Our borders are too loose, too relaxed. And those dead bodies, they're just a scam."

A flash of angry memory, hauling in that dead woman, and then eventually finding her drowned infant, fastened to her chest.

"A scam?"

A firm, knowing nod. "That's right. You see, these bodies, they're either fake, or folks that died in a hospital or nursing home or something. They get tossed in the water, wash up ashore, and then it starts people feeling sorry for 'em."

"You mean, the refugees?"

"The illegals," he said, gently correcting me. "Yeah, it's just a scam so that the locals see all those dead bodies ashore, they feel like they need to do something. Like welcoming them all in, give 'em instant welfare, food stamps, cellphones, free healthcare and stuff like that."

"And your patrol, you're trying to do what, catch them in the act?"

"That's right," he said. "Catch them offloading the bodies, make a citizen's arrest, get the real news out about what they're trying to do."

I was tempted to ask Josh who "they" were, but my head was already spinning with what I had heard. He eyed me closer and said, "Looks like you don't like what we're doing."

"It's an interesting theory," I said. "But I helped bring in one of the drowning victims, the other day. With her dead baby strapped to her chest. I don't think it was a scam. She seemed pretty real to me."

"Yeah, but do you know where she was from?"

I said, "Sorry, she wasn't wearing an Epcot Center T-shirt. I have no idea where she came from."

Josh gently kicked at one stone in the water, and then another. "That's an attitude you've got there."

"Thanks," I said. "It's all mine."

"Yeah, well, you look like you think I'm trespassing. Right?"

That question was a trap, which I generously decided not to enter. "Some might say that," I said.

"Hah," Josh said. "If you've lived here as long as you said you have, then you know there's no such thing as private property on the shoreline. It's all open to everyone. Anyone can walk up and down these eighteen miles and it's all legal."

"That's what I've heard."

"Yeah, well," and he turned, "back over there a ways, somebody's put up some 'No Trespassing' signs. There's no law about trespassing here."

"Maybe it's a suggestion, and not an order."

Josh didn't seem to know what to say about that, so he said, "Well, I need to get back to my patrol."

"Must be rough, walking up and down here."

"Well, I work nights at the Walmart distribution center, so all I'm giving up is some sleep. But it's important, for my kids and their kids, to have a country that controls its borders. Don't you agree?"

I started to walk back to my house. "Enjoy your day."

"Oh, I will," he said. "You can count on that, Mister Cole."

BACK HOME I made sure I knew exactly where my 9 mm pistol was located and found out I had a phone message waiting for me. I thought it was Paula but after I checked the sole message, it certainly wasn't.

"Hey," came the voice of Felix Tinios. "You know who this is. That place that has the piano, let's get together. At one? Call me if you can't make it. But I think you'll want to make it. I've got something for you. Later."

I could make it.

I went around to the kitchen to get a quick drink of water, and then I looked out the window and saw a member of the Wentworth County Free Militia stroll by, armed and ready for whatever black plot was about to reveal itself to him.

17

At one p.m. I parked my Pilot at the Lady Manor House, a cute little inn up in North Tyler, the mostly ignored small community next to Tyler and its famed beach. Like my house, it's situated on an isolated cove on the Atlantic, but that's where the similarity ends. My house is old, battered around, a mix of building and re-building styles over the years, and the Lady Manor House is elegant and compact, sort of like a smaller version of the Lafayette House.

The dining room was about a third full, and the glassed-in piano alcove with a view of the rocky shore and the distant Isles of Shoals was empty. Felix was already there, a glass of San Pellegrino before him, wearing light gray slacks and an open neck blue Oxford dress shirt. Unlike some of his ethnic brethren, Felix isn't into wearing gold jewelry or necklaces nestled into his prominent chest hair.

I sat across from him and he said, "Still wearing that bit of gauze?"

I reflexively touched the side of my temple. "I guess I am."

"Trying to impress the ladies, then?"

I sat down and said, "Doubt it. Doesn't seem to be working."

"Anything develop on the police end about that shooting?"

"No," I said. "No witnesses, the surveillance cameras from the Lafayette

House didn't show anything, and as much as she's a lamb, Diane Woods and the Tyler Police Department currently have their hands full."

An enthusiastic young man named Ken, wearing black slacks, white dress shirt and a tiny black bowtie, took our order. He hovered around Felix, smiling, occasionally touching his shoulder, making lunch recommendations, and then going back out to the kitchen.

Felix and I exchanged quiet looks, and then he said, "You're still poking around about these drowned refugees. Correct?"

"I am."

"Any progress?"

"Lack of progress, I suppose. I've talked to the local head of Homeland Security, Diane Woods, a woman who wants to welcome them with open arms and gluten-free cheesecake, and a guy who's part of a local militia who wants to fight them on the beaches and send them back."

"Hell of a mix."

"Yeah. Plus Alice Hackett, that cable TV talking head, she and her assistant want me to appear on her cable show. I told them no."

"You don't like TV?"

"I don't like her."

"Anything else?" Felix asked, and there was a gentle inquiry there, but also a deep seriousness. He told me he had something, which meant he did. Felix wasn't one for playing games. But what he was doing now, I figured, was seeing what I knew and how that was going to tie into his later reveal.

I said, "I've talked to two brothers involved in the fishing business. One seems to be nice, the other doesn't like me at all. Neither one is saying that they're seeing darkened freighters coming in at night, shoving people off into life rafts and small boats, and then scooting away."

"Fishermen never like to talk," he said. "Not surprising."

"And you?"

He ran a thick finger around the rim of his water glass. "Hearing things. I've done some quiet poking around. I'm figuring you'd like to know more."

"I'd love to know more," I said.

A pause. "All right. I pass this along with the usual fair and thorough warning that this is an area I don't deal with. So my...influence and importance is near nil."

"I hear you."

"I know you hear me," Felix said. "I want to make sure you understand me. That means if I give you some information and you dive in with your usual attitude of truth, justice, and what passes for the American way, I might not be there to help you."

"All right."

His face seemed to darken. "Just to be clear, that means me intervening on your behalf, accompanying you into danger with my rugged good looks and heavy firepower, or riding to the rescue just about the time you're going to be shoved into a woodchipper, feet first and wide awake so you're alive and conscious until your lower legs are flying out in front of you in bloody dust and bone fragments. Lewis, I just might not be able to help you."

My mouth was dry, and I realized our enthusiastic waiter hadn't brought my drink.

"Okay," I said.

"Okay," he said. "Shall I proceed?"

"Please."

A formal nod. "It's a quiet, powerful, and well-financed group. A mix of Russians and Turks, with a few Greeks tossed in for flavoring. They've been bumped out of the Mediterranean, and they're hoping to set up shop here. But mistakes have been made."

"Yeah," I said. "Bodies washing up. Big Federal presence up and down the seacoast. Lots of news media attention to round things off."

"And that's only what's out there in the public."

"Oh, there's more?"

He rubbed at his chin. "Lots more. If you have the time, check out the obits in the *Boston Globe* and the *Providence Journal* for the last couple of months. A fair number of young men have died suddenly, unexpectedly or without warning."

"Usually that's code language from somebody dying from an overdose."

"Well, among some families, it means someone having a closed casket at the funeral service because his head was missing."

Our late lunch thankfully came in to break up the mood, a sautéed vegetable and linguini dish for Felix, a thick bowl of clam chowder for me. Thick means putting a spoon in the middle of the chowder and seeing if it stands up or not. Mine did. There was also no tomato in sight. Whatever that's called, mixed in with clams or fish, it is not a chowder.

Ken dropped my food off and then went back to Felix, making sure everything was in order for him, brushing off a piece of invisible lint from his right shoulder, laughing too loud at Felix's quiet remarks.

He left before I could remind him of my iced tea. Felix raised an eyebrow, and I got up, found my way to the far waiter station, found some water glasses, and filled mine from a tap.

When I got back, Felix said, "Heck of a place."

"Nice service," I said.

"You think?"

We didn't say anything but we didn't talk about the elephant sitting comfortably on the other side of the room, and when we were done and coffee was ordered and delivered, Felix rubbed at his chin again and said, "I have a cousin on my dad's side. She has a son that has...challenged her. Nico's been in a few scrapes, here and there, and I always told her that I could help out with things, get him away from the life. But Cora said no, she could handle it."

"And now she can't handle it?"

"She's too afraid to handle it," he said. "So it's now my turn."

"Is Nico involved with some maritime activities?"

"True," Felix said. "What he saw, what he was involved with, scared him out of what little wits he has. He's stuck somewhere. Cora asked me for help, and I said I'd do it, on one condition."

"What's that?"

Ken came back, gently deposited the check in a black leather case, and gave Felix a cheery, "Hope to see you again."

Felix waited until he was out of earshot and said, "That Nico would tell me and a friend of mine what's going on, and who's running the support crew on shore," Felix said. "These people aren't being dumped ashore without somebody to greet them. He gives us the name and address, he gets a new life where his previous friends can't find him."

"Did he agree?"

"He certainly did," Felix said. "Didn't even wait for me to stop talking."

"Scary times," I said.

"You know it," Felix said, and he paused, looked out at the Atlantic, and said, "What's going on here and now...I think of my folks, coming over here from Sicily and Greece. It was a time of poverty that was part of the system, year after year, generation after generation. They came here with hope to make something better, if not for themselves, but then for their kids."

I kept my mouth shut. Listening to Felix talk philosophically was an unusual event. He said, "Those folks out there now...it's hope, but they're mostly coming here from fear. Towns and villages being bombed, machine-gunned, hit with gas. That's understandable. But the folks who step forward and take advantage of them...they're not to be crossed, Lewis, or encountered, or angered. So after we meet with Nico, tread carefully."

"Any idea when?"

"Tomorrow," he said. "Or maybe the day after. I'll let you know. You going to pay the bill?"

"I can't see how I can avoid it," I said, going into my wallet, pulling out a credit card. "Thanks."

I took the check out, signed the bill, and added a nice tip. Behind the bill was a business card for The Lady Manor, and scribbled on the back was a phone number and a handwritten note.

Call me!

I gave the business card over to Felix. He looked at it and I said, "Must be nice, being so popular, no matter which side of the aisle you reside on."

"You have no idea," Felix said.

18

I called Paula Quinn at the office and on her cellphone, and both calls went to that mysterious part of cyberspace called voicemail, where messages from romantic to tragic lived forever.

It was mid-afternoon, and I decided to go for a road trip, and since I was north of home, it seemed logical to head north, and I did so until I reached the gates of McIntosh Air Force Base and then rolled up to the buildings occupied by Homeland Security. I parked in the same spot I used last time, and I entered the building and went up to the same glassed-in counter as before. And speaking of before, the severe-looking woman in a two-piece gray suit was sitting at her station.

I recognized her, but being the professional she was, she pretended she didn't recognize me.

"Yes?" she asked.

"I'd like to see Agent Mark Stockman," I said, sliding my driver's license and press identification through the opening at the bottom of the thick glass.

She didn't bother looking at my identification.

"He's not in."

"Are you sure?"

She looked as insulted as a Catholic nun being asked about her dating habits. "He's not here."

"Do you know when he'll be back?"

"No."

"Do you know where he is?"

"Yes."

"And...I guess you won't tell me where he is."

A slow nod. "That's correct."

Right then my cellphone rang, and trying to be courteous, I stepped out into the afternoon air and sunshine to take the call.

It was Paula.

"Sorry I've been missing your calls," she said. "How's your day going?"

"Still poking around, still trying to find stuff to write in my magazine column."

Paula paid me the favor of not laughing. I said, "And you?"

"Appointment after appointment," she said. "Over at the town hall, trying to track down some missing petty cash funds, and then an interview with the town manager about a personnel matter involving the school department that everyone is pretending doesn't exist, and, oh yeah, trying to squeeze out any more news about the drownings."

"I'm up at McIntosh Air Force Base, trying to talk to Agent Stockman."

"Really?" she asked. "Is he there?"

"Officially, no," I said. "But I might hang out for a while, see if he rolls back in. What do you have going on?"

"A selectmen's meeting that's starting in just over an hour," she said.

"Wait, I thought they usually met at seven p.m."

"They do," she said. "But tonight's an experiment, see if they get more public input at five than seven. Problem is, you start at seven p.m., most meetings don't get wrapped up until midnight or so."

"As we both know," I said.

A gentle laugh that pleased me, and I said, "Maybe I can take you out to a late dinner when the meeting is over."

"Maybe you can," she said. "Gotta run."

She clicked off and I looked back at the sad-looking and grim concrete cube behind me. Lots of cubes like this were scattered across our fair land, like an archipelago of secrets kept and guarded. I had once been part of this hidden world, had loved it, then missed it, and now?

It was different from when I had been at the DoD. Back then, there was One Enemy, and despite all of the new history books and re-thinking, it was still a foe worth reckoning. Now, the Enemy's numbers and faces changed year after year.

The door to the near cube opened up and Brady Hill—assistant to cable personality Alice Hackett—came out, dressed well, carrying a slim brown leather briefcase, looking pretty happy with himself. He glanced at me and with an exaggerated motion, looked away, doing a pretty lousy job of pretending not to see me.

But I wasn't in the mood for pretend games.

I strode over and got in front of him. "Hey, Brady, how's your day going?"

He stopped, changed his briefcase from one hand to the other. "Going well."

"Glad to hear it." I noted where he had come from. "How's things in Homeland Security? Agent Stockman in a good mood?"

"Agent Stockman is—" and then he stopped, glared at me.

"You've got to do better, Brady. If someone tells you to keep a secret, you need to keep it a secret. Otherwise they won't be your best friends anymore. Or best friends with your boss, Alice Hackett."

"You have no idea how many friends Alice Hackett has. In the street, in the news media, in the government...but not in Homeland Security."

"Goodie for her. Does she want a cookie?"

The briefcase changed hands once again. "People who are her friends are rewarded. Those who aren't...aren't. And that includes Homeland Security." He looked back at the blank concrete cubes. "Especially Homeland Security and its representatives that won't cooperate."

"Did you or she think that up all by yourselves?"

"In a day or two, Alice is going to hold a prime-time town hall from Tyler on cable, about the refugee crisis and how it's impacting small-town America," he said. "Our offer to appear as her special guest still remains. Think about it."

He brushed past me, and I said, "Think about what?" but that was that.

. . .

I STARTED BACK to the Pilot when I heard a growl and *chuff-chuff* of a tractor-trailer truck taking off from behind an adjacent warehouse-type structure. The truck moved by, gaining speed, and I noticed how odd it was when it rumbled by. For one thing it was white, with no company logos, and even license numbers weren't stenciled on the driver's side. The trailer was as blank as the cab, and then as it went by, there were also no markings on the rear doors.

But the license plates said U.S. Government and were blue and white, and at the forward end of the trailer unit, just behind the cab, was a refrigeration unit.

A blank tractor-trailer truck, hauling a refrigerated trailer.

I ran to the Pilot, jumped in, and started it up.

There was no grocery store or warehouse nearby, but I knew what that refrigerated unit was carrying.

Drowned bodies.

Maybe even the body of that poor mother and child that drowned within sight of me and my home.

I KEPT up with the truck as it merged onto Route 16, just across from the malls in Lewington—which changed their names every few years to drag in more unsuspecting customers—and then we went south along I-95, heading towards Massachusetts. I checked my gas gauge. Nearly topped off. I could keep a long chase if I wanted to.

And why the chase?

Because I was tired of all the questions I was facing, and this little chance meeting meant at least I could have one puzzle answered.

The truck was moving right at the 55 mile per hour speed limit, and I had a brief moment of sorrow for the hired driver ahead of me. As a government employee he could get away with lots of things, but exceeding the speed limit wasn't one of them. There was a GPS system in there somewhere that kept track of his or her driving time, and woe be upon the driver if it was found that he had driven faster than the speed limit.

The driver might be hauling bodies in a classified attempt to keep secret whatever was going on here off the New Hampshire coast, and that was fine, but he or she would definitely be in trouble by contributing to the death of the planet by going too fast.

But it made my job tailing that much easier, although I kept a couple of car lengths behind, just so I wasn't too obvious.

All right, I thought. Decision time was coming up in a few minutes. We were both quickly approaching the Tyler tollbooths, one last chance for the State of New Hampshire to grab some money from tourists and visitors before crossing into Massachusetts. The tractor trailer truck up ahead could continue south to Massachusetts or take a right at the tolls for an exit that would bring the truck and its sad load onto Route 101, which traveled east to Tyler or west to a good chunk of the Granite State.

Either way, I planned to stick close behind.

And then what?

Well, find out where the bodies are being stored. And maybe...

My Beretta was still in the front seat.

I was getting angrier and angrier with each passing mile, and a sweet dark fantasy started bubbling up, of tailing the truck until it came to a stop sign or stoplight, and then stepping out with my 9 mm, going up to the driver, and demanding that the rear of the truck be opened up. Demanding that in the collection of body bags back there, I retrieve that poor drowned woman and her child, and take her away, and present the remains to Diane Woods, so she could conduct her own investigation, and in the end, ID who she was and where she came from, and then put her and her infant to rest somewhere.

Sweet little fantasy.

I was trying to talk myself out of doing something so drastic—really, drive up to the Tyler police station and happily point out the two bodies in the back of my Pilot to Detective Sergeant Woods?—when the truck started signaling it was making a right turn.

Onto the exit for Route 101.

Apparently, there wasn't going to be a visit to the Bay State today.

All right, then. That worked out for me. Massachusetts cops tend to get all spun up if they cross somebody's path who's carrying a weapon, while in New Hampshire, the same's not true.

Score one for Cole.

Traffic bunched up at the exit as the truck, me, and about a dozen other vehicles slowed down for the three open toll gates ahead of us. Two were for the EZ Pass, one was for the dinosaurs still using coins and paper currency, and another on the far left was closed, with a red stoplight glowing on top and an orange traffic cone blocking the way.

The refrigerator truck was inching its way up to the EZ pass lane on the far left. I was in the near lane, keeping an eye on things. Once we both got through, it'd be a simple task to catch up with him and keep on following.

Simple indeed.

A woman tollbooth worker wearing a bright orange vest stepped out from one of the booths and casually walked over to the blocked lane, picked up the traffic cone, and stepped to one side.

The tractor trailer truck immediately cut left, passed through the now-open lane—even with the red stoplight still glowing—and zoomed out.

The worker placed the cone back into position and went back to her booth.

By the time I got through the lane and electronically paid my toll, I had lost sight of the truck, save that I knew it had gone to the right, where Route 101 headed west into New Hampshire's interior.

I got onto Route 101, hammered the accelerator down and got up to 80 miles per hour for a while, and by the time I got outside of Manchester, the state's largest city, I gave up.

The truck and its load were gone.

And even with my disappointment, I had to admit that whoever was driving the truck had done a good job losing its tail.

Like me, he or she had been trained well.

19

I did a couple of housekeeping chores—ATM cash withdrawal, getting some weather stripping for the doors leading out to the rear deck in preparation for the upcoming winter storms, getting a container of orange juice —and it was near five p.m. when I was done, so I decided to go over to the Tyler town hall and keep Paula company during the upcoming selectmen's meeting.

That's when I faced the second big surprise of the afternoon—the first being that truck slipping away from me at the tollbooth—as I pulled into the parking lot next to the town hall.

There wasn't a spare parking spot to be seen.

I slowed down and someone behind me honked his or her horn in irritation. There were cars, SUVs, and pickup trucks packed in tight. There were also two television vans, one from the local Manchester station WMUR and the other from a Boston station. I drove out of the town lot and made my way to a church parking lot adjacent to the town hall, found a space, and then walked to the town hall.

The town hall was not much of a building and was designed that way. It looked like a large Cape Cod-style house with two single-story wings, and it had white clapboards, black shingles, and black shutters. It was in stark contrast to its neighbor to the south, Falconer, which could afford a town hall three times the size because of the tax revenue it got from the Falconer nuclear power plant.

When I got up to the entrance, there was a knot of men and women, some smoking, and others carrying homemade cardboard signs.

AMERICA FOR AMERICANS

SEND 'EM BACK

SECURE BORDERS NOW

I went up the stairs, nodded at a couple of acquaintances, and I had to push my way into the selectmen's meeting room. I've said before to Paula and others that while I'm a firm believer in small-town participatory democracy, that didn't mean I'm an enthusiastic engaged citizen, so I've only attended a few selectmen's meetings over the years. The meeting room had a long wooden table at the far end where the five selectmen and the city manager sit during a meeting, and two rows of folding wooden chairs, holding a hundred people in the rest of the room.

Until tonight, I'd never seen a hundred people in total during my attendance, and not only was every chair taken, there were people standing up against the wall and near the exit. Other signs were being held as well.

OPEN ARMS TO OUR NEIGHBORS

HUGS, NOT GUNS

WE ARE ALL ONE PEOPLE

American and New Hampshire state flags were on poles at each far corner, and there were plaques and framed certificates on the walls, including an old one declaring that Tyler had been declared an official Bicentennial Community. There were also two photographs of past Presidents of the United States who had visited Tyler during long-ago campaigns. A few years back there had been some debate about which portrait should go up, but after a bout of good citizenship and compromise, one President from each political party was displayed, thereby letting the selectmen off the hook for being charged with favoritism.

That was then, this was now. There didn't seem to be much room for compromise and good citizenship in the room this afternoon.

Up in the front row to the left were a row of chairs reserved for the news media, and on other times I've been here, I've sat with Paula Quinn, my press pass giving me permission to be there. It used to be that reporters from other papers, like the *Porter Herald*, would drive here to attend, but since most meetings were broadcast over local cable television, those reporters from the *Herald* preferred to stay home, play with their cats, and watch the proceedings from afar.

Paula once had told me how much she hated that.

"That's not journalism," she had once said. "For *The Porter Herald*, that's being a stenographer for those who run things. Real reporting is sticking it out in the meetings, with the politicians and people, so you can ask questions in person and be a pain in the butt."

Tonight Paula's pretty butt was sitting in her usual place, but the rest of the reserved row was filled. Two television cameras had been set up, and when the clock reached one minute past five, the chairman of the board of selectmen, Bruce Acquin, rapped the ceremonial gavel on the table and said, "All right, let's begin."

Bruce was a retired shipyard worker from Porter, a native of Tyler, and who had been a selectman for six years as part of those local volunteers who work to give back to their town. There were four other selectmen—a female retiree from the Post Office, a woman who ran a gift shop at the beach, a man who was an American Airlines pilot, and another man who ran his own landscaping business—and both women had once pronounced that the three-hundred-year-old phrase "selectman" bothered them not one bit.

Two other folks were up with the selectmen as well, Ray Perry, a chubby young male who worked as a legal aide for one of the law firms in town and who was the clerk—even though everything was being videotaped—and Clarissa Townsend, a former model from the Ford Agency who was the town manager this year. She had flawless skin, a pretty smile, and a brain that could crunch numbers and make budget recommendations as fast as I could clip supermarket coupons.

Bruce said, "Let's start with the Pledge of Allegiance," and everyone stood up, and as hokey as it sounded, there was something precious about having the entire room recite the pledge.

As it turned out, that was the positive highlight for the night.

It was about to get much, much worse.

20

Bruce Acquin sat down, with a little standing plaque saying CHAIRMAN before him on the long table, and someone called out, "Can we start, Bruce?"

He shook his head. He had a jowly face and a short haircut that would have looked stylish on a 1956 episode of *Dragnet*.

"Nope," he said. "We're going to follow regular order. First thing on the agenda is the review of the minutes from the last meeting. Anyone have any edits or comments?"

As it turned out, the other selectmen didn't seem cowed by the large and increasingly unsettled crowd. About ten minutes went into making sure that the right speakers were identified, that a budget review of ten thousand dollars was corrected to reflect the real sum of ten thousand five hundred dollars, and other civic matters were correctly recorded.

When that was completed and the minutes from the previous meeting were approved—by a unanimous vote—then came a review of any old business, and while an issue involving the use of the selectmen's meeting hall for the local Boy Scout troop was being reviewed, another voice called out, "C'mon, let the people speak!"

Bruce used the gavel in a sharp report. "Enough of that," he said. "People are going to be allowed to speak, but we're not going to be stampeded. We're following regular order tonight, and if you don't like that, you can leave."

A few mutters and one man raising his voice to a guy sitting next to him about how this was all political bullshit, and then the Boy Scout discussion continued.

But I could sense a change of mood in the room. There was an edgy hum, like being outside in an open field underneath under a dangerous high-tension wire. There was a sense of expectation, that something would break, that voices would be raised, that violence would break out at any moment.

The last time I had felt this was last year, at a large demonstration against the Falconer nuclear power plant, when a large peaceful grouping was hijacked by a violent contingent and there was tear gas, gunshots, and bludgeoning, and one of my best friends, Diane Woods, was nearly murdered.

I didn't like it.

I was near the exit door if something were to happen, but Paula was up front, at least ten rows away from me.

I didn't like that either.

The selectmen chairman rapped the gavel one more time when the Boy Scout discussion was finally wrapped up, and he said, "There was a speaker's list that we asked folks to sign before the start of the meeting. It's a pretty long list. We ask that you keep your comments to three minutes, and per our rules of order, residents get to speak first. Okay, first up, Lynn Turner."

Lynn Turner was an older woman who walked slowly and with some difficulty, and when she stood in front of the selectmen, she said, "Lynn Turner, Highland Avenue, and I want to talk about the speeding that goes on near the school."

Moans and groans followed her words, for most of the people here wanted to talk about something else, but she pressed on, and when she was done, it was Mo Walsh's turn, the open borders representative I had met earlier.

She strode up there with determination and energy and got right to it.

"Mo Walsh, Barnes Road, and I want to know why this board is letting

Homeland Security trample all over our rights and responsibilities, and your duties as the governing body for this town."

The five members sat there, stone-faced, and Bruce Acquin cautiously said, "I'm not sure what you mean, Mo."

"You know what I mean," she shot back. "Twice in three weeks, the drowned bodies of these poor refugees—"

"Illegal aliens!" a brusque male voice shouted from the crowd, interrupting her, but she persisted, and said, "—poor people have landed on our shores. Basic human decency should allow that our police investigate the matter, that their remains be treated with respect, not bundled into some government warehouse. The Tyler selectmen should inform Homeland Security that the town's laws and ordinances take precedent, that we are a decent, caring community, and that we welcome these poor people from away."

Another shout, "Then put 'em up in your house, Mo," and that brought cheers, jeers, boos, and a couple of guys standing up, pointing fingers at each other, and then Bruce gaveled everyone back into order. Clarissa Townsend, the town manager—meaning she was the one responsible for the day-to-day operations of Tyler and its departments—took out an iPhone or something similar, and started texting someone, which struck me as odd. A few of the older and dumber men in Tyler thought that because she was an attractive young woman that she could be a pushover, and that false premise lasted right up to the time when they all ran into the buzz saw that was her sharp mind and sharper tongue.

Seeing her calmly texting someone seemed off.

Mo spoke for a bit longer, and then it was the turn of another resident, Dave Tyler, who was a member of the long line of Tylers that went back to the first settlers, back in 1638, headed by one Reverend Bonus Tyler from England.

He was in his sixties, stooped, with a big belly and he liked to wear both a belt and suspenders, and he looked over his reading glasses at the board. He was nearly bald, save for a fringe of white stubble around his skull.

"Dave Tyler, Perkins Road," he said. "You all know me. Most of the people in this room know me. I've been a selectman, have served on the budget committee, the planning board and—"

A woman yelled out, "And don't forget the militia! You're one of those gun nuts, aren't you?"

Bruce gaveled and Dave turned, defiant, and said, "Sure, I'm a member of the Wentworth County Free Militia. We're not breaking any laws. We follow state and federal rules when it comes to firearms, and we're here to protect all of us, even those who don't agree with our positions."

A big round of applause at that, with more boos and hisses. He turned back to the selectmen. "I served twenty years in the Navy, and when I was done, I came back home to Tyler. Because it's a special place, the best place in the world. And it's ours. And it should be protected."

Dave's voice choked some for a moment, and the room became quiet. "I've gone all over the world. Asia, Africa, Europe...and there's not one place I'd rather be than Tyler and our beaches. I've seen things, lots of things. Incredible poverty. Crowded, filthy cities. Starving folks. And I feel bad for 'em, honest I do. And I can see why they'd want to come here. If I was in their place, I'd do the same. I'd hock everything I own for a chance to bring my family over here. That's what I'd do."

A quick pause. "But that don't make it right! We worked hard, we sweated, we bled, and we built a place that's the envy of the world. But if we open everything up, if we don't protect what we have, then Katie bar the door, everyone will try to come here. Everyone! And what will be left when they come here, not speaking the language, not knowing our rules, looking to live off the welfare and not pull their part, and—"

More shouts, more applause, more yells, and when Bruce managed to gavel some sort of order back into place, Dave said, "Okay, I'll wrap up. Like it or not, we're gonna get overwhelmed if this stuff keeps on happening. I'm sorry those folks drowned. Other, nastier folks took advantage of 'em. But charity begins at home. We need to protect what we can. And we love our police and first responders, but we know they can't be everywhere at once."

Murmurs and some whispers. Dave cleared his throat. "As the secretary for the Wentworth County Free Militia, we're putting a request before the Tyler Board of Selectmen, asking that you recognize us as a defensive force in the town, and that you tell the chief that—"

Lots of shouts, people standing up protesting, others standing up as well, protesting the protestors. A couple of the wiser townspeople decided enough was enough and slid out the door, but they were quickly replaced by new folks, who had to be briefed by those standing in the rear. Two more young men pushed their way in, and I recognized their faces. They were Tyler police officers, and they were dressed in civilian clothes.

Now I know why the town manager had been texting earlier. It was a rare sight to have any police presence at the selectmen's meeting, except for the chief's monthly report, but this had quickly changed into something more than a standard meeting.

More gaveling from Bruce and some voices of "quiet, quiet, shut up folks," and just as the residents crammed into this meeting room were finding their way back to some sort of order, the door opened up and it all went to hell.

I HAD to look twice to make sure I was right, but yes, it was Brady Hill, confidently strolling in, calling out in a strong voice, "Mister speaker, mister speaker, if I can have a moment of your time, sir."

Heads all swung back and near me an older woman muttered, "He's the chairman, not the speaker, you moron," and Brady, dressed well and carrying his briefcase, walked right up to the front of the room, and again, that poor gavel was used until most of the voices quieted down, and Bruce said, "Excuse me, who are you?"

Brady smiled. "I'm Brady Hill, personal assistant and adviser to writer and commentator Alice Hackett, and—"

Cheers, boos, applause and hisses swept through the room, and a few minutes later, after he once again managed to wrestle the room into some form of quiet, Bruce said, "I'm sorry, who are you, and who's Alice Hackett?"

A few folks laughed at Bruce not knowing, but that didn't seem to bother him. Bruce was of the old school who thought that when you crossed over the border down in Falconer that lead into Massachusetts, you were entering a terra incognita where the taxes were high and the gun permits were low. And except for parts of Maine, no other part of the Republic was worth listening to or considering. Once upon a time New Hampshire had a state holiday called Fast Day, and he said we should keep it in place, despite the absence of the holiday in other states. "We're the ones keeping step," he had said back then. "The other forty-nine don't know what they're doing."

But Brady Hill seemed stunned at the question. He stammered and said, "That's Alice Hackett. She's a writer...she's on all the cable networks. She's an adviser to the President. She's—"

A shout: "She's a bitch on wheels, that's who she is!"

A few boos were overwhelmed by applause and laughter, and Brady pressed on. "She's outside at this moment. She'd like to come in and address the council—"

"Selectmen," Bruce corrected.

"Ah, yes, she'd like to address the council about this immigration crisis that's tearing your town apart, and there's a camera crew with her as well, and it would be..."

He kept on talking about how this would be a wonderful chance for the hardworking and God-fearing people of Tyler to make their views known to the entire world, and it was a grand opportunity that really shouldn't be ignored.

I checked my watch. It was coming up on six p.m.

Sure. Six p.m., right at the top of the hour, Alice Hackett could stride in here and speak live to the rubes of this small-town New Hampshire, and have her voice spread to millions. A wonderful opportunity indeed.

Bruce waited until Alice's assistant caught his breath, and he said, "Sorry, sir. We have a regulation here for our selectmen's meetings. Town residents get to speak first. That's the right way to do things. Visitors and out-of-towners have to speak last. And according to the speakers' list...Ray, do you mind?"

Ray Perry, the secretary, passed over a sheet of paper and Bruce looked at it. "Yep. According to the speakers' list, we already have thirty-four people in front of her, so—"

"Let her speak!" came a yell, and somebody else shouted, "No!" and then it deteriorated into shouts of "Let her speak!" to counter-shouts of "Follow the rules!" and Bruce hammered the gavel so hard that it finally split into two, with the head flying off into the front row where Paula Quinn and the other journalists were sitting.

"Okay, okay," he said, breathing hard, as a young male reporter I didn't recognize brought the loose head of the gavel up to him. "That...is...it. We're gonna follow the rules. I don't care if it's Alice Hackett, or the First Lady, or the Empress of the Known Universe. The speakers' list is the list, and we're going to follow it."

Then I think most everyone in the room was surprised when Marcia Owens, who owned the Tide and Shore Gift Shop on Tyler Beach, leaned over and said, "Mister Chairman?"

Bruce turned. "Yes, Marcia?"

Marcia said, "I think we should let her speak."

Some gasps from the attendees, and then Roland Putney, the airline pilot, spoke up as well. "I agree with Marcia."

"But the rules," Bruce said, exasperated.

Marcia said, "We could suspend the rules."

"But—"

"There she is!"

The door at the rear opened up, and Alice Hackett walked in, followed by the glare of a television crew, and there was a great movement of people surging towards her, applause, cheers, jeers, calls of "Let her speak!" followed by "Follow the rules!" followed by a tumble and crush of people, and then there was a gunshot.

21

Shouts, yells, punches thrown, elbows shoved, chairs collapsed, a few screams, and I forced myself against the crowd, half of which was trying to go out the rear door, the other half that was trying to force its way past the selectmen's table to the right, to the interior of the town hall. There was the sharp scent of spent gunpowder and pepper spray in the air. My feet were stepped on, I caught an elbow in the chin, but I fought my way to the left of the room, and there was Paula, wide-eyed with her back against the wall, camera in hand, and I grabbed her free arm and pulled her down to the floor and covered her with my body, as the shouts, yells, and chaos ensued.

At 1:03 a.m. the next morning, a bleary-eyed Bruce Acquin looked across the near-empty meeting room and then said with a tired voice, "All right, Tommy, thanks for that." And Tom Vasquez, the building inspector for the town of Tyler, got up from his chair and made his way to the rear of the meeting room.

Bruce coughed. "Do I hear a motion to approve the report of the building inspector?"

Willy McMahon, owner of McMahon Landscaping, sat there with arms crossed, nearly dozing, and he lifted his bearded head and said, "I so move."

"Is there a second?"

Tilly Heston, the retiree from the Post Office said, "I second."

"All in favor?" Bruce asked.

The motion was passed unanimously, five to zero.

But after what had happened some hours earlier, the board was not unanimous, not at all. Marcia Owens and Roland Putney, who had urged the suspension of the rules to let Alice Hackett speak out of turn, sat by themselves about three feet away from Bruce and the two other selectmen. After the room had been cleared, after the windows had been opened to air out the gunpowder and the pepper spray, and after the shooter had been arrested—a young man from the Wentworth County Free Militia whose pistol had accidentally gone off—Bruce had resumed the meeting, even against the advice of Clarissa Townsend, who had suggested that the meeting be postponed and rescheduled.

"Hell, no," Bruce had bellowed. "For more than three hundred years we've had selectmen meetings in Tyler, through wars, the Depression and bad weather, and they've never been canceled, or postponed. I'll be goddamned if I'm going to be the first chairman to break that record."

Then he had taken the broken head of the gavel in his hand, rapped it on the table, and said, "Meeting called to order."

And that had been that.

Paula was sitting next to me, fighting to keep awake, and she was the last reporter left. Alice Hackett had never gotten her chance to speak, but a strong dozen or so had stuck around to make their viewpoints known, and two uniformed Tyler police and two county sheriff deputies had taken up places at both ends of the room.

Now Bruce took a breath, looked down at the agenda, and said, "It appears a motion to adjourn is in order."

Again, Willy McMahon made the motion, it was seconded by Tilly Heston, and Bruce gave one last hit of the gavel head—"Meeting adjourned"—and then picked up the broken handle of the gavel and shook his head.

Paula got up and so did I, and she said, "I need to write this story now."

"Paula, please..."

"If I don't do it now, I'll fall sleep and I'll be fuzzy headed and worthless when I get up. I write it now, I can file it, crash, and have a good solid sleep before getting to the paper."

"I'll join you, keep you awake. You heading to the office?"

She yawned. "Silly man. Haven't you heard of the Internet? I'll write and file it from home."

"I'll still come along."

"Oh, please do," she said.

OUTSIDE IT WAS A CRISP NIGHT, the overhead stars pretty bright despite the streetlights illuminating the parking lot, and the lot was nearly empty. I heard some voices out there in the ill-lit lot, and I said to Paula, "Hold on for a sec."

I walked closer and saw two men nearly toe to toe, arguing with each other. Paula followed me.

One was Brady Hill, briefcase at his feet.

And the other was Agent Mark Stockman, of Homeland Security.

"Lewis?" Paula asked.

Either her voice caught their attention, or something else, but both Brady and Agent Stockman looked our way, and then they quickly separated. Brady ducked down a grassy path leading out from the lot, and Stockman moved quickly to a black Chevrolet Suburban, starting it up, and driving out.

"What was that?" Paula asked.

"Something weird," I said.

"Weirder than what just happened at the selectmen's meeting?"

"I'd say it's tied."

"Who were those two guys?" she asked. "I didn't get a good view before they ran off."

"Brady Hill, Alice Hackett's gofer, chatting it up with Mark Stockman of Homeland Security," I said. "Then again, it looked like they were arguing."

"What do you think they were arguing about?"

I took her hand. "Beats me. Alice is having a town hall here in a couple of nights for her cable show. Maybe she wanted her best boy to convince Stockman to make an appearance."

"Well, your best girl is about to fall asleep standing up, so let's get a move on."

I walked her back to her Ford Escort, thinking of something else I could note but decided not to.

What was Agent Stockman doing here in the first place in Tyler, at this time of the night and thirty minutes away from his home base?

AT HER CONDO on High Street, about a five-minute drive from the town hall, Paula went straight to her kitchen table, swept a tumble of envelopes and old newspapers to one side, and got to work on her laptop.

"Lewis, be a dear, make me something to eat," she said. "And coffee. But the decaf. I want to sleep when this is done."

I got a tea kettle filled with some water and set it on the stove, and I rummaged through her refrigerator, found some eggs, grated Parmesan cheese and some deli ham. I pulled out a frying pan and immediately washed it again—Paula had done a good job, not a great job, bless her—and in a bit, I made some scrambled eggs with parmesan cheese and torn pieces of ham tossed in. In the freezer I found a solitary English muffin, defrosted it, and about fifteen minutes later, we were both eating. I had a glass of orange juice and she had decaf coffee, and she insisted on sharing the English muffin with me.

She licked some butter off her thumb. "After all, a man who makes me a meal should get an equal share."

"Thanks," I said.

"Especially when I'm going to invite said man to spend the night."

I smiled. "Not sure how much night we have left, but I'll take every minute."

"Smart boy."

As we were nearly finished up, I said, "Funny you'd wait until now to write your story."

"Say what?"

"The action took place hours ago. Too bad the *Chronicle* won't have an exclusive."

"That's too bad," she said. "A while back you were a smart boy. I'm afraid I'm going to have to take that back."

"Excuse me?"

She wiped up her plate with the last of her English muffin. "The town hall has wi-fi access. I filed about a half-dozen bulletins and stories to the Associated Press and *The Boston Globe* without leaving my chair. Plus a couple of photographs."

"You techno girl you."

"We try," she said.

I picked up the plates and did a quick wash, and when I turned back, she was flicking through her laptop. "Though sometimes I hate this new quick business."

I sat down and she said, "Now the story's all over the world, within seconds, that the good people of Tyler are torn over immigration, that they're full of bigots and ignorants from all stripes, and that they're prone to violence at any second."

"That's what happened," I said.

"Doesn't make it right," she said, her fingers from her right hand still flickering across the keyboard. "I've been here nearly all of my life. All in all, the people of Tyler are good people. But this whole immigration mess, and the refugees coming here, and the bodies washing up, and Homeland Security stomping over everything...it's a complex story. And at the bottom of it, people are scared. That's all. Scared that there's a threat out there that they can't understand, scared that a civil war a half a globe away will wash up here, and scared that their government is sliding to fascism. Lots of fear, lots of complexity, and who cares about complex stories nowadays?"

"I do," I said.

"No offense, big whoop," she said. "You're a minority of a minority." She shook her head again. "This is when I say, what's happened to us? How did we get here?"

I yawned and she followed suit, and then she said, "Crap, what time is it?"

I glanced at my watch. It was ten after two in the morning.

"Time for bed."

"After you," she said. "I need a quick shower, just to get the scent of that place off my skin."

"Promise you won't snore?"

She pushed her chair back. "Can't promise you that, chum. How about you?"

"I plead the Fifth."

I stood up and went over, we kissed, and then I moved left to her bedroom, and she moved right to the bathroom.

Inside her bedroom I stripped and crawled under the covers. My bed was larger, more comfortable and the bedroom had great views of the beach, but Paula's bed had the scent of her, which was a winner. I rolled over and listened to the water run, and then I didn't hear much after.

Though I did wake up when she crawled in and kissed me, and her hair was wet, and she whispered, "There's a time for loving, and a time for sleeping."

I wanted to ask her which time it was, then I fell asleep again.

IN THE MORNING I scratched at my face, woke up, and found myself alone in bed. I rolled out, got dressed, called out, "Paula?"

On her small kitchen table was a note, a small brown paper bag and a cup of coffee.

The note said:

L—

You still don't snore. Thank you.

Here's your breakfast.

Dinner tonight at your place?

—P

I checked the time. It was 10:31 a.m.

"Getting old," I said to myself. The paper bag contained a fresh maple square, and the coffee was still warm. I ate standing up, washed and dried the dishes, and scribbled a quick postscript to her note:

Yes

. . .

A WHILE later I picked up the day's newspaper, plus my mail from the Tyler Post Office, and I was stunned to see that last night's events at the town hall had made the front page of *The Boston Globe* and a small news item in *The New York Times*. The Greater Tyler Chamber of Commerce would no doubt be thrilled.

I called the Tyler police station, made a later lunch date with Detective Sergeant Diane Woods, and drove home. Outside the Lafayette House there were two television trucks from Boston networks, and the parking lot was nearly full. If anything, at least this crisis was providing a boon to the hospitality industry of Tyler.

I maneuvered my Pilot through the line of parked cars, heading to my dirt driveway at the other side of the parking lot, and there were three guys sitting on the boulders marking the north end of the lot.

As I approached, they got up and gently blocked my way, with the guy on the left making a motion with his left hand.

Interesting.

I slowed down and stopped, lowering the window.

Two of the guys moved to the right, pushed their jackets to the side, revealing each was carrying a holstered pistol. A surprise to many visitors is that my fair state is an "open carry" state, meaning anyone can carry a weapon in public without a license, like the young clown the night before at the selectmen's meeting. Odd, but that's how my state works. So seeing these two men—one with a thick moustache and the other working on a beard—carrying holstered pistols in the open wasn't illegal, but it was certainly off-putting.

The man approaching the Pilot was friendly enough, with a warm, smiling face and black-rimmed glasses, wearing a tan coat and a Red Sox baseball cap.

"How's it going?" he asked.

"Going fine," I said. "How are you doing?"

"Great," he said, and his head moved, and I could tell he was peering into the rear seat and cargo space of the Pilot. "My name's Glen Forsyth."

"Lewis Cole," I said.

He didn't offer a hand, and neither did I.

A few seconds passed, and he said, "Where are you going?"

"Straight."

"Why?"

I was getting irritated. "That's where I live. Why do you care?"

He nodded to the other two armed men on the other side of my Pilot. "We're from the Wentworth County Free Militia. Just doing our job."

"Really?" I asked. "What job is that?"

"Protecting our land when the government can't—or won't—do it."

"Oh," I said. "That's pretty considerate of you. I guess nobody's stolen anything yet, am I right?"

He looked puzzled.

Good.

"What?" Glen sked.

"The land," I said. "You said you were protecting the land. I guess no one's stolen any land since you've been here."

He didn't seem to like that, and he leaned in a bit more. "You're that smart-ass magazine writer, aren't you?"

"That's me."

"You think you're so smart."

"Most days, yeah."

One of the two men on the other side said, "Hey, Glen, this is the guy who dragged in those two drowned illegals the other day."

Glen looked back to me. "That true?"

"Every word."

"Well, let me tell you Lewis Cole—"

I took my foot off the brake, slammed my foot down on the accelerator, and in a few seconds, I was pulling up to the shed near my home that was my garage.

As I got out, Glen was up at the top of my driveway, with his two buddies next to him.

I waved up at them.

They waved back, with a grand total of three fingers being extended in my direction.

. . .

IN THE HOUSE I sorted through the mail, did a bit of tidying up, saw I didn't have any phone messages nor emails of note—would Nigeria always be a country cursed by its spamming industry?—and I went back up my drive-way. The well-armed trio of the Wentworth County Free Militia was caught by surprise as I drove by, which caused me to smile and feel disappointed.

Not much of a militia. I thought the old militia types from the 1700's could have taught them a thing or two.

22

Diane Woods and I went to Massachusetts for lunch at the famed Markey's on Route 286, and we had seafood—fried shrimp for me, baked stuffed haddock for her—and we took a corner seat that gave us a view of the Salisbury marshes.

As we ate, Diane said, "Not that I don't love Tyler and New Hampshire, but it's nice to get out and about where the snobs and gossips don't see you and count the number of minutes you take for lunch."

"Aren't we in a grumpy mood," I said.

She kicked me under the table. "I have a right. You were at the selectmen's meeting last night, weren't you?"

"Not much of a meeting," I said. "More of a brawl. Just lucky that bullet went into the roof and nobody's head. The shooter still in jail?"

"Nope," Diane said. "He got bailed out by his parents, with a half-dozen charges attached to him. I wanted to add one more, but the county attorney said no."

"What charge?"

She dug into her late lunch. "Felony stupid."

We talked about this and that for a while, and I said, "How's Kara doing?"

"My lovely is doing just fine, thank you," she said. "Though sometimes she makes me feel like an old dumb lady."

"You're not that old," I said.

That got me another kick from underneath the table. "She loves computers, loves software, loves solving puzzles. A long time ago I could keep up with her, back in the day when everyone used to get AOL CDs in the mail once a month. My computer knowledge then leveled out, and she's gone into outer space."

"Does she send back messages from orbit?"

A smile came from that, and she said, "Messages, and if I've been a good girl, massages as well."

"How goes the wedding planning?"

"Nice to get it up and going again," she said. "Still on for next May. Finally."

Diane and Kara had planned to get married four months ago, but Diane was still recovering from a severe beating she had received while on duty, and as she had said at the time, "I'll be goddamned if I'm going down the aisle like some limping monkey."

"Good to hear that."

A smile still on her face, she said, "And when's your wedding date?"

I nearly choked on a piece of fried shrimp, and when I recovered, I said, "That's up orbiting with Kara. No talk yet."

"Yet."

"That's right."

"You're not getting any younger," she said.

"Gosh, what a detective you've turned out to be," I said. I moved my fork around and said, "Truth is, she was spending quite a few nights at my place. But now she's not."

"Why? Too many girlie things in the bathroom? Her hair clogging the shower drain? She make you watch Lifetime instead of the History Channel?"

"Nope," I said. I touched the side of my head where the bandage was still there. "Recent events. She's been at my house once when there was gunplay. She doesn't want to be around if it happens again."

"Smart girl."

"I like to think so."

We ate for a few more minutes, and Diane said, "Anything else going on with you?"

"You tell me," I said. "Head's healing nicely, but I still feel like someone's out there who wants to do me harm. Anything more into what happened?"

She shook her head. "Nope. We sent about a half-dozen Explorer scouts marching in a line, up and down where the shooter might have been, and no joy. No cigarette butts, scribbled hate notes to *Shoreline* magazine, or shell casings."

"A revolver."

"Sure sounds like it."

"Not much of an assassination weapon," I said, "even with a good shooter. Clumsy."

She gave me a look. "Take a glance around. Lots of clumsy people stumbling into each other lately. Now it's my turn. You get anything threatening after those shots were fired?"

"Not really," I said. "Although members of our local militia are hanging around at the Lafayette House parking lot, defending the purity and essence of our water. Three of them gave me a lookover as I went home."

"I can see why," she said. "You're an intellectual. An enemy of the people. Plus, there's word that you're part of the grand conspiracy to bring in refugees."

"Say that again?"

"You heard me," she said. "That poor woman and her child...they were supposed to meet you in your little cove, and then you were to hustle them off to wherever they could steal good jobs and medical care from the local citizens."

"Good Lord, for real?"

She wiped her fingers on a paper napkin. "For real. If you had told me a few years back that the good people here in Tyler—friends, neighbors, relatives—would be tearing themselves apart over illegal immigration, I would have never believed it. What would be the point? But the world is tearing itself apart on the other side of the globe, and its refugees are coming ashore here. Poor old Tyler is just part of the greater picture."

I said, "So far, all that's come ashore have been the drowned ones. There must be a number of survivors. Where did they go?"

"Good question," she said. "Why don't you ask your new best friend Agent Stockman of Homeland Security?"

"He's not my new best friend," I said. "More of an acquaintance. And I went up to see him yesterday and he was there but wouldn't see me."

"Poor little fella," she said, smiling at me. "Did it hurt your feelings?"

"For about a second or two," I said. "But funny thing, I was there and saw Brady Hill. And then I saw the two of them again, right after last night's selectmen's meeting."

"Am I supposed to know who Brady Hill is?"

"He's the go-to guy and gofer for Alice Hackett."

Diane smirked. "You know why Alice Hackett wears slacks all the time?"

"Beats me."

"To hide her cloven hooves."

I couldn't help myself and my smile matched hers. "So much for the sisterhood."

"Assuming facts not in evidence, amateur counselor," Diane said. "That she's a sister. But still...that's odd."

"That's what I thought," I said. "From the little I've seen and read, Alice isn't a fan of immigrants, illegal or otherwise, and is definitely not a fan of the Administration, ICE, Homeland Security and any other federal agencies out there. So why would her number one best boy be visiting the local Homeland Security rep? Not to mention, why is he here anyway?"

"What do you think?"

"Because of the drownings," I said.

She gave me a look like she had found a thick bone in her haddock.

"Well, that's the official story."

Diane said, "Lewis, for real? Homeland Security has a nice big chunk of Federal office space over in Concord, with lots of nice restaurants within walking distance. Why ship yourself all the way over to what's left of McIntosh Air Force Base to respond to a few drownings?"

"That sounds cold."

"That sounds accurate, and you know it," she said. "He's up there with a couple of his minions, and that's it. Why?"

"He's waiting for something."

"I agree."

I finished off my last fried shrimp. "He has intelligence or information that something big is heading our way, bigger than the earlier drownings. And he wants to be in a position to be the first responder, to take over the scene."

"And get all the nice headlines, stories, and increased budget requests. With maybe a nice shiny promotion to get him out of New Hampshire and to D.C."

"I've been here, and I've been in D.C.," I said. "I should tell Agent Stockman that D.C. is a wonderful, fulfilling and exceptional place."

"Why in the world would you do that?"

"To make sure he leaves," I said.

The waiter sauntered by and dropped off the check, which I seized before Diane could grab it, and I said, "So something big is coming. Agent Stockman wants to head it off before it happens. And having Alice Hackett's best boy visit…"

"Means she's in on it, too," Diane said. "Gives her publicity, maybe another book deal. I read somewhere that her ratings are starting to tank. It would give her a boost, wouldn't it, being on the scene. And that's why she's here, too. Waiting."

"All the while an overcrowded and leaking boat is heading this way, filled with frightened refugees," I said. "Not knowing they're about to be used in some political drama."

"Thanks for lunch," she said. "Funny world we're in, isn't it?"

I slipped out some cash and she said, "You ever meet up with Billy Bragg?"

"In a manner of speaking."

"Oh, stop with the big phrases," she said. "What happened?"

So I told her about my encounter at the Lafayette House parking lot and his threats and sharp words, and Diane narrowed her eyes. "Sometimes guys like that who have very little to call their own tend to get violent if they feel threatened. Either by you or by my brothers and sisters in law enforcement. And just so you know...Fish & Game are looking for him with a fresh warrant in hand. So I'd expect the next time you see him, he'll be in a fouler mood."

We both got up and I said, "Thanks for the warning."

"Why?"

"Because I'm going out to see if I can find him again."

23

I drove down the bumpy dirt road of the Tyler River Campground and pulled in next to the boarded-up office. The place looked pretty much as before. I stepped out into the cool afternoon and heard chainsaws operating a number of yards away.

Nearby was the tent belonging to Fran Dependhal, the woman overseeing the place. I got up to the tent and didn't know the custom of how to get someone's attention from inside. I couldn't knock, and I didn't want to unzip the flap, so I leaned in and said, "Fran? Are you in there? It's Lewis Cole, the magazine writer."

No answer, but a tall and thin woman strolled by, her auburn hair loose at her shoulders, the roots about two inches pure white. She had on a patched dungaree jacket, black tights, red sneakers, and she was carrying a child wrapped up in two or three blankets.

"You looking for Fran?"

"I am."

"You a cop? Or from the bank?"

"Nope," I said. "I work for a magazine. I was just looking to talk to her."

She lifted a shoulder in the direction of the chainsaw noise. "There's a work crew out there, making new campsites for the spring. I think she might be there."

"Thanks," I said.

"You have a good day, now," she said, and I returned the greeting, not sure what kind of day faced her and her child.

It was an easy stroll going along the paths and cleared places where the trailers, RVs and a few large tents were parked or set up. There was the smell of wood smoke and burnt wood and wet clothes. A dog barked. I put my hands in my coat pockets and came up to Billy Bragg's place.

The stretch of dirt at the side of his trailer that looked to be used for a parking spot was empty. No rusty truck with bumper stickers. But the lobster traps and two 55-gallon drums were still there, as well as the blue tarp covering the roof of the trailer.

I went up and knocked on the side door anyway.

Nobody answered.

I stepped out on the dirt road, walked away from the trailer, got to the point where the chainsaws were louder, and I could hear raised voices. The road curved left and there was Fran, smoking a cigarette, watching three young men at work. Two had chainsaws in their hands, and the other had a set of clippers. The man with the clippers worked alongside the two with the chainsaws. They were working along a rectangle that had been plotted out with foot-high stakes and orange strips of tape. The chainsaw men cleared away the heavy brush and saplings, while the third one did cleanup. The cut brush and branches were tossed in the center of the dirt road. It looked like there were three other rectangles marked out farther down the dirt road. They worked hard, smiling and sometimes shouting at each other as they made good progress.

Fran jerked her head back, like she had sensed my approach, and she dropped her cigarette, ground it out with her booted heel, and came back, holding an arm out, like she was trying to escort me away from the worksite.

But it was too late.

I'm no expert on anthropology, ethnicity, or the history of the human race, but those three workers were speaking in Spanish, and it seemed like they were all from Central America.

· · ·

WHEN WE GOT out of reach of the loud noise, Fran said, "What are you looking for?"

"Billy Bragg," I said. "Is he around?"

"I saw him head out this morning."

"Any idea when he'll be back?"

Fran gave me a look. "For real?"

I shrugged. "Always ask, just in case I get surprised."

We walked a few feet and she said, "I can explain."

"I'm sure you can."

"Don't sound so snotty, or judgmental."

"I'll try."

She stopped and so did I.

"Where are they from?" I asked. "Guatemala? Honduras?"

Fran sighed. "El Salvador."

"How's their documentation?"

"Non-existent," she said.

I looked at her and she stared right back, and Fran said, "You're probably thinking about what I said last time we met. About illegal immigrants. The way they steal jobs from the poor folks around here."

"Yes, I thought about that," I said. "At least for a moment or two."

Fran said, "I didn't have a choice."

"I'm sure."

"There you go, sounding snotty again."

"Sorry, just my style sometimes. You were saying you didn't have a choice?"

"I didn't," she said. "My cousin Bonnie came to me, saying her idiot husband Paul was giving her grief over me being here and having the campsite opened all winter. The locals seem to be doing a good job pretending nothing's going on here, but Paul's concerned that the state or some charitable outfit will learn differently. Then the town will have no choice but to shut us down."

"Go on."

"So Paul said to Bonnie, if I could open up six more campsites for spring —bringing in extra money—he'd shut up for the rest of this fall and winter. He'd even pay for it. But the money he gave me..."

"Not enough to hire the locals."

"Nope," she said. "I tried, but the work is too hard and doesn't pay enough. I couldn't get anybody here or elsewhere to take the job."

I said, "So you had no choice."

"I had no choice."

"It happens," I said.

I turned away from her and walked back to the campground, and she didn't go back to her illegals working, and she didn't follow me either.

She just stayed there, in the middle.

BACK AT BILLY BRAGG'S trailer, there were now two pickup trucks in the small yard, and I recognized one that was Billy's. I walked up to the door and it swung open, and Glen Forsyth of the Wentworth County Free Militia was stepping out, followed by Billy Bragg.

"Afternoon, gents," I said. "Going out hunting? What's the bag limit for refugees?"

Both Billy and Glen gave me foul looks, and Billy said, "Glen's just leaving, ain't you Glen."

He turned to Billy and said, "Hey, c'mon, Billy, don't say no so quick, all right? You know how it is, and—"

Billy gave him a not-so-gentle push to his shoulder. "I said my piece. Now get off my property."

Glen snorted. "Some property."

"Yeah, but it's still mine. Get the hell out."

Glen stalked off and made a point to walk past me so he could bump into me—hard—with his left shoulder.

I kept my spot and as he left, I said, "I'll let you have that one."

Glen turned back. "Let? What the hell do you mean let?"

"I meant what I said," I pointed out. "I'll let you have that one. Try it again, or even think of trying it again, I'll knock you flat on your ass."

He glared at me, said a couple of naughty words, and got into his Chevy pickup truck. He started it up, roared back in reverse—I think trying to intimidate me, which didn't work—and then he drove off and skidded through a turn, and was gone.

A chainsaw still chattered and roared out there in the woods.

"Hey Billy," I asked. "How's your day going?"

He stepped down, rubbed at his bearded face. "What the hell do you want?"

"Cable television bills that don't go up every two months," I said, "but a little information would be nice."

"Why should I talk to you? What do I get out of it?"

"Some information that you might find useful."

"What's that?"

"Tsk, tsk," I said. "That's not being fair. It has to be a trade. I ask you a question or two, and if I like the answers, I'll give you something in return."

"What do you mean, if you like the answers?"

I said, "If you just grunt, or say no, or yes, then that might not make me happy. And I won't say a word."

He shifted his feet. "How's that bullet wound doing?"

"Healing."

"Guess it didn't scare you off too much."

"So far it hasn't."

He said, "Okay. You ask a couple of questions, and we'll see where it goes. And I'll tell you, if you piss me off, we'll see how tough you are. Glen looked impressed. I'm not."

"That's a deal."

"Go."

I said, "I'll start right from the beginning. You know these waters, you know them too well, according to the state and federal fishing authorities. There have been two instances of bodies washing ashore, refugees, illegal immigrants, migrants, whatever you want to call them."

"That a question or a statement?"

I had to smile. The rough guy had gotten me.

"All right, here's the question," I said. "The refugees that have drowned coming ashore, they had to have come here by freighter, or some sort of mother ship. Have you seen anything like that?"

"In the daylight? Nope. Nothing. Only thing I've seen is the regular freighter traffic going in and out of Porter Harbor."

"I didn't ask about the daylight," I said. "Have you seen anything strange at night?"

"You think I go out at night all the time? Dangerous time for a fisherman. Plus you can't do some fishing at night, like lobstering."

"I got the impression that rules didn't quite apply to you."

He laughed. "Yeah, I'm guilty of that."

"So what have you seen at night?"

He took a step toward me, but I wasn't concerned. It seemed like he was coming toward me to take me into some sort of confidence.

"At night?" he said, his voice lowered. "You can't believe the things I've seen at night."

"Try me."

"At night...there's the glow of lights along the coastline...the farther out you get, the softer and dimmer they get. You start out saying, hey, that's Porter, and that's Tyler Beach, and that's Falconer, and then Salisbury...and before you know it, there's just that faint line of illumination that marks everyplace you've ever been or seen."

The chainsaws kept chattering. "Then you spot the other lights. The Isles of Shoals. On a clear night, maybe some of the Maine lights, or Cape Anne. And the stars at night...so hard and bright you think you could take a pole and knock them around. You see little moving dots of satellites, and sometimes, the little flare of meteors burnin' up in the atmosphere. Then there's the red and green of the navigation lights of other ships out there...and you can pick them up on your radar screen, see what size they are."

He seemed to be enjoying himself. I let him talk. "There are times you see ghost shadows out there, flitting around, trying to be quiet, blocking out what ambient light is out there. And twice...twice, I tell you, so you know I wasn't drunk, twice I've seen underwater vehicles, all lit up."

"Submarines?" I asked.

He shook his head. "You don't read enough, do you. Nope, if the skies can have their UFO's, then the water can have their unidentified objects. I served some years in the Navy. I know what submarines look like. Those weren't submarines."

He stopped talking and even the sound of the chainsaws had died off. It got so quiet I could hear the low hum of traffic on the Interstate, or on Route 101, the state highway.

"Well?" I asked.

"Well, what?" he replied. "It's your turn now."

"But—"

"But what? I answered your questions. You might not like the answers, Mister Cole, but I answered your questions. And I'm done."

I hated to admit it, but Billy was right. I had wanted to ask a couple of questions, I had done so, and just because I didn't like his answers didn't mean I couldn't keep up my end of the bargain.

"I'm waiting," Billy said. "Or are you gonna get pissy on me and sulk away. You said you had something for me. What is it?"

I hoped Diane Woods would forgive me, for I said next, "Fish & Game are looking for you."

He barked out a laugh. "For real? That's it? Christ, those green goblins are always looking for me."

"I know, but I got word, they've got something new, and they're coming after you soon."

"How soon?"

"Soon," I said.

He folded his arms, rocked back and forth. "That good info?"

"The best," I said.

"All right then," he said. "We're through. Why don't you head out."

I started off and then turned back once more. "What are you protecting?"

He was halfway up the steps to his trailer, and he turned as well. "Me? What am I protecting?"

"That's right," I said. "Are you getting a pay-off? Some sort of consideration? How and why are you protecting whoever's out there?"

He quickly stepped back from the leaning little staircase and came back at me, and I prepared myself for a swing or a punch, but he came up and said, "Moron."

"I've been called worse."

"Fool," he said, lowering his voice again. "What kind of people you think are out there? Hunh? I know, I know, dangerous people. But that's just words. It's like you sitting on your warm ass in your warm ass house when a Nor'easter is pouring through, and you think about us fishermen out on the water, and you go outside for a minute to scrape some ice, and you think you know what it's like. No, you don't know what it's like. You don't know what it's like, working on an ice-covered deck, knowing one slip will put you into the drink and you'll be dead in seconds 'cause of hypothermia. Or having to knock ice off the gunwale and other equipment, so you don't get top-heavy and turn turtle. So you don't know what it's like."

He took a breath. "Again, you sitting in your fine home, driving around in your fine Honda, nice fat bank account, and you know shit. You think you know these smugglers are dangerous. Shit, man, these are guys with brass and enough money to outfit a freighter, shove it full of desperate people, and sail 'em across the Atlantic, and then dump their sorry souls on the doorstep of the land of the free. And they don't give a crap about humanity, about being civilized, and doing the right thing. You get in their way and you...are...dead," he added, spacing out each word for emphasis.

Another pause, and he said, "Yeah, you are dead. And to them, it's a business expense like paying extra for postage. They rightly don't give a shit about anything here, except a place to dump their cargo and make millions."

"Billy..."

He said, "You damn fool, if I'm protecting anyone, it's you. Now get the hell out, stop poking around. Other folks got it covered. You're too weak, too stupid."

Then he quickly walked up the stairs and went back into his trailer, slamming the door shut behind him.

I GOT BACK to my Honda Pilot, started up the engine, and feeling warm and not as comfortable as before, I turned around and headed out of the Tyler River Campground. I was halfway up the dirt road, heading back to Route One, when I slowed down due to a dark green pickup truck coming from the other direction. It had state license plates marked FG and on the side of the passenger's door as I drove by, I noted the simple seal of the N.H. Fish & Game Department.

Two wardens were in the crowded front seat of the truck, and I gave them both a wave—which they returned—and then I was on Route One and started my way home, feeling out of sorts and maybe just a bit of guilt over having given Billy Bragg his warning.

TWO MEMBERS of the Wentworth County Free Militia were sitting on the boulders at the north end of the parking lot, drinking coffee, rifles leaning up against adjacent rocks. I wonder how they would react if I were to quickly drive up to them and start gibbering Russian or some other foreign language.

Instead I slowly drove by them, and then something odd happened: the one on the left took my photo with his handheld phone, while the other one made a notation on a clipboard.

My own private security force. Lucky me.

I drove down, parked the Honda, saw that a couple of storage cardboard boxes on wooden pallets at the far end of the shed had fallen over. I left the boxes for later, got out and into the house.

Billy Bragg said he was protecting me. That was a concept indeed.

Was he lying?

And did I do the right thing, giving him the warning about the Fish & Game officers heading his way? That was solid, actionable information. All I had gotten in return was a lecture of the old fishermen and strange lights in the sky and in the water, mysterious shadows, and the sense of isolation out there in the near Atlantic.

I PUTTERED around the house a bit, answered those few bits of email that hadn't originated from Lagos or Mumbai, and Paula Quinn called.

"My day is nearly at an end," she said. "Feel like inviting a lonely working woman over for dinner and a recreational nap?"

I said, "Hey, Paula. Why don't you come over, have something to eat, and maybe fit in a recreational nap if that's okay?"

She laughed. "My, you do come up with the best ideas," she said. "I'll be over in under an hour."

"Say hi to the militia when you walk by."

"God, they're at your house?"

"At the upper end of my driveway," I said. "Taking photos and taking names. I guess I've been designated an enemy of the people or something like that."

"I've always thought that about you," she said. "Okay, so they're going to take my photo you said?"

"They're keeping track of who's coming and going into my house."

"Then I might pose for them," she said. "Show off my new French cut panties."

"That'll make their day."

"Maybe yours, too, if you play your cards right."

I CLEANED up the house around the kitchen area and then realized I was short on supplies for making the two of us dinner. Usually our meals at my house were hit or miss, with the life supply of bachelors, i.e., take-out, being my usual default, but I wanted to cook tonight.

After rummaging through my supplies that made me feel like a Wehrmacht supply sergeant in Stalingrad in 1942, I came up with the necessary supplies for something called a hunger beater that Felix had introduced me to last winter. It was similar to a quiche except it had more of a firm flour bottom, and was a thicker mix, with bacon chunks and lots of egg in the center, and with a cheese crust on the top.

At the time Felix had said, "My Greek grandmother taught me to make this years ago, a simple peasant dish, and a week ago, it was a feature recipe in *The Wall Street Journal*. Goes to show you almost anything is a gourmet meal if it sticks around for a while."

Usually it's served with a salad, but I was hoping we both could eat it and Paula wouldn't notice the difference.

I got the plates and silverware out and checked the time, and Paula was right on the dot when I got the cast iron skillet out of the oven and put it on top of the stove to cool. There was a knock at the door, and I called out, "Give me a sec," and then I washed my hands and went across the small living room and wondered if I had locked the door. At this stage Paula could just walk in without any fuss from me, and I got to the door and easily spun the knob.

So it wasn't locked.

And Paula wasn't there.

It was a man in his thirties, standing there, shivering, with a woman next to him, her head bowed, her two hands on the thin shoulders of a little boy standing in front of her, pressing against her sopping wet skirt. The woman looked a bit younger than the man. The boy was about six or seven. He was wearing a dark orange life vest.

The man's eyes were filled with fear and pleading.

"Help?" he asked. "Sir? Help?"

24

I opened the door wider and waved them in, and then I leaned outside to see if we were being spotted, and I couldn't tell. It was dusk and I was sure my two armed members were still up there, and then I closed the door and the man spoke to me rapidly and shook my hand, and the woman—whom I guessed to be his wife—started bawling, and then the little guy started whimpering.

"Okay, okay, okay," I said, "you're safe, you're safe," and at least I resisted the all-American urge of speaking louder and slower so my foreign visitors would better understand me.

I motioned to them to take off their sopping wet coats, and mom's fingers were shaking so much that I took over getting the life jacket off the little boy. When it came off, he started sniffling and bawling, and the woman was trying to hush him, and dad was working on his coat as well. I fell back and went to the thermostat for my oil furnace and cranked it up. I usually keep it at sixty-eight degrees this time of year—I get a lot of sunlight in the morning hours that helps heat up the joint—but I boosted it to seventy-two degrees.

I next went into the coat closet adjacent to the stairway, yanked the door open, and at the top shelf took down three heavy black wool blankets that I keep in case I lose power and the fireplace can't keep up.

Back in the living room, I draped one blanket over my couch, gestured to the family to sit down, and then gave the other two blankets to mom and dad. They sat their child between them and draped the blankets over themselves. They kept on shivering. Their sodden and cold coats were on the floor. I didn't care.

It would take a bit for the oil furnace to kick up the temperature, and I went to my fireplace, about eight feet away from the couch and my visitors. I opened up the flue, crumpled up old copies of *The Tyler Chronicle*, and in a few minutes, a fire was underway.

I checked on the three refugees. Where in God's name had they come from, and where had they been these past few days? The mother had her blanket up to her chin, her dark eyes staring at me. She had thick black hair and eyebrows, and an olive complexion. Dad had a thick black beard, same dark eyes and hair as mom, and he was talking softly to his boy, who was now grinning.

Kids. Sometimes they were damn near indestructible.

With the fire going and the furnace chugging along, I went to the kitchen, drew two tall glasses of water, and went back to the family. Mom and dad took the water, with mom offering a glass to her son first, and the son murmured something, moved his hands underneath the blanket, and then took out a plastic glass, cracked at the top. It was of an odd slender design, and I knew I had seen and held its mate a few days ago, and I also knew the name of that German manufacturer was on the bottom.

RITZENHOFF

Dad poured some of his water into his boy's glass, and they drank some more. I went back and forth into the kitchen one more time, until they had their fill of water.

On my third trip to the kitchen, I decided to go back with something else.

THE EGG, bacon, chive and cheese dish had cooled down enough for me to slice it, and I didn't know what kind of dietary restrictions my visitors might have, and at this point, I don't think either of them would care. I held the still-hot cast iron pan with an oven mitt and cut the hunger beater into three huge triangles. They came out reasonably well, and I plated them and took two out at first, with a knife and a fork. In front of my couch was a coffee table, and I pushed aside old copies of *Smithsonian* magazine and *The New York Times*, and then I put the plates down, went back to the kitchen, and soon the three of them were eating, talking low among themselves, mom still looking at me with suspicion, son now giggling and shoving food into his mouth, and dad smiling and looking at me, whispering, "thank, thank, thank."

I said nothing, just smiled in return, and then went up to my office, and came back down a few minutes later with a thirty-year-old atlas, with wildly outdated maps and city names, but I never could allow myself to throw it away.

When I came back, the three of them had finished eating, and mom had carefully placed each used plate on top of each other, with the silverware on the top plate.

I moved the plate and squatted down and opened up the atlas and got to a map that showed the northeast United States, and I tapped on the tiny smudge that marked the New Hampshire coastline, and then pointed out the sliding glass doors to my deck.

I got nods from mom and dad, and then son had retreated back under the covers, gingerly sipping water from one of my glasses.

I then opened up the atlas to a wider view of North Africa and the Mediterranean, including the regions of the Middle East and I pointed to them, and then I pointed to the atlas, and again, I pointed to them, and made what I hoped would be a universal quizzical, "hey, mind telling me where you're from" look.

Dad nodded and reached out a hand, and mom barked something and slapped his hand back. He looked hurt and said something, and then mom replied in a long rattling sentence that I was sure translated, *Are you an idiot, telling this stranger where we're from? For all we know, he's already called the Army or police to come pick us up.*

I smiled at mom to show there were no hard feelings, and I closed the atlas, took the dishes away, and dumped them in the sink. I came back with a couple of stools that I used around the kitchen counter, and I draped their coats over them and backed them up to the fire, so they could dry off some.

Then I gestured to them to follow me. Mom and dad exchanged worried looks, and there were whispers, and then dad said something sharp, mom replied with something sharper, and then dad got up from the couch, and took his son by the hand.

Mom said something else, like, *I can't believe you're doing this, why in hell did I marry you in the first place,* and then all three were up, the blankets over their shoulders. I walked slowly up the stairs and dad led the way, followed by mom, and then their son, who was looking around with wide eyes.

At the top of the stairs, my large bedroom with a much smaller deck was off to the right, and to the left was my office with its too many books and not enough bookshelves. Before me was my bathroom, and I led them in.

Besides the sink, toilet and large bath/shower unit, there was also a compact washer and dryer for laundry. I turned on the hot water in the tub, switched the shower off and on, and then I went to a nearby closet and pulled out lots of towels.

More whispers and then I thought through, ducked into my bedroom and went to my closet, and grabbed some sweatpants from a time of lunacy when I thought I could actually get into a regular scheme of exercising, and some heavy shirts and T-shirts that I was sure would fit mom and dad.

As for their boy...there was nothing, save the dryer.

It was the best I could do.

I went back in, and mom was playing with the water going into the tub, and dad was standing there, looking relieved and confused, and then I put the clothing in his arms and nodded and smiled, and backed away, closing the door behind me.

I went downstairs and was two steps from the bottom when there was a knock at my door.

I DIDN'T LIKE the sound of the knock and I spent a quick minute or so tossing the now-wet blankets and wet coats into the closet, and after the third door knock, I was ready.

I opened the door, and I wasn't too surprised, for one of the militia members was there, standing on my stone steps, looking eager and happy, and with a semi-automatic rifle slung over his shoulder. He had on a bright red L.L. Bean jacket and a navy black watch cap.

"Everything okay?" he asked.

"Perfect," I said.

"You need any help?"

"Gee, I got some dishes in the sink, but I think I can take care of it."

He smiled some more and leaned left, and leaned right, trying to look beyond me.

"That's not the kind of help we're offering."

"The only kind I need," I said.

The militia member said, "Thing is, Jerry back up there, he thought he saw a couple of folks run out of your garage over there, and then go through the front door."

The storage boxes at the end of my shed, the ones I thought had fallen. No, they had been moved earlier to provide a hiding spot.

"He thought he saw? Really?"

"Yeah," he said, sounding foolish. "We've got a nice pair of night vision goggles, and Jerry was trying to see if he could see anything across the street, up in some of those guest rooms, all the while the idiot should have been looking down here."

I started to close the door. "Well, when you work with idiots, don't be surprised by the results."

We both heard some laughter and singing coming from upstairs, and I said, "Damn TV always gets louder when the commercials come on, don't they."

Then I shut the door in his face.

I WENT BACK UPSTAIRS and there was still some laughter coming from behind my closed bathroom door, and I decided to leave the family alone. Lord knows how long it had been since they last had a chance to laugh at anything.

In my bedroom I switched off the lights, retrieved a nice pair of Zeiss 7 x 50 binoculars, and looked out one of the windows to see what I could see up at the top of the driveway.

A few more people, it looked like.

A pickup truck coming to a quick halt, armed people coming out.

I lowered my binoculars.

I could call the Tyler cops and eventually they'd get here, and eventually they might be able to convince them to go home or at least not block my driveway, but that was a lot of eventualities.

After all, they weren't breaking any laws.

I put the binoculars back on top of my bureau, went around and then started downstairs, and like I was in some sort of live action Looney Tunes cartoon, when I got downstairs, there was yet another knock at the door.

Thank goodness I had never installed a doorbell. The sound of the chimes would have driven me crazy.

I got to the door and Paula was there, fumbling with her leather bag and a plastic grocery bag, and she said, "Wow, the militia folks sure are gathering up there. They practically asked for my ID after I parked my car and started down here."

I took both bags from her hands and when she came in, and after a brief kiss, I kicked the door shut with a loud slam. She took off her coat and said, "Jesus, Lewis, are you freezing? The place feels like a sauna."

"Thought the fire would add some romance."

"It's adding degrees, that's what it's adding," she said, and then she sniffed. "Damn, that smells good. What's for dinner?"

I put her bags down. "Nothing for the moment."

"What, it's not ready?"

"Well, it was ready about a half-hour ago, and then it was eaten."

She looked at me like I was trying to joke with her, and she was not in the mood for joking. "Lewis, I'm hungry, and I don't understand you. Did you eat it?"

"No."

"What?"

More singing from upstairs. "My visitors did."

She lifted her head up to the ceiling. "Visitors?"

"Refugees," I said. "Illegal immigrants. Undocumented aliens. Whatever phrase is in vogue nowadays."

Paula said, "You're kidding."

"Can't you hear them singing?"

"How many?"

"Three," I said. "Mom, dad and young boy. They came by about forty minutes ago, knocking on the door."

"Where are they from?"

"I don't know," I said. "I tried to find out, but they're scared out of their wits. They were also cold, thirsty and hungry. I got the fire going and boosted the heat, gave them something to drink, and sorry to say it, gave them our dinner."

"I get it. What are they doing upstairs?"

"Showering and changing," I said. "Let's see."

We went up the stairs and at the bathroom door, and after a slight knock and "Hello?" mom answered the door, wiping her long hair with a towel. She had on gray sweats and was wearing a Red Sox T-shirt, while dad had on a blue pair of sweatpants and was wearing a Space-X T-shirt. The young boy was wearing a plain blue long-sleeved T-shirt whose hem reached just above his chubby knees.

I smiled and showed them Paula, and to give them an idea of who Paula was, I hugged her shoulder and kissed her cheek.

"Lewis..."

"Yeah, I know."

Mom and dad smiled at us, while the young boy was carefully drying off his toes.

"No," she said. "You don't know."

"What?"

But she went forward to the pile of wet clothes, and started sorting them, and opened up the top of my clothes washer. Mom started helping and I felt like a dolt, and dad smiled at me and said something I didn't understand, but I think the general tone was, *Our women think we're idiots, right?*

In a few minutes the laundry was going, and we ushered the family out of the warm and moist bathroom and then downstairs. I stripped off the damp blanket on the couch and they sat down, and I went into the kitchen and rustled up some apples, oranges, and Hershey's chocolate bars.

I brought the food back on plates and Paula said, "You got coffee? Tea?"

"Only instant and the tea is in bags."

She started through my cabinets. "We need to change that, friend. You need to get a coffee maker, at least enter the twentieth century."

I said, "In some ways the twentieth century was overrated. Here, I'll help."

I got a wide wooden tray and as the kettle started to get heated up, Paula said, "If you can handle the rest of this, I can get to work."

"What work?"

She gave me a surprised look. "The story."

"The story?"

Paula gestured to the three family members, warm and dry on my couch, munching on my dessert plate. "This story, silly. About these three refugees, washing up ashore, alive and well."

"Paula..."

She went out to the living room, got to her bag. "I'll get some photos, find out where they're from, interview them using Google Translate, and—"

I put my hand on hers.

"Paula."

"What?"

Mom being mom, she sensed something was off and stared at me, while dad was busy unwrapping a Hershey's bar for his excited little boy.

"Would you join me in the kitchen for a bit?"

"Sure," she said, her voice edged with frost.

In my kitchen Paula said, "Lewis, don't you dare tell me not to write this story."

"I'm not telling you, I'm asking you."

"You have no right!"

"No, I have every right," I said. "These people are my guests. They're here illegally, they're just starting to figure out what's what, and—"

She folded her arms tight. "Lewis Cole, I've interviewed car accident victims, folks whose homes have burned down around their ears, and mothers and fathers whose children have shown up dead, either through drowning, gunshot, or opioid. I think I have the sensitivity to interview these folks and get their story."

"You do that, you'll be putting them in jeopardy."

"Like crossing the Atlantic and getting to your house without drowning in the process?"

"No, like telling the smugglers that they made it here alive, that they didn't meet up with their coyote to bring them wherever they had to be, and that they're in a position to tell investigators what they know. If that happens, they'll be dead in a day."

"I won't reveal their names, and the photos won't show their faces."

"So all that will go out will be a story about a family of three from some country in the Mideast who arrived here within the past couple of days? You think that won't identify them?"

"Don't you dare tell me how to do my job."

"I'm not," I said, feeling my temper rise. "I'm telling you how to be a human being first, and a hard-nosed journalist second. You can do this story and get it out, and make a difference, and get nice coverage, and put those three over there in danger. Or you can help in getting them out somewhere to safety, and not do a story about them in my house."

If her voice earlier had been frosty, now it was particularly Arctic.

"Why can't I do both?"

"Paula, we don't have time."

"You looking to kick them out?"

"No," I said. "I'm looking to get them someplace safe."

"And your home isn't that place?"

"No," I said, "It's not. You saw what was up at the parking lot. The local militia members know something is up. They're calling in their friends, reinforcements. In a while they're going to start talking, maybe start drinking, and they're going to decide to take care of things themselves. And when that happens, they're coming down that dirt driveway and to my house, and even if I don't answer the door, they're coming in."

Paula kept quiet. On the couch mom and dad were now looking over at us, knowing from our tone that something was going on.

I said, "When they come in, there's going to be some shouting, pushing, some punches. Maybe a gunshot. And then they're going to leave with that family with them. I'm not going to let that happen. I'm getting them out of here, and I'm sorry, that doesn't leave time for you to interview them here."

Paula kept quiet. Mom and dad were quiet, too. The little boy sitting between them was talking or singing to himself, devouring a Hershey's bar between lines.

The teakettle started to shriek.

25

In about thirty minutes, we were ready to leave. The family's clothes had been washed and dried, and through gestures and hand waves, I insisted mom and dad keep on what I had donated. Paula had quietly and efficiently made ham and cheese sandwiches for the trio—at least knowing they weren't Muslim or Jewish by seeing how eagerly the boy munched on a piece of sliced ham when it was offered to him—and I put together three water bottles.

Throughout it all, Paula was quiet and did what was necessary, but I knew from bitter experience that she was going to give it to me later, good and hard, and without any mention of her undergarment status.

Their freshly washed clothes and food went into old plastic grocery bags, and I gathered our little group in front of the door. The boy looked fine, but mom and dad were concerned. I knew why. For a brief while they had been here, warm and safe, no concern for food or water.

Now they were on the move again, out to uncertainty and fear.

Paula said, "What's the plan?"

"Get them the hell out of here," I said.

"Thanks for clearing that up," she said, voice sharp. "I had no idea."

"I'll get my Pilot, back her around to here, and then we'll get in and head up the driveway."

"The militia is up there."

"I know."

"They have weapons," she said.

"I know that too."

Paula said, "Why not call Diane Woods? Get them out of here, in police custody?"

The three faces of my guests looked at me.

"I can't do it," I said. "If they were just going to be in Diane's custody, well, she'd treat them right, she'd treat them fairly. But now it's changed. Diane is a cop. She's tough, fair, and friendly, but to these three...she's a cop. And chances are, at some point, these three will be taken by our local Homeland Security folks, and then they'll be caught up in the fine gears of the federal government."

"And you have a better idea?" she asked.

"Maybe not better, but it's mine," I said.

Dad reached over, touched my arm. "Sir? Help?"

I touched his arm right back. "You got it. Help."

Paula looked to him, managed a smile. "Yes. Help."

THE FRONT of my house and shed were under surveillance by the brave men up on the parking lot, and I positioned Paula with the family, and she said, "You know I'm coming along, right?"

"But of course."

"One of the smarter things you've said tonight."

I opened the door a bit and said, "Hang here until I back up, and then shove everybody in the back."

"It'll be crowded."

"It'll work," I said. "We won't have time for everyone to climb in like they're heading off to dinner."

"Okay."

"And Paula?"

"Yes?"

"Thanks," I said. "I'm counting on you to get these three out and in my Pilot without hesitation."

She said, "I'll do it. I just hope you know what you're doing."

I grabbed my jacket, made sure the keys to the Pilot were in the pocket, and then went to the rear of the house, switching off the lights to the kitchen. I unlocked the sliding glass door, removed the length of wood that blocked the runner, and then slid the door open.

I stepped out into the cold darkness, and then slid the door behind me. I wanted to take a quick look up at the top of my dirt driveway before leaving out the front door.

It looked crowded up there.

Damn.

I went back into the house.

"Change of plans," I said.

I WALKED over to a downstairs closet, reached up to a top shelf, grabbed a pistol grip, and then removed what was up there. Mom and dad were looking at me with fear.

I didn't blame them.

Paula was standing next to the young boy, hand on his head, bag over her shoulder.

"What now?"

"Feel like driving my Pilot?"

"No," she said, "but I'll do it if it's important."

"Very important," I said. "You're going to drive the Pilot with the family in the back, covered with blankets."

"And you?"

"I'm taking the lead, driving your Escort. Stick right behind me, don't turn on the headlights, just follow your car's taillights. From the parking lot, I'm taking a right and heading north on Atlantic Avenue."

"What are you going to do when you get to the top of the hill?"

I hefted up what I had just taken out of my closet.

"Give them one bright surprise," I said.

WE MOVED QUICKLY.

Paula's car was parked near my shed, so I pulled that around so the engine was running, lights off, but I parked it so I was at least blocking part of the view from the militia members. I then backed the Pilot out of my shed and rolled it to the rear, near my front door.

I left the Pilot's engine running, switched off the interior lights, and then got out, leaving the driver's door and near passenger door open. The refugee family came out, followed by Paula, who closed the door behind her.

The dad started whispering something to me and I just patted him on the shoulder, and then pushed him in. The boy jumped in with glee, like he was looking forward to tonight's adventure in America with a full belly and warm clothes on him, and mom was last, and I couldn't tell what she was feeling.

Paula got in. I leaned in, kissed her.

"For luck," I said.

She managed a smile.

"It'll take some luck for this to work."

"I know."

"Just don't bang up my Escort," she said. "She's an old bird but she's paid for, and reliable."

I gently closed the door to the Pilot, went up and into Paula's Escort.

I buckled in, checked that my pistol was in its place—shoved in between the front seat and center console—and that my other weapon was within reach, over there on the passenger's seat.

I lowered the driver's side window.

It was cold.

I glanced up to my rearview mirror. Just my Pilot and some shadows contained within.

I shifted the Escort into drive, switched on the parking lights, and then started up the bumpy dirt path. I've driven this roadway hundreds of times and know every bump, ripple and pothole, so even with the dim amber beams from the Ford's parking light, I had no difficulties.

But it was time to pass some on to the militia members crowded up there, a couple with flashlights.

I punched the accelerator, switched on the headlights, hit the high-beams, and then grabbed the handheld spotlight next to me, held it up to the windshield, narrowed my eyes to slits, and then switched it on.

Instantly about 6,000 lumens of light glared out, enough to light up the lighthouse over at the Isles of Shoals if I wanted to, and I heard yelps and shouts as the light blinded the armed men, including those unfortunate few who were using night vision goggles and who just had their optic nerves dazzled.

I blasted through, horn blaring, and the brave men scattered, and I switched off the spotlight—my own vision slightly dazzled as well—and then I drove through the parking lot, up to Atlantic Avenue, and calmly switched the headlights to low-beams and turned on the right turn indicator.

I got onto Atlantic Avenue in Paula Quinn's car, and then I looked again to the rearview mirror, and I saw a vehicle depart the parking lot and catch up with me.

It seemed to be my Pilot, but I wasn't sure, and then the driver flicked the high beams three times at me, and then backed away some, and I knew it was Paula, right behind me.

I tapped the brake lights twice to let her know I had seen her message, and the two of us sped through the night.

LESS THAN TWENTY MINUTES LATER, we were in North Tyler, and I parked Paula's Escort in the dirt parking lot of the Grange Hall, having enjoyed the experience of driving her car, even though the rear seats were cluttered with old newspapers, empty coffee containers, and crumpled bags from McDonald's and Dunkin' Donuts.

The Grange was a two-story building with black shutters and a black shingled roof, and the white paint was flecked and peeling. More than a century ago, Grange Halls were established post-Civil War to provide a fraternal and support organization for farmers, and in some places, it still lived on, providing other community activities.

Like renting tonight's hall for a group of immigration activists.

I parked Paula's Escort at the far end near a spot where there was a green Dumpster, and I got out and waited for Paula to show up in my Pilot, which happened about ninety seconds later.

I stepped up and she was smiling, which cheered me. "Well, that was a special ride."

I peered in and saw my three visitors clustered in the back seat. The young boy waved at me and I waved back.

"Glad for your help."

Paula said, "What now?"

"Inside the Grange Hall is a meeting of the Open Arms Coalition," I said.

"Really?" she asked. "Good call. If anyone would be up to helping these people out, it'll be them. Do you have a contact?"

"I do," I said. "Look, I'll duck in there and you find a place to park." I handed over her car keys. "Thanks again. And by the way, your car really needs a good cleaning out."

Paula said, "If I ever do that, I'll never recognize her."

I bent down, gave her a quick kiss, hoping that her earlier Arctic anger over me asking her not to do a story was maybe melting away, and then I started to the front of the Grange, and saw Paula take my Pilot to an empty space underneath some oak trees.

INSIDE THE GRANGE it was loud and bright with lights and burning zeal in the justice of their cause, and about sixty or so people were sitting on brown folding chairs that had N. TYLER GRANGE stenciled on the rear. A large table had been set up near me with drinks and homemade cookies and brownies—I hate brownies, always thinking of them as a waste of perfectly good chocolate—and there was the gentle hum of conversation. The closed windows were tall, like that of a Congregational Church, and it seemed every spare bit of the walls was filled with framed black-and-white photos of old farms and stern looking men and women in nineteenth century clothing.

There was a small stage up front, flanked on each side by American and State of New Hampshire flags, along with a lectern, and a polite older man wearing sandals with socks and bearing an Amish-style beard came up to me.

"Looking for someone?" he asked.

"Mo Walsh," I said.

"Hold on, I think I saw her a couple of minutes ago. Mind if I ask who's looking for her?"

"Lewis Cole," I said.

There were also handmade posters hanging near the refreshment table, with familiar slogans I had seen from the other day at my not-so-friendly neighborhood riot:

LAND OF THE FREE, NOT DEPORTATIONS!
BORDERS AREN'T RIGHT!
WE'RE ALL HUMANS HERE!

"LEWIS?"

I turned and Mo gave me a big smile, held out her hand, which I shook. "Wow, so you've decided to come to speak to us after all."

"Um, not really—"

She looked down at her clipboard. "I'm not sure where I can fit you in. Reverend Slayton isn't here yet, but I think he wouldn't mind if—"

"Look, Mo, you don't understand—"

"And if he does show up, he can—"

I gently took the clipboard from her hands, and she looked at me with shock.

"Mister Cole, what in the world are you doing?"

I gave her clipboard back. "Trying to get your attention. I need to speak to you, in private."

A knowing smile. "Please. This is an open organization. We have no secrets from each other. It's only when we start keeping secrets from each other that oppression and tyranny enter our lives."

"That's nice," I said, giving a quick glance to see if anyone was near us, open or not. "I need your help."

"Of course," she said. "What can I do for you?"

I stepped a bit closer, lowered my voice. "I've got three refugees that need help."

"What?"

"Refugees," I said. "Mom, dad, little boy. They came to my door a couple of hours ago, looking for help."

"Refugees?"

"Refugees, undocumented migrants, illegal aliens...whatever you want to call them. They're far from their original home, and they're out in there in my Honda, and they're scared out of their wits. Can you take care of them?"

It seemed like a long wait, as there was more chatter and talk from these concerned citizens, and then Mo looked at me with determination.

"No," she said.

26

I said, "What? Did you just say 'no'?"

"God, yes," Mo said, holding up her clipboard. "That's what I said. Why in the world did you bring them here?"

"You're the 'Open Arms Coalition,'" I said. "The supposed good guys in this nasty debate. You say you're open to people crossing into the States without borders."

"We are," she said.

I gestured to the cheery posters. "Well, for Christ's sake, here's the chance for you folks to do what you say you want. Take in three refugees, provide them assistance."

"But we're not set up for that!" she said, then looking behind me, like she was scared that the refugees had followed me in. "We're a pressure group, an organization to raise awareness, get the laws changed, improve the functioning of the immigration courts. We...we don't have the resources to actually take in people."

I said, "Look, I'm not asking you to make a prison raid or something. Just take three people in, shelter them, and then work something out."

One and then another member of the group—both elderly men with suspicious looks—stepped in behind Mo.

"Is there a problem?" the near one asked.

"No," Mo said. "I believe Mister Cole was just leaving."

This was getting ridiculous. "All your bravery, all your bold talk, all your slogans...just that, am I right? Just a chance to get together and have protests and tell each other how pure and noble you are. But when something real comes up, you won't do a thing."

Mo started moving away. I guess the important rally was about to start.

"You can call the North Tyler police," she said, not sounding embarrassed at all.

"I do that, and they'll probably be with Homeland Security in less than a day and sent to some prison somewhere."

She turned her head away from me and walked into the hall, joining up with her dedicated and self-satisfied group.

I WENT OUTSIDE. The air had gotten colder. The parking lot was full and then a dark blue North Tyler police cruiser slowly rolled in.

It just sat there, engine rumbling, its headlights switching off. There were two police officers sitting up front.

Time to get out of here.

I went around to the rear of the Grange and saw something I hadn't expected.

An empty spot where Paula Quinn's car had been parked.

NOW I WAS at my Pilot, and I opened the door—the interior lights still switched off—and the dad said, "Watch, watch."

Watch what?

There were two lumps on the front seat. I felt them up, realized it was my spotlight and my pistol. I picked them both up, slipped the pistol into my shoulder holster, and got into the Pilot.

"Here," the man said, and he pressed a slip of paper in my hand. I reached up and switched on an interior light, instantly recognizing the handwriting.

. . .

Lewis,

Sorry I ran out on you. Work and duty calls.
P

PRETTY STRAIGHTFORWARD NOTE.

I crumpled it up and dropped it on the floor.

What now?

And why were the North Tyler cops here? Expecting trouble? Or did my militia friends raise a fuss, and Tyler dispatch sent out word to local departments to look for me and possible refugees?

I started up the Pilot.

The three were still sitting back there.

I couldn't imagine being in their position, in a strange and frightful country, depending on a stranger to take care of them...if that's what he's doing.

I didn't know where to go, but I knew we couldn't stay here.

I started up the Pilot and started out of the parking lot, and—

One of the cops was now standing outside his cruiser, looking in my direction.

The woman behind me uttered a soft cry.

Her husband tried to shush her.

The boy was quiet.

I waved at the cop, he waved at me, and I drove out, heading back to Atlantic Avenue, not knowing where I was going, but at least knowing that for now, I was driving these folks in a place where the police usually couldn't stop you because you didn't speak the language or looked differently.

I STOPPED ONCE AT DUNKIN' Donuts in Porter, looking for directions—I knew the name of the street, but not the exact address—and within five minutes, I was pulling the Pilot into a paved lot near the Porter Harbor. In front of us was a small white building with curves, and a small dome with a cross above it. Dad and mom leaned over their boy to look out the windows.

I got out, gave them a cheery smile that didn't represent what I was feeling, and walked out, past a wooden sign saying that this was a Greek-Orthodox church—St. Gregory the Theologian—and went to the rear, to where I hoped the rectory was located. The grounds were well kept and I easily found my way due to the lot's utility lights. At a rear door I rang the doorbell, knocked, and rang the doorbell again.

The door opened to a friendly looking yet wary bearded man in his mid-30's, wearing black trousers, white collared shirt and black vest.

"Yes?"

I said, "Are you..."

And damn if my mind drew a blank right then. My face felt warm, like I had stood up to speak in class and had forgotten the name of my teacher.

"Father Bob," he said, smiling. "And you are?"

"Lewis Cole, from Tyler Beach," I said. "Father, excuse me for bothering you...but you know a Felix Tinios, am I right?"

His expression changed, instantly becoming more reserved. "I...do. And how do you know Mister Tinios?"

I was in a spot. I was meeting a religious man at night, hoping he could help me and those three folks in my car, but he had asked me how I knew Felix. A man who was legally a security consultant, but who had many bloody years working for what passed for the Mob in Boston and Providence.

How would this priest react? What should I say?

I took a breath.

"Felix is a friend of mine," I said. "I've known him for years, know what he's done and the experiences he's had. That's how I know him."

Father Bob nodded. "That's him."

I said, "I also know that off and on he's donated to this church over the years. Because it's the closest Greek-Orthodox church to where he lives."

The priest folded his arms. "Or perhaps he's made donations because he's trying to assuage his guilt over what he's done to his fellow man over the years."

I didn't know where this was going but I decided I had to go along for the ride for the sake of my passengers.

"That's not Felix," I said. "He's not wired to feel guilt. Regrets or sorrow, absolutely, but not guilt. Now, excuse me Father, but it's getting cold out here and I've got three very scared foreigners who need help."

He reached back and took an old jacket off a rack. "Yes, that's Felix all right. Let's go help them."

"Just like that?"

Father Bob shrugged on his coat. "Just like that. Or why else would I be here?"

He followed me back to the Pilot and I put on my best smile and relaxed attitude, and I opened the rear door and mom, dad, and young boy came out, eyes blinking, looking around. Father Bob said, "Welcome, welcome," and then repeated the same in Greek, but I couldn't tell if they understood it or not. He shook the man's hand, gave a little bow to the woman, and rubbed the top of the boy's head.

Dad turned around, grabbed my right hand in two of his.

"Thank," he said. "Thank."

I shook his hand back.

"Yeah, thank," I said.

I SHOULD HAVE FELT satisfaction with getting the refugee family to some safe harbor, but I was grumpy and out of sorts as I drove home. There were various things rocketing through my head, from the militia members playing guard duty at the top of my driveway, to the knowledge that another freighter was out there close to shore and coming in with scores more migrants like the ones I had saved and had dragged ashore, and then there was Paula.

Not like her, to bail out like that. What was going on? Still pissed about how angry I had gotten over her idea of using these folks for a story? Or did something else come up at the newspaper?

I thought of calling her but it was too late and I was too tired, and I made the turn back into the parking lot of the Lafayette House, and I decided to try to play nice for a couple of minutes, so I drove right over to my driveway, headlights on regular, and there were four or five militia members, standing around an empty 55-gallon drum with wood burning in it, like they were steelworkers in Pittsburgh working on week two of a strike, and they all looked at me with hate as I drove by and got to my driveway, and two of them gave me the traditional one-finger salute.

I pulled into the shed and then went back into the house and spent a few minutes just cleaning up and tidying things, and then I spotted the plastic glass that the boy had kept in his jacket.

RITZENHOFF.

If I had been a fully-fledged private investigator within the Granite State instead of a magazine columnist with too much time and guilt on his hands, I would consider this a clue. Important, no doubt, but how? All I knew was that this was the second time I had seen such a plastic glass in my hands, and somehow it got from Germany and ended up here.

I placed the glass on my now clean kitchen counter, and thought that if this was one of those criminal forensics shows on television, the investigators would bring this glass into their super-duper ill-lit laboratory with futuristic equipment and gizmos, and they'd retrieve some latent fingerprints from the plastic, and they'd run the fingerprints through The System, and since the plastic cup came from Germany, they'd trace it back to the manufacturer, and when they did that, they'd get a hit on the prints.

That would ID a player in the smuggler ring, and he'd be picked up and sweated out, and then the entire smuggling ring would be exposed, and armed Coast Guard special forces would be rappelling out of helicopters onto a rusty crowded freighter, about to sink, and all would be solved and happy in forty-six minutes, complete with a cheery and smiling epilogue.

I went upstairs.

No television was on in my house.

I picked up a pair of binoculars, looked up at my neighbors, spotted the flickering flames coming from the steel drum. I picked up my phone, dialed a number from memory, and it was picked up on one ring.

"Tyler police and fire dispatch."

"This is Lewis Cole, from Atlantic Avenue," I said. "It looks like there's an illegal fire burning in a drum at the north end of the Lafayette House parking lot."

I gave her a bit more information, and then hung up the phone and took a shower.

When I was dried and dressed, I went back to my bedroom window, picked up the binoculars again.

The fire was out. All I saw were flashing red lights from a Tyler Fire Department pumper truck.

"Good job," I said.

I went into the kitchen, grabbed two Hershey bars from my pantry, and went back out to the living room, putting on a heavy jacket and a knit cap Paula once made for me a few years back when she was temporarily seized by the knitting bug, and with Beretta in hand, I went out to my laughingly small and rough front yard, until I found a nice place where I could sit down against a boulder, being partially hidden.

I put the pistol in my lap and pulled out one of the Hershey bars, unwrapped it and gave it a good bite. It tasted good. For some reason chocolate tastes better outdoors, especially in the cold, and very especially at night. It reminded me of my long-ago youth when I delivered newspapers on bicycle, and one customer would pay me every Friday late afternoon by putting that week's money in a little jar, with a Hershey's bar to go along with it.

Fond memories.

I leaned back and looked up at the bright stars overhead, and I felt ashamed that I couldn't remember the last time I had hauled out my telescope to do some serious stargazing. Time to change that, before it got too cold.

I ate half of the Hershey's bar before I caught movement coming down my driveway, and I folded up the bar and put it into my jacket pocket.

I took my Beretta out and continued waiting, easing my breathing.

Three shadows appeared, walking slowly but confidently toward my house. I could see two were carrying weapons over their shoulders.

They stopped in front of my door, and I saw them huddle together, like they were considering what to do next.

I decided to speed up their decisions.

I pulled back the hammer on the Beretta, which made a loud click in the stillness of the night air.

The conversation over there instantly ceased. The men slowly turned in my direction, although I was confident they couldn't see me, as hidden as I was.

I called out, "Guys, I could drop all three of you right now, and there's not a jury in New Hampshire that would convict me for shooting three armed trespassers. So turn around and get the hell off my property."

I waited, holding the Beretta in my hands, and then the armed trio turned and went back up my driveway.

I kept on waiting.

Then I slowly let the hammer back down on my pistol, waited a few minutes more, and then got up and went back into my house, locked the door, and went to bed.

27

It didn't seem like much time had passed when the ringing of my upstairs phone woke me up. I fumbled my way across my bed to the near night-stand, grabbed the phone, and a woman's voice said, "Morning."

"Paula?" I asked, rubbing at my eyes.

A loud laugh. "In your dreams, writer-boy."

I checked the time. It was 8:01 a.m.

"Sorry, Diane," I said. "It's early."

Tyler's most famous detective sergeant said, "Nice to be a civilian. I've been on the job for more than an hour."

"As a taxpayer, I thank you. What can I do for you?"

"Asking a favor."

"Ask away."

She said, "Come on down to my office. Have some coffee and blueberry muffins."

I yawned once more. "Diane, that's a great offer, but can I take a rain check?"

"No," she said, and there was something in her voice that woke me straight up.

"Diane?"

"It's like this, Lewis. Come on down for a little coffee and breakfast, and a talk about recent events, or I'll have to send up a uniformed to take you in. Don't make me go official on you."

I sat up in bed. "Let me guess. The members of the Wentworth County Free Militia didn't appreciate me last night."

"Or your friend. Or friends."

I checked the time. It was 8:03 a.m. It seemed like more time than one hundred-twenty seconds had passed between us.

"All right. Give me time to get dressed and such."

"Not a problem," Diane said. "Take your time...but get here soon enough. All right?"

"All right."

AFTER SHOWERING AND DRESSING, I went out to my Pilot—still carrying my Beretta in a shoulder holster—and got in and backed up, and then up the driveway. At the top where the dirt driveway meets up with the Lafayette House parking lot, two sad looking sorts were sitting on the open tailgate of a dirty white Chevy pickup truck. They had open sleeping bags over their shoulders, their hands were in their coat pockets, and the pair didn't seem to have the energy to say or do anything.

I drove by without a wave on my part, and when I got to the parking lot, drove across and to the Lafayette House. I parked in a NO PARKING zone, got up and went into the gift shop where I picked up the morning newspapers—*New York Times, Boston Globe, Wall Street Journal, Boston Herald*—and two coffees in cardboard caddies, and some Hostess breakfast pastries.

Burdened down some, I went back out to the Pilot, and just as I was maneuvering my way in, saw a black Chevrolet Suburban slide out to Atlantic Avenue. A young man was driving, and for a second, I caught a glimpse of his front-seat passenger.

Agent Mark Stockman of Homeland Security.

BACK AT THE PARKING LOT, I pulled in next to the pickup truck and stepped out, holding my breakfast offerings to these two dispirited members of our local militia. One had a thick brown mustache, the other hadn't shaved in a couple of days.

"Hey," I said. "You guys looked like you could use a breakfast."

The guy with the mustache just frowned but his friend got off the tailgate and came over. "We was supposed to be relieved an hour ago."

"What happened?"

"Who knows," he said, taking the coffees and breakfast from me. "I think people are just getting tired of it all. I mean...no offense, we're supposed to go down there and walk up and down the coast but Jesus, what's the point, hunh?"

I went back to my Pilot. "Smartest thing I've heard in a while."

At the Tyler Police Department I stashed my Beretta underneath the front seat of my Pilot and went into the station, and a minute or so later, I was back in Diane Woods' familiar office. She looked tired and had on blue jeans and a black polo shirt with the Tyler Police logo embroidered on the upper left side, and I took a chair across from her. The view outside was still obscured by scaffolding, but the hammering and drilling noises seemed to be on the other side of the building.

"Before we start, I just wanted to let you know that there's nothing new concerning the potshots that were taken at you," she said. "No brass recovered, no other witnesses came forth, nothing on any surveillance cameras in the area. Things okay with you? No threatening phone calls? Emails? Severed horse heads in your bed?"

"All quiet," I replied. "Seems like...well, nuts to say, it seems like a one-off in some way. I've not felt threatened, nobody's following me or tossing bricks through my window at three in the morning."

"Let's hope that's what it was," she said. "Hold on, I'll be right back." Diane got up from her cluttered desk and went up the hallway to the small kitchenette the station has, and she came back with a coffee mug and a tray of bite-sized blueberry muffins. She sat down and I grabbed two of the muffins and I said, "I guess I'm on the enemies list of the Wentworth County Free Militia."

"A good guess," she said. "Two members have filed criminal complaints against you."

"For being mean?" I asked, munching on one of the small muffins. It had a crunchy exterior and a buttery interior, and I wished there were more on the small plate. I picked up my coffee mug, knowing Diane had fixed it just the way I like it, black with two spoons of sugar.

Diane took a sip of her coffee, glanced down at her notes. "A few others have done as well."

"Such as?"

"Former Selectman Dave Tyler, of the famed local Tyler family," she said. "I'm sure you know of him."

"Hard not to," I said. "What's his beef with me?"

"It's with his son Roger, who's one of the leading members of our militia," Diane said, head down, still reading from her notes, like she didn't want to look at me in the eye. "He and others are claiming that you tried to run down members of the militia who were peacefully gathered in the Lafayette House parking lot last night. He told his dad and dad rang my bell about an hour ago. True?"

"I don't know," I said. "I didn't listen in to your phone call."

Diane looked up and said, "Usually your above-it-all wiseass nature is amusing, but not today. He seems like an old Navy vet, working for his town and fellow residents, but he's sharp and he feels like he's representing more than three hundred years of Tyler history. So stop with the attitude. What happened last night?"

I took her warning. "It was late at night. They had harassed me when I came into the lot on my way home, and later two of them knocked on my door, giving me grief. Later that night, Paula and I left in our respective vehicles, and I wanted to make sure we didn't get held up. So I flicked my high beams on and shone a spotlight in their faces. Seemed to work."

"Partially," she said. "When you lit up the militia members, a couple of them panicked and fell down."

"Not very well trained, are they."

"One sprained his ankle, the other fractured a wrist in the confusion. They're pretty much pissed at you, and so is former Selectman Tyler. He wants me to press charges against you."

"What do you want to do?"

"Not do that," she said. "But can you promise to be a good citizen and tone things down?"

"Depends," I said. "What do you mean by tone things down?"

Diane looked like she was struggling. "You're a smart fellow. You know what I mean. With the bodies washing ashore, the near riot at the selectmen's meeting the other night, and armed clowns marching up and down Tyler Beach and elsewhere, there's too much tension in the air. Please be a friend and don't add to it."

"I'll do my best," I said. "But I won't be bullied."

Diane kept quiet for a long, long moment, and said, "About last night and the drive out of your driveway."

"Yes?"

"You said it was you and Paula, right?"

"That's right."

"And Paula still drives a Ford Escort, right?"

Damn.

"That's right."

"But Roger Tyler is sure you were the one driving an Escort last night, and Paula was behind you, driving your Pilot. Sounds pretty funny, hunh?"

"It does."

I kept my mouth shut. I didn't like the feeling. This conversation had taken a turn, and I was no longer talking to my friend Diane, but Detective Sergeant Diane Woods of the Tyler Police Department.

We both stayed quiet, and she said, "Care to tell me why you both drove each other's vehicles?"

A number of snappy and wise-ass answers suggested themselves to me, but I just shook my head. "Not at the moment."

"Another funny thing," Diane said. "When the Pilot drove by, being driven by a woman—and I think we both know it was Paula—another militia member said he was certain that two or so people were trying to hide in the back seat."

I nodded. "Okay. I promise to tone it down, best I can. I don't want to make your life any more difficult."

Diane didn't seem happy or triumphant. Just tired.

"Are you making that promise to me or to the Tyler Police Department?"

I popped the other muffin in my mouth. "I'll guess we'll never know," I said. "Just put it down to my good mood for the morning."

She said, "I guess you haven't seen *The Tyler Chronicle*'s website this morning, then."

I was glad I had swallowed.

Things felt tight around my throat.

"No, I haven't," I said. "Care to show it to me?"

She swiveled the display screen of her laptop around so I could see what was up there, and what was up there wasn't good. There was the standard Tyler Chronicle banner, but what was underneath was anything but standard. A large headline announcing that "Refugee Family Washes Ashore at Tyler Beach", and below that was a photo of the family that I had taken care of last night.

They were huddled together, looking at the camera, trying to smile, and their heads were lowered so that they couldn't easily be recognized.

But I recognized them.

I stared, barely reading the news story next to it, the one written by PAULA QUINN, CHRONICLE STAFF WRITER, starting with the sentence, "The continuing migrant crisis along the New Hampshire seacoast continued last night with the discovery of a refugee family who had ended up ashore on Tyler Beach."

Diane quietly said, "Not to be too snarky, Lewis, but that sure looks like the rear seat of your Pilot."

I turned the computer screen back to Diane.

"It sure does," I said.

28

It took me about ten minutes to get to *The Tyler Chronicle* from the police station and I don't think I consciously made a single turn or acceleration in my brief journey, relying on my muscle memory to get me there. Traffic was light and I easily found a parking spot in the newspaper's lot, and I slammed the Pilot door and went right through the main entrance of the *Chronicle*.

The door to Paula's office was closed and I gave it a brief knock before swinging it open.

Paula looked up, surprised, and so did two women of a certain age that I recognized as freelancers from the outer part of the *Chronicle*'s circulation area.

"Paula, a minute?" I asked.

She said, "Well, I'm in the middle of wrapping up something, and—"

The far woman gathered up her purse and iPhone and said, "Paula, I think Marcy and I are okay...we'll be going."

Marcy quickly nodded, like she was a rear-echelon supply sergeant hearing the approaching rumble of artillery, and she got up as well, both of them sliding past me. When they were out, I closed the door and said, "Paula, for God's sake, what the hell were you thinking by running that story?"

Her face flushed as she slowly sat up straighter. "I was doing my job."

"You said you weren't going to run a story about them."

Paula's face got redder. "That's not true."

"It certainly is," I said. "I asked you last night not to do a story about that family, and I just saw your online story."

She said, "Then your memory's starting to slip, Lewis. I said no such thing."

I felt incredibly frustrated, like indeed something was starting to slip away, and it wasn't my memory.

"Paula..."

She picked up a pen, dropped it on her desk, and said, "I agreed that I wouldn't do a story about that family at your house. That's exactly what I did. When we were at the North Tyler Grange, that's when I did the story. So I kept my word."

There was more slippage. I felt wrong, out of place, and in a terrible state.

"You...you put those people in jeopardy."

"Their faces were hidden."

"You just told their smugglers that they survived."

"So what if I did?" she asked. "The whole purpose of smuggling them across the Atlantic was to get them to New England. They're in New England. Alive. I had an opportunity to tell their story, and that's what I did."

"You...Paula, you didn't have the right to put them in danger. And you knew what I was asking for, back at my house."

Her eyes narrowed and she picked up the pen again and didn't let it drop. "Speaking of rights, where do you get off telling me how to do my job?"

"I wasn't—"

She plowed right over me and said, "I've been running down sources, doing good reporting for more than a decade. I've had weeping parents in this office, embarrassed town officials and victims of crimes knocking on my door, all asking me to do the same thing: not do a story about what happened to them. And I had to tell those folks what I'm telling you, that

I'm a goddamned journalist, doing my job, and I can't make an exception for anyone, anyplace."

"But you saw how scared they were."

"Of course I did," she said. "And I've talked to dads who had to ID their kids at the hospital after getting killed in a drunk driving accident, and businessmen whose lifetime work was wiped out by arson, and a town clerk who froze when I asked her about discrepancies in the petty cash account. They were all people having the worse moments of their lives, and even more unfortunately for them, it was all news, and I was there."

"Still, I mean, you saw them, how could you..." My sentence dribbled off.

"How could I be so cold-blooded to take advantage of them, is that what you're saying? I did it because it's my job, and I'm good at it. I reported on them, and the story's been picked by the local and national wire services, and the cable networks. It means more clicks on our website, and more newsstand sales, and maybe a few more subscriptions. Which means that in addition to doing my job as a journalist, I'm also doing my job as an editor, keeping this newspaper alive and jobs for a fair number of folks."

"Paula, please," I said. "You could..."

I didn't finish my sentence.

She jumped on that, too.

"Could what?"

I was about to say that she still had time to pull the story down from the *Chronicle*'s website and not set it for print publication later this afternoon, but I knew that was a non-starter.

"Nothing," I said.

Her phone started ringing.

She said, "Are we done here?"

"We are," I said, and I left her office.

I RAN A COUPLE OF ERRANDS, gassed up the Pilot, stopped at the Post Office to find I was too early for my mail, and when I got back to the Lafayette House parking lot and the start of my dirt driveway, there was only one militia member seemingly on duty, and he was sitting in a green-webbed folding lawn chair with a blanket over his lap, along with what looked to be a single-shot .22 rifle.

I drove by without him even looking up from whatever game device he was holding in his hands.

Seeing the drop-off in militia members guarding my driveway was about the only positive thing going for me this day.

LATER IN THE afternoon my phone rang, and I was hoping it was Paula, so we could at least find some common ground for peace—or at least a truce —but it was Felix, with news that I wasn't anticipating.

"Hey," he said. "You know that thing we were talking about? And the family relation?"

"Hey," I snapped back. "You know what? You really think all this double-talk and code words actually means something?"

Felix breathed and said, "Boy, somebody's having a bad day."

"Like you wouldn't believe."

"Are you standing up?"

"Yes."

"You breathing?"

"Yes."

"Bleeding anywhere?"

"No," I said, "and you can stop the lecturing. Okay. I know what you're talking about. There's a development?"

"Yeah," he said. "There's a meet tonight. Hook up with me at the Round-about Restaurant...say, eleven p.m. Come along and we'll see what we can squeeze out of this knucklehead."

"I thought this knucklehead was a member of your family," I said. "That must be disheartening."

Felix said, "Well, that's part of history, isn't it. Powerful and strong families get diluted over the years. Who's afraid of the Borgias nowadays?"

"Not me," I said.

"Nor I," Felix said, and then he hung up.

. . .

THE AFTERNOON DRAGGED on and on, and two phone calls to Paula went unanswered and straight to voicemail. The first message I left was a simple one, identifying yours truly and hoping we could talk. I didn't leave a second message, because that would be edging into stalking or begging territory, lands I didn't want to visit.

The sky was graying out with clouds rolling in, and I took a few minutes to go out on my rear deck and check out the Atlantic, my nearest and fiercest neighbor. The surging water was reflecting the gray overhead and my mood. The waves were sweeping into my small cove, and I was haunted with the thought that for now and forever, this little slice of sand and rock would ever be overlaid with the memory of bringing the dead mother and her child up to shore.

The wind picked up. I wasn't dressed for being outside, but I waited.

Out there beyond the horizon was one more crowded and decrepit tanker, biding its time until the sun set either tonight or tomorrow or the day after, and then it would make a high-speed run into this shore, to rendezvous with someone, somebody, and then bring their human cargo ashore.

They were waiting out there.

Here, others were waiting as well. The various police agencies. The thinned-out Coast Guard. The Wentworth County Free Militia. The local residents who were either violently opposed or enthusiastically supportive of the refugees stumbling ashore. And Alice Hackett, making news and ratings by riding this story for as much as she could. Not to mention Mark Stockman of Homeland Security, doing his job.

Whatever that job was.

I shivered once and then again, and then went back into my house, sliding the glass door behind me. It was good to be warm, it was good to be safe.

I checked the time.

I had six hours to kill.

And I didn't want to kill them here, alone in my old house.

So I decided to do something else.

. . .

FROM WHERE I had parked my Pilot, I had a good view of the Homeland Security offices at McIntosh Air Force Base. Earlier I had called and asked for Agent Stockman, and surprise of surprises, my call was routed right through, and I hung up when he answered.

Meaning he was still there, over in that concrete cube.

I had parked a block away, in the parking lot of a restaurant that claimed it was an Irish pub. One day I had taken Felix there for lunch and he had frowned and said, "If this is fake Irish food, I'd hate to meet the real deal."

I accused him of being anti-potato and left it at that, but the place was popular, which meant my Pilot shouldn't stand out while I conducted my little surveillance. I had a monocular viewing lens at my side, because bringing up a pair of binoculars can catch people's attention, and that can lead to a cop coming by at some point and asking why I was sitting here, spying on someone.

I used it a few times, watching figures amble out of the building, while traffic went around me and two KC-135s of the N.H. Air National Guard practiced take-offs and landings at the near runway.

Somebody familiar stepped out and I took a gaze, and what do you know. It was Alice Hackett's best boy, Brady Hill, walking briskly out of the Homeland Security office, walking over to a white GMC sedan that I was sure was a rental. He didn't have anything in his hands, but he walked oddly, like something was weighing him down.

What was going on?

He unlocked the door to the sedan, took something familiar looking out of the right pocket of his gray suit jacket, slid it under the front seat, and then got in and drove off.

I was tempted to follow him but no, I had another target in mind.

Stay on target.

The fifth time I had my monocular up to my right eye, I lucked out.

There was Mark Stockman, briefcase in hand, walking out to a black Chevrolet Suburban. He got out of the lot and took a right onto Aviation Lane, and I followed him.

It wasn't much of a surveillance.

He drove four more blocks and then parked his car in a lot for a medical device company that had taken over one of the single-story brick buildings from back when this place belonged to the Strategic Air Command, and foreign policy and objectives were a hell of a lot simpler.

I passed by and went to the parking lot next door, belonging to Southern New Hampshire College, and waited.

Not long at all.

He parked his Suburban, got out, and then walked over to a red Toyota Camry. From there he started it up and drove out, and I kept pace with him.

ABOUT THIRTY MINUTES later we were in a part of Porter that was relatively rural and near the border with Wallis, and we were on Atlantic Avenue, within view of the ocean and about a twenty-minute drive from my home.

There, Stockman parked his Camry with New Hampshire license plates at the cracked asphalt parking lot of the Worldwide Inn, a one-story motel with an office attached at one end.

Interesting.

I drove down Atlantic Avenue, made a U-turn, and pulled into a small lot for the South Porter Condominium project, and despite the warning signs telling me I needed a permit to stay here, I fought the law and stayed right where I was.

But I was too late, or Stockman was too fast.

I couldn't tell where he was.

Hunh.

I looked around and there was an Irving gas station a block up the way. I went there and purchased two newspapers. Then I got back in the Pilot and drove back to the Worldwide Inn. I pulled in front of the office and went in, a bell on the door going *jingle-jangle*, and I went up to the counter where a manager was working.

She was an attractive woman of a certain age, with thick close-cropped brown hair. It seemed I interrupted her evening meal, for it looked like a half-eaten Philly cheese steak sandwich was on a sheet of wax paper before her. There was a small television at her elbow that was showing an episode of "Call the Midwife."

There was a nameplate that noted ROSALIE GREEMAN before her, and on the side of the counter was a stack of mystery novels. I tilted my head and saw they ran the gamut from Lee Child to Sara Louise Penny to Ann Cleeves.

"Can I help you?" she asked.

I smiled back. "Quick question...how did your place get the name?"

She leaned back in her chair, pointed to a number of framed color photos on the walls behind her. "See? I've been fortunate in my life to have traveled to all seven continents. How many people can say that? Look at that photo...one of my favorites."

The photo showed her smiling and looking down at an ice cream cone, and a little plaque underneath said *Ushuaia, Terra del Fuego.*

"Very impressive," I said. "I'm afraid I'm only up to three."

"Well, do it as soon as you can," she said. "And you still haven't answered my question: how can I help you?"

I placed that day's copies of *The New York Times* and the *Wall Street Journal* on the counter, next to a small brochure stand advertising whale watching trips from nearby Wallis Harbor. "Hey, I was wondering if you could help me out. My boss just got here a few minutes ago and I forgot to pack this in his briefcase. Would you mind dropping them off at his room?"

"Who's your boss?" she asked.

"Mark Stockman."

She took a peek at what looked to be a register and shook her head. "I'm sorry, no one's here by that name."

Of course, I thought.

"Well...he works for the Federal government. He's a prominent official in Homeland Security and sometimes he likes to go out anonymously. He's driving a Toyota Camry with New Hampshire plates...and he's about this tall—"and I used a hand to indicate the height "—and he's got gray eyes, and what little hair he has is shaved pretty close on top."

The woman nodded. "All right, I think I know who he is. But I can't tell you his room number."

"I'm sure," I said. I gently pushed the papers over and said, "When you have a chance, could you take them over? Please?"

Her smile was pleasant and wide. "Sure. Once I finish my dinner."

I went to the door. "Good for you," I said. "It looks tasty."

. . .

I PULLED out of the parking lot and parked farther down the street, out of
sight of the motel, and then walked back up along the side of the road.
There was no sidewalk here, just a rough path of crushed stone and gravel,
with a big dirt berm on my right and the increasingly busy Atlantic Avenue
on my left. Near a dumpster by one of the small condo parking areas, I
scooted in and waited.

And waited.

And waited.

It was dark and getting colder, and the smell of the dumpster was
pungent and sickening, and in between the engine sounds of traffic going
by, I was sure I could make out rustling noises of four-legged rodents
moving around and dining in the trash.

I brought up the monocular. It didn't have night vision capabilities but
the streetlights in the motel's lot gave pretty good illumination.

There.

The friendly and world-traveled Rosalie Greeman stepped out of her
office and walked down to the row of units. The monocular was powerful
enough so that I could see the black paste-on numerals, and I saw her stop
at Room 9.

She knocked on the room's door.

Knocked again.

The door opened up, and she passed the newspapers over to the person
standing there.

Alice Hackett.

29

When I got to the parking lot for the Roundabout Restaurant in Porter, Felix was already waiting for me in his Mercedes-Benz sedan. I was five minutes early and saw that, once more, he'd followed his rule of arriving at a meet earlier than the other party.

"It gives you a small advantage," he had explained to me once. "It makes the other person a bit nervous, unsettled, like they're either late or that I'm a hard-ass, wanting to get there early because I have better things to do."

The October night was crisp indeed and I made the quick walk from my Pilot to Felix. The Roundabout restaurant, years and years ago in a simpler time, used to be one of the many Howard Johnson's restaurants stretching across the nation. Now, somewhere out there is just one remaining. Still, this building maintained a bit of the architectural structure of the old HoJo's. Before us was the Porter traffic circle, with an endless loop of cars and trucks heading over to Porter, or to the east to Maine, or farther north into New Hampshire.

I got into the front seat of Felix's car, and he said, "Carrying, correct?"

"I am."

"Good," he said, shifting his car into reverse. "Don't think we're in any peril, but Nico is traveling with a very rough crowd. The Boy Scout approach is always the best."

Be prepared, of course, which—by the by—is not their slogan.

Felix drove us with caution and assurance through downtown Porter, which was first settled back in 1623. It has an ongoing feud with its neighbor to the north—Dover—which also claims it was first settled back in 1623, and the arguments over who was first have gone on since then and will probably go on for another century or so.

Years back, downtown Porter was a depressing collection of rundown buildings and sketchy bars serving sailors and marines from the nearby shipyard. The actions of berserk developers flattened lots of 1770s-era homes in the name of progress, but through some civic action, many of the old homes were saved. And lots of the bars that offered cheap drinks and working women who charged their male customers by the hour for their companionship were now boutique shops and very pricey restaurants.

But the civic minded residents remain, though they've changed as well over the years. As Paula Quinn once told me, "Once upon a time the concerned citizens of Porter worked hard to preserve their history and community. Now those citizens have been replaced by a chattering mob that latches onto anything that offends them and destroys people's lives and reputations."

I didn't like thinking of my last meeting with Paula, so I said to Felix, "Where are we going?"

"The proverbial abandoned warehouse."

"Really?"

"Well...abandoned for now. But there's plans to change the building into a craft brewery if the local planning board votes its approval."

It was nearing midnight and I admired Felix and the way he handled the Mercedes. No GPS, no printed-out directions, no hand drawn map of where we were going. Among his many skills was the ability to know where he had to go and how to get there.

And no GPS. GPS signals can be tracked, and Felix was not one to be tracked.

We were in a part of Porter that bordered the North Mill Pond, with homes dating back to the 1700s and 1800s, tightly clustered together and with narrow roads that were barely a lane wide. There were old brick warehouses, train tracks, wide stretches of gravel, and marshland leading off from the pond. Along the side of the railroad were piles of ties and old iron rails.

It was a bumpy ride and Felix pulled in behind a two-story brick building with boarded up windows on the first floor, and gravel, trash, and knee-high grass scattered around in clumps.

"Well," he said.

We got out and I let Felix lead the way. I spared a quick look back at the lights of downtown Porter, imagining all the locals and tourists and others having fun at the restaurants and bars and clubs over there. Yeah. Over there was innocent fun. Here, in the dark with the stench of the near pond and the sound of a train in the distance, it felt like we were in a place where anything bad could happen with no witnesses.

Felix had a small penlight in his hand that lit the way to a crumbling loading dock. He scampered up a set of steps and went to a splintering wooden door that was secured by a combination lock. Felix spun the dial, and, in a few seconds, the lock was undone and we were in.

He flicked the light around, showing a concrete floor and soggy piles of crumpled cardboard containers, broken bottles, and empty beer cans. The brick walls were covered with graffiti in white and black paint. I thought I could hear water dripping somewhere.

There seemed to be a glowing light down at the other end of a brick hallway.

"This way," Felix said.

The air felt damp, and the stench was nearly overpowering, of urine, stale smoke and beer, and decaying, wet trash. As we walked down the narrow brick hallway, a voice called out, "Who's there? Who's there?"

"Shut up, Nico," Felix said.

The hallway opened up into a square room with battered metal desks and broken chairs shoved into one corner, and a scared-looking young man was sitting on the floor, back up against a brick wall, on a foam mattress with a couple of blankets over his lap. There were crumpled-up paper bags from McDonald's and Dunkin' Donuts at his side. Another dark hallway led off to the right of the room. A battery-operated lantern wasn't doing a good job lighting the place, and the corners of the room and the other hallway were barely visible.

He seemed to be in his early twenties with shoulder-length brown hair and scraggly beard and mustache, wearing a dark blue sweatshirt and holding a knife in his hand.

"God, Uncle Felix," he said, putting the knife in his lap. "I'm so glad you're here."

Felix pulled a chair from the mess of broken furniture, dragged it over, and then got another one for me. We both sat down, and Nico started talking.

"Uncle Felix, this has been a big screw-up, please, can you help me out? Can you? I mean, I don't think—"

"Nico, shut up," Felix said.

He shut up.

Felix rubbed his hands together, unbuttoned his wool Navy peacoat, pulled it aside, revealing a holster and pistol. My coat was open as well, but I didn't feel like showing off like Felix.

He said, "You've made your mother very unhappy."

Nico nodded. The poor guy looked pathetic.

"How in the world did you get involved with these people?" Felix asked.

And he started weeping, wiping at one eye and then another with one trembling hand. "My buddy Carl, he was running a lobster boat out of Gloucester. He needed a deck hand. Good money, cash, paid under the table...so things were going well for a while. We both got dinged and bumped up after a while, though, and we needed painkillers to keep working. Goddamn doctors. So I drained my checking account and ran up the credit card bills and—"

"Shut up," Felix said. "Spare my friend and I your medical concerns. I want to know how you got hooked up with these human smugglers."

He wiped another hand across from his face. "I owed Carl money. A lot of money. And he said he was going to tune me up so not even the strongest shit I was taking would ease the pain. And I said I couldn't find work, so he sent me to a guy, who sent me to another guy."

"Who was it?"

Nico violently shook his head. "Man, I didn't want to know, for Christ's sake, I didn't want to know. I don't know most of the names, and that's fine. We met somewhere down south, Rockport, maybe, and we were in the back of this store, and this big guy—shit, must have weighed nearly three hundred pounds—he sat in a corner, eating cheeseburger after cheeseburger. And he had this weird accent, almost like Russian, and he said, 'Couple of question for you. You need money, can you work on boat, can you keep mouth shut?'"

Felix said, "I take it you said yes all three times."

Nico said, "Shit right I did. So right after that, we were on this stern trawler, had all this gear stripped off, and we went off one night. No running lights, no interior lights, nothing. And we went out for an hour, met up with this rust bucket, and they lowered a net overside, and we took on about fifty folks. I mean, we were crowded, and good thing the water was smooth as silk that night, otherwise, we would have gotten swamped."

I said, "Where did you bring them to?"

He looked to his uncle and said, "Ah, crap, do I have to answer him, too?"

Felix said, "You give any of us any problem, right now, I'll leave you behind. Including not listening to my friend here. Got it?"

Nico didn't look happy, but he said, "Back to Rockport. Some isolated dock. There were these long passenger vans, engines running. We got the folks off, in the vans they went, and that was that. I spent some time hosing down the boat—lots of them had puked on the way back—and I got a nice grand in cash for a night's work."

"How many times more did you do this?" I asked.

"Twice more," he said. "Then the last one, the set-up for the fourth time..."

The tears started up again.

Felix said, "What happened?"

"We...we were back at that store in Rockport. They had maps and charts and shit, and they said they had another trip set up for in few days."

"When exactly?" I asked.

"Tomorrow night," he said.

Felix said, "Go on. Don't leave anything out."

Nico wiped at his tears again. "So there was arguing, from this other guy. Never saw him before. I couldn't tell what they were saying. Again, sounded like Russian. But the big fat guy, he was sitting on a stool, just eating his goddamn cheeseburgers, while this other guy got worked up. There was maybe eight or so of us there. And the guy caught his breath, the fat guy put his cheeseburger down, reached under his napkin and picked up a pistol and shot the other guy in the face. Just...like...that."

He stopped talking. Felix kept looking. I could sense the fear and terror coming up from his nephew and it was making me nervous. I so wanted to leave this place, with or without Nico, get away from this stench and the fear and the dampness in this old brick room. More sounds of water dripping.

"What happened then?"

"The fat guy picked up a fresh cheeseburger, some other American I just know as Skip, he told me, 'come on, let's clean this joint,' and he and me, we dragged the guy out of the room."

Nico swallowed. His voice shook.

"You know, it's nothing like the movies, or the TV shows, or anything like that," he said, voice still shaking. "Me and Skip, we drug him out to another room, and the blood was smeared...and his face and jaw were so messed up...we had to go back and pick up a couple of teeth...and then Skip made me help him roll the guy up in a tarp...and shit, I thought he was still alive, there were gurgles and sighs..."

"Dragged," Felix said.

"Hunh?"

Felix said, "You dragged the body out. You didn't drug. Get back to the point, Nico. When and where is there going to be another exchange?"

Nico rubbed at one wrist, and then the other. "Tomorrow night. Midnight."

"Where?" I asked.

"Not sure," Nico said.

Felix reached out and gave his legs a swift kick. "Then be sure. Where is the rendezvous?"

"Ow!" Nico folded up a leg, rubbed a shin. "It just sounded weird, that's all. Smooth Dome. I saw a note on a map, you know, one of those ocean maps that show the islands and depths. Written there was Smooth Dome."

"What's Smooth Dome?"

"How the hell should I know?" he shot back.

"Who's going to be there?" I asked. "Same crew from Rockport? Or somebody else?"

Nico kept on rubbing at his leg. "There's gonna be a fisherman helping us again. Some guy from Tyler. I guess he's been there from the beginning."

It was like my eyesight and hearing suddenly got enhanced, because I could hear Nico breathing and see red blotches on his skin.

"Who's the fisherman?"

"Some guy."

Felix kicked at him again. "We know it's some guy. Tell us his name."

The one syllable name sounded as loud as an old brick falling into the room.

"Bragg."

Felix said, "That it?"

"Yeah. Don't know his first name, but I know the first name initial. 'W.'"

I said, "W. Bragg, then?"

"Yep."

W. Bragg.

Like William Bragg?

Like Billy Bragg.

I was going to ask him more when a heavy-set man with a thick black beard came in from the other side of the room, through the dark hallway, carrying a pistol.

30

I was surprised and Nico shrieked with both recognition and fear, and Felix spun in his chair, his own pistol out, and he got a shot off just as the guy was lifting up his own weapon. Felix missed but I knew he wouldn't miss with his second shot, but as he got up, the old chair he was using collapsed, and Felix fell back.

The man fired a shot at Nico—also missing—and as he was turning, I had my Beretta out and the man and I locked views for the briefest of a split second, and we both shot at about the same time.

Something tugged at my left shoulder.

The man stood still, then seemed to be aiming at Felix, and then he dropped the pistol.

Looked down at the cement floor.

I was about to pull the trigger again when he slowly collapsed, like one of those Macy's Thanksgiving Day parade balloons, deflating.

The air smelled of burnt gunpowder.

Felix kicked his legs, freeing himself from the broken chair, cursing in very loud Italian.

"Where's Nico?" he asked, standing up.

I slowly turned.

"Gone."

"Damn it."

Felix strode over to the man I had shot, kicked his pistol away. Squatted down and examined the man for a few seconds. From where I was standing, I saw black sneakers, black jeans, and an open leather jacket.

"Well?" I asked.

Felix stood up, gave me one hard and knowing glance. "He's dead."

Felix moved quickly, examining the floor, picking up three shell casings. "You sure you didn't see where Nico went?"

Dead.

The man was dead.

"Lewis?"

"No," I said. "I don't know where Nico went. Felix...he's dead. You sure?"

"Yeah, I'm sure. You okay?"

"Yes."

He came over, touched my shoulder, pulled a few times on a fresh torn spot. "His round ruined your coat. Sorry about that."

Felix looked around the room and said, "That damn Nico...bailed right out on us."

He went to Nico's meager belongings, started poking at them with his right foot. I went over to the man on the floor. His eyes were open, his mouth was open, and foamy blood caked his lips and beard.

Nothing moved.

There was blood on his khaki T-shirt, the cloth torn.

I felt like a child who had broken a valued vase belonging to his parents, and who was now desperately thinking of where the glue was, could the pieces be sorted soon enough, would the glue fix the broken pieces so that no one would ever, ever, notice.

The dead man was still dead.

Not enough glue in the world to fix this, to change this.

Someone grabbed my other shoulder. I jumped.

Felix said, "We've got to get going. I've got our shell casings."

"I...I killed him."

"Yes, you did."

"I killed him."

He took my left arm. "And the more we wait, the better the chance that we'll both be telling that to the Porter cops in a few minutes. I've checked Nico's junk. There's nothing there with his name on it. We've got to go."

I followed him out of the building and then outside, and as we went back to his Mercedes, I said, "Don't you want to look for Nico?"

"No," he said. "Get in the car."

I opened the passenger side door and Felix started up the engine and had us moving before I got the door closed.

When we were on the pavement and Felix sped our way out of the neighborhood, I said, "You sure you don't want to find Nico?"

Felix kept his speed at the limit and made complete stops at each intersection. "No. This is going to sound harsh and brutal but it's the truth. I came to see Nico for two reasons. One was to milk him for whatever information he had that might help you. The other was to save his worthless skin. I got the first part down. I was in a position to save him, and he decided to bail out on us. His decision."

Now we were approaching I-95. Felix said, "We're going to make a quick trip to Maine. Then I'll get you home."

I looked out at the lights and cars and people out there having fun and relaxation.

"Felix...the man I shot..."

Felix didn't answer.

We took an exit onto I-95 and started heading north, going into Maine via the Piscataqua River Bridge.

"Okay," Felix said. "Quick lecture time. He's dead. I'm alive. You're alive. That's an equation I'm happy with. You should be happy, too."

"But—"

"Lewis, he wasn't there to talk to us, to negotiate, to reach a fair and equitable arrangement," Felix said. "He was there to kill Nico. He was there to make sure Nico couldn't say anything to anybody about the refugee smuggling. If we had been fifteen or so minutes later, we would have walked into the building and found him dead. We got there first. You got information you were looking for. And before he could kill Nico, you, or me, you got him first. I'm fine with that. You should be fine with that. Anything else?"

Felix was right.

But I still didn't like it.

"No," I said. "Nothing else."

WE WENT up the span of the Piscataqua Bridge and Felix said, "This is going to be quick. I'm going to pull over and put on the blinkers, and you're going to jump out and look like you're vomiting over the side. And you're going to dump my pistol, your pistol, and the shell casings. Got it?"

"Got it," I said.

Felix checked his sideview and rearview mirrors, turned on the right hand directional, and braked hard and pulled us over. "Here," he said.

I took his pistol and the shell casings, and he said, "Make it quick."

I got out into the cold salt air and went up to the waist-high metal railing, leaned over, and dropped his pistol, the shell casings, and with a hint of regret—I've owned this particular Beretta ever since moving back to New Hampshire, and it's gotten me out of some tight jams—I let her drop the hundred-plus feet into the cold and deep waters of the Piscataqua River.

I stood there, felt my hands shaking. Out beyond me were the bright lights of Porter and the Porter Naval Shipyard, and two other bridges spanning their way into Maine from New Hampshire. In the space of my eyesight were hundreds upon hundreds of innocent people, none having done anything wrong tonight, none having done anything approaching the murder of another human being.

I glanced down to the wide and dark waters of the river and harbor below me, and right then I had the briefest hint of the temptation that can enter one's mind, just to slide on over and let it all end, to let the voices and guilt and sights and sounds go away forever.

A horn honked.

It was Felix.

I turned around and got into his Mercedes. I shut the door and fastened the seatbelt, and then he drove off, and in about ninety seconds, we were in Maine.

"You okay?" he asked.

"No," I said.

· · ·

WE DROVE in silence for a few minutes, and then Felix got us to a Dunkin' Donuts on Route One in Kittery, a chain restaurant that used to sell doughnuts made on site, and now sells good coffee and lumps of fried sugary fat and breakfast sandwiches. He got us both cups of coffee and backed his Mercedes into a parking spot at the far end of the lot.

He left the lights off but the engine rumbling. The interior was warm.

Felix said, "You get home tonight, make sure your shirt, pants, and jacket go in the washer. Give them two good washes before putting them in a dryer. Then it's your turn. Give yourself a good scrub down."

I took a sip of the coffee, stopped. It was too damn hot.

Felix said, "We've been through some things, you and me, over the years. A couple of guys have been killed in our vicinity. I think it'd be fair to say that their absence has made the world a better place."

He was trying so I went along. "Probably."

"Thing that's different tonight, you were the one pulling the trigger. You were the one doing it. You were the one who dropped that guy. Still doesn't make you feel better."

"Understatement of the decade there, Felix."

"Sure," he said. "It's like driving along Atlantic Avenue, up by the line between North Tyler and Wallis. Late at night. Guy's walking across the street. You brake, but you won't make it in time. So you swerve and go over the cliff...or you hit the guy. Tough choice. But you had to make the choice."

"Hell of a difference between a Mercedes and a 9 mm Beretta."

A few seconds passed.

"Trust me on this," he said. "You're going to have a rough night. And tomorrow night will be rough, too. You'll be overthinking things, my friend, the way you usually do. And you're going to feel guilt at what you did, at taking that man's life, taking away everything he had in front of him, all of his dreams and actions and hopes. Chances are, there's a family out there, or some friends, who will mourn him."

I didn't feel like answering him, so I didn't.

Felix said, "All those thoughts are natural. Are part of what has to be dealt with. But remember this, okay?"

I kept on not saying anything.

He turned and said, "Lewis, listen the hell up, and now. That guy came in that room with the intent of killing Nico, then you and me. No witnesses left behind. This wasn't an accidental shooting, this wasn't something that could have been avoided through good intentions or negotiations. Got it? He was there with the intent to shoot to kill. Thank God you killed him. You're not thinking that tonight, but some day you will."

I tried for another coffee sip. This time I was successful.

"Felix?"

"Yes?"

"Take me back to my car."

31

Felix took us back to Porter by taking back roads and side streets, and we exchanged not a word when he dropped me off at the Roundabout Restaurant. I got into my Pilot and that little imp of the perverse spoke up—the voice that whispers to you, "Go ahead, jump," when you're standing at the edge of a precipice—since I had the slight mad idea to drive back into the city to see if the Porter cops had gotten to the scene of the shooting, but no, I headed home.

The scene of the shooting.

The murder scene.

And I was the murderer.

AT HOME I checked through every room and closet, and then locked the front door, and got the shakes for a few minutes—suppose the men who had been sent to kill Nico had me on their list as well?—so I tightened up the house by taking a wooden chair and jamming it under the doorknob to the single door leading outside, and then I turned on the television, wanting to hear humans talking.

I took off my jacket and looked at the torn cloth and threads from my left shoulder, from the bullet fired by the man who had come in shooting. A few inches down and I would be in a hospital somewhere, with a shattered shoulder and blood loss. A few inches to the right and my body would still be back at that abandoned warehouse, with Porter cops looking down at me, measuring and taking photos, digging out my wallet and later seeking in vain to notify any next-of-kin.

The jacket got tossed on the floor in my downstairs closet. I would never wear it again.

Out to the living room now, I turned the channel to Turner Classic Movies, where a black-and-white film from the 1930's I didn't recognize was playing, and then I went upstairs. From underneath my bed I slid out my Remington 12-gauge pump action shotgun settled on a piece of foam, and then I took the shotgun with me into the bathroom. The next part of a half hour was taken up by following Felix's washing instructions, and then I got out and put on fresh clothes and checked the time.

It was almost two a.m.

I felt wired, tight, nervous and irritable, and I knew there was no way I was going to sleep. Shotgun in my hands, I went back downstairs and sat down on the couch and watched the television for a while, but the memories of what I had done a couple of hours ago kept on playing and replaying in my mind.

At one point a wave of nausea came over me, and I made it to the sink before bringing up the bitter remains of my Dunkin Donuts coffee. I cleaned up and stretched on the couch and threw a blanket over me, and with the shotgun on the coffee table within easy reach, I turned down the volume and dozed off and on until the morning sun lit up the inside of my living room and woke me up for good.

I stayed on the couch, head facing the door, feet facing my sliding glass doors and the morning view of the beautiful and deadly Atlantic Ocean, and I knew that out there, beyond the horizon, a freighter was slowly beating its way in with frightened and seasick refugees, full of hopes and dreams and fear, and that I had to do something about it.

So I did.

. . .

I TOOK another shower because sleeping on the couch made me feel like I needed another one, and in the daylight, things didn't look quite as scary, so I stopped walking around the house with shotgun in hand like I was an actor in a bad zombie television series, scared of being attacked for somebody's next meal.

I was jumpy, feeling out of sorts, like my skin didn't quite fit over my body. I fixed a simple meal of coffee, scrambled eggs and toast, and then walked around some more, tidying up a few books, getting rid of a couple of old magazines, tossing three days' worth of *The Tyler Chronicle* next to the cold fireplace, in preparation for a cheery fire, maybe in a year or two.

Seeing the *Chronicle* and Paula's byline prompted me to grab the phone and make three phone calls: to the newspaper, to Paula's home number, and to her cellphone.

None of the calls were answered.

All went straight to voicemail, and I left the same message three times.

"Hey, Paula, just wanted to see how you're doing."

And that's exactly what I wanted to do. I couldn't tell her what I had done the previous night, could not even consider the words I could tell of how I felt right now. I just wanted to hear her voice, get some slight comfort from talking to someone who had no idea that I was a murderer.

I put the phone down, looked at the shotgun and what it represented, and what I did some hours ago.

And again I looked out at that wide ocean.

Time to get to work.

I WENT UPSTAIRS to my office, fired up my MacBook Pro, and then flicked up the homepage of the Great God Google, and did some searching, and then made a phone call to a place about thirteen miles north of my home.

Unlike my previous three attempts, this call was answered after the first ring.

"Coast Guard Station Porter Harbor, Petty Officer Palmer," came a strident young male voice. "How may I assist you?"

"Petty Officer Palmer," I replied. "My name is Lewis Cole, and I'm a resident of Tyler Beach. I have some information to pass on."

"Sir."

Suddenly what I was about to say seemed ridiculous, from sitting here in my dry and safe office. Was I certain? Was I about to send the Coast Guard out on the proverbial wild goose chase?

"It's about the human smuggling that's been going on the past several weeks along the seacoast," I said. "I've got information that there's going to be another attempt later tonight...at midnight, somewhere off the New Hampshire coast. A freighter is going to be dropping off a number of refugees to try to make it to shore."

"I see," he said, keeping his voice even. "Do you know the name of the craft?"

"I don't."

"Do you know where it departed from? And when?"

"No."

"Sir...do you know where it's going? Is it attempting to dock in Porter? Or somewhere else?"

"No," I said. "I believe it will be dropping anchor somewhere in the Gulf of Maine, perhaps near the Isles of Shoals. At a location called Smooth Dome."

"Smooth what, sir?"

I closed my eyes, rubbed at my forehead with my free hand. "Smooth Dome. It must mean a shoal or something prominent."

"Well, sir...I don't know about that. Do you have any idea what vessels might be rendezvousing with this vessel?"

I was tired of saying no.

"I'm not aware of that information."

"Well, can you tell me the source of your information? Was it reliable?"

Not in the least was the truth, but I didn't want to say that.

"I'm afraid I can't say any more than that, Petty Officer Palmer."

"I see. And your name again? And phone number?"

I passed that along and he said, "Sir, thank you for the information. I'll make sure it gets passed on."

. . .

AFTER HE HUNG up on me, I waited for a few moments, went back to Google, and a few minutes later, I made a phone call to the Coast Guard's First District Office in Boston. A few moments of phone play later, I was talking to a Lieutenant Santiago, a very polite woman who asked the same questions as Petty Officer Palmer, and then asked, "Mister Cole?"

"Yes, Lieutenant?"

"May I ask why you're calling us with this information?"

Lots of reasons, I thought, including doing some good to make up for the killing I had committed some hours ago, and I said, "Being a good citizen, I guess."

"But you are unable to verify this information."

"True."

"Can you tell me any more of who provided this information to you?"

"Someone involved in the smuggling operation. He's gone out three times. Tonight is supposed to be number four."

"I see," she said. "And where is he now?"

I hesitated for a long second. "I don't know."

Then it was her turn to pause. "Mister Cole, I'm sorry, I don't know if we can do anything about this...claim of yours. Do you understand?"

I said, "But don't you have any craft on regular patrol?"

"Not as many as we should," she said. "I'll pass this on, that's the best I can do."

And for the second time this grim day, the Coast Guard disappointed me.

And I couldn't blame them.

ONE MORE TIME to the telephone, and I called Homeland Security up at McIntosh Air Force Base and asked for Mark Stockman.

"He's not here at the moment," the officious woman said, with no doubt years of practice.

"Are you sure?" I asked.

"Yes," she said.

"Positive?"

"Sir, stop wasting my time."

She hung up.

Guess she didn't appreciate my sense of humor.

Then I had a thought.

Waited a few minutes.

Played with my phone so that my number was blocked, and then I called back, and got the same woman as before.

"Mark Stockman's office," she said.

I spoke fast and held the phone away a bit from my mouth. "Yeah, Brady Hill here," I said. "Is Alice there?"

"Excuse me?"

"Yeah, is Alice there? I need to reach her. It's an emergency."

A pause. "I haven't seen her today."

My turn to hang up.

Interesting.

I paced around the house for a few minutes, and then tried Paula Quinn again, seeking a brief moment of comfort, and had no joy again.

Damn.

It was time to stop making phone calls and start doing things.

WITH MY BERETTA on the floor of Porter Harbor, I left my house with my sole remaining handgun, my .32 Browning pistol. It wasn't the right size for my Bianchi leather shoulder holster, so I had to shove it in a coat pocket. It was a cold and overcast afternoon, and I was still thinking about last night, when I killed a man, and I was also wondering if his co-workers were out there, searching for me.

I got into my Pilot, backed up and drove up the driveway, and for the first time in a long time, there was no longer anybody standing—or sitting —guard up at the parking lot.

When I got to the pavement, I glanced out at the Atlantic, knowing that if the county militia members knew what I knew, there might be a change in policy.

But they weren't going to get that from me.

. . .

ONCE MORE AT McIntosh Air Force Base, and back in the parking lot of the heavy concrete buildings that belonged to Homeland Security. I didn't see Agent Stockman's Suburban, and I also didn't see any tractor trailer trucks with a refrigerated trailer, ready to receive the bodies that might be washing ashore later tonight.

My session inside was brief and to the bitter point.

The woman that had been there before during my earlier visit, and who I probably had harassed earlier in the afternoon, just looked exasperated when I asked to see Agent Stockman.

Behind the thick glass separating her office from the lobby, she looked up at me with disdain and said, "I'm sorry, Mister Cole, but he's not here."

"But I need to talk to him."

"He's not available."

"I need to tell him about a freighter coming in tonight, carrying migrants. It's arriving at midnight."

And once again, for the third time that day, I wasn't able to answer any of her questions to her satisfaction.

BACK IN THE PILOT, back home to Tyler, and I got off I-95 and drove to the reduced offices of *The Tyler Chronicle*. The receptionist desk was still empty, and the heavy bass from the music being used by the dance studio next door could be felt through my feet.

The door to Paula Quinn's office was closed, and I knocked twice, and with no answer, I opened the door and looked in.

Paula was behind her desk, with two older women sitting across from her, with notepads in their hands. I felt terrible but I couldn't remember their names, only that they were the dependable and very underpaid free-lance reporters who kept the paper alive.

Paula had on jeans and blue-and-white UNH sweatshirt, and her face was not a happy one.

"Lewis?" she said. "You're interrupting a staff meeting. Again."

"Sorry," I said, and I really was. "Can I have a minute?"

She looked up at a wall clock. "In about twenty minutes, yes."

I said, "Paula, please. I really need to talk to you."

One of the women said, "Paula, really, I—"

Paula held a hand out. "Joan, no, it's okay."

Then she looked to me and said, "Can it wait?"

What to say? I wanted to apologize for how I had tried to prevent her from doing her job, and that I realized she was doing what she had to do, and that I had no right to do otherwise. I also wanted to tell her about the freighter out there that was due to appear off our shores in a few hours, and that she might be able to get more photos of drowned bodies tomorrow.

And also...

I wanted to take her aside and sit down in a quiet place and tell her that I had killed a man, and how it happened, and why it happened. But that...I couldn't do that to her. Not now. Maybe not ever.

"Lewis?"

"No," I said, walking out, hand on the door handle. "Paula, it can't wait."

32

At the Tyler Police Department, Detective Sergeant Diane Woods was in a mood.

I caught her in her office just as she was putting piles of papers and folders onto one corner of her cluttered desk, and she was standing up as I came in.

"You've got about a minute or two before I head out," she said. The hammering and drilling for the building's renovations was back again, even louder than before.

"I might need more than just a minute."

"You're wasting whatever time I've got for you," she said. "So what's going on?

I wanted to sit down but I had a feeling doing so would make this session get more tense, so I said, "I've got information about a freighter coming in tonight, probably off the Isles of Shoals. At midnight. They're going to drop off a load of migrants."

Diane didn't seem impressed. "Then contact the Coast Guard. Or Homeland Security."

"I did," I said.

"Then you've done your duty."

"But I don't think they're taking me seriously."

Diane glanced up at me, and the old scar on her chin looked white indeed, always a warning sign. "So? What do you want me to do?"

"I don't know," I said. "I was hoping you could contact Fish & Game, or the harbormaster in Tyler or Falconer."

She put down one last pile of paper. "Why not the Sea Scouts while you're at it?"

"Diane..."

She picked up her leather coat from the rear of her chair. "Lewis, hate to be abrupt and direct, but here we go. For the past week, I've been putting in twelve and fourteen-hour days, all thanks to folks in Homeland Security and the Coast Guard not doing their job. Plus those clowns not doing their job has made my work even harder...for shit's sake, we nearly had a riot at a selectmen's meeting. A selectmen's meeting!"

Diane was on a roll, and I was about to try to get in her way.

"Tonight, Kara has made me my favorite meal, a nice roast beef with homemade gravy and twice-baked potatoes," she said, shrugging on her coat. "That's about a ten-minute drive away, and in fifteen minutes, I'll be sitting on our couch, drinking a nice glass of Cabernet Sauvignon, while Kara gives me a neck rub. So unless you're telling me that there's going to be a robber at First National of Tyler, or somebody has shot somebody in the middle of the Common, I really don't give a crap. That freighter out there isn't my problem. Got it?"

I got it. "All right," I said. "Look, one more quick question, and then I'm out of here."

"You've already used up your time. But I'm feeling generous because I've got hot roast beef and a hot gal waiting for me."

"Porter," I said. "Have you heard any news about a shooting up there?"

"Have you seen anything on the news?"

"No," I said.

"Then neither have I," she said.

Diane grabbed a leather bag, and I followed her out to the rear of the police station, and out in the cold air of the rear parking lot, Diane briefly clasped my hand and said, "Sorry I was a werewolf back there. Feel like coming over for dinner? I'm sure there'll be plenty for three of us."

"Thanks," I said, heading away to my Pilot. "But I've got a full night ahead of me."

"What are you going to do?"

"Try to stop that freighter," I said. "Or at least make sure it's greeted by some kind of law enforcement agency."

"How are you going to do that?"

I said, "I have no idea."

THE SUN HAD SET when I got to the entrance of the Tyler River Campground. The gate was open, and I drove in and then parked near the shuttered gatehouse.

It was dark and when I switched off the Pilot's lights, it got even darker. I grabbed a flashlight from the glove box, stepped out, and shivered in the cold. Through the trees and brush there were the flickering flames of open fires, and the scent of wood smoke was strong. A couple of dogs were barking, and there were voices and music playing. I switched on the flashlight and went down the nearest dirt road, and I was being watched, and I felt like I was in a movie set representing some post-apocalyptic America, with its good citizens living in tents and leaky motor homes.

I shaded the flashlight with my left hand and tried retracing my steps, but in the darkness, nothing was clear.

Ever.

I went down one dirt road, came to a place where it dribbled out to some low brush, and then I walked back and shivered more in the cold. Time was just slipping away, and I felt like I was in the middle of one of those anxiety dreams where someone is breaking into your house, and you can't find the phone, and when you find the phone, it doesn't work, and when it finally works, the nine-one-one call can't be placed.

I always hated those dreams.

A dog ran past me, followed by another one.

There.

Up ahead was the trailer belonging to Billy Bragg, but his truck wasn't there.

I kept walking.

I flashed the light around and saw his trailer seemed to be in worse shape than earlier. A window was smashed, the door was gently swaying back and forth. I took the steps up, poked my head in. "Billy? Anybody here?"

No answer. The interior was tossed around, and it looked like violence of a sort had happened here.

Which brought me to thinking again of last night, of the pistol in my hand, the shots fired, the man falling back, dead by my hands.

I didn't want to think about that.

Out on the steps a shadow was there. "Who's that?" came a familiar voice.

"Fran?" I asked. "Fran Dependhal?"

"The same," she said.

I stepped back on the ground, kept the flashlight pointed to the ground. The light illuminated her tired clothes and tired face. She smelled of stale marijuana smoke and shifted from one leg to another.

"Looking for Billy?" she asked.

"That's right," I said.

She kept on moving restlessly. "Then you're the third one who's come by, seeing if he was around."

"Who were number one, and number two?"

Fran came closer to me. I could smell beer on her breath.

"Number one were a couple of tough looking fellas," she said. "Didn't say much, and what they did say, it sounded Russian, you know? They broke into his place, spent a couple of minutes, and then they left."

"You call the police?"

She laughed. "Didn't have to. They were group number two. Number of Staties and Fish & Game. Rolled right in and up to his trailer. Spent a bit more time in there than the Russians, and that was it."

"Do you know where Billy is?"

"Nope."

"If you did, would you tell me?"

"Nope once more."

I took one more look around at the campfire lights and the dim illumination coming from the other trailers and tents.

"Anything else?" I asked.

"Sure," she said. "I'm a weak woman. I've gone back to my demons. And I'm not proud."

"I'm sorry."

"Not your fault. My fault. And other shit."

"Like what?"

She opened her arms wide. "All of this. I've been running for years and I thought I had found my little slice of respite, my refuge. This place worked for me, Mister Lewis Cole, and I was content. The world was out there, and I was in here. And tonight...the world came back in. Those Russians...I had one look at them and their voices, their manners, put ice in my spine. I can't remember ever being so scared. And when the Staties and Fish & Game showed up, the good guys with guns, I thought, you know, those two Russians...they could handle those uniformed men without breaking a sweat."

I stood there and she said, "I don't very much like the world. It broke in tonight...and it broke me."

BACK IN MY PILOT, I started up the engine and turned up the heater. I grabbed my cellphone and worked my way through the screens until I found the phone number of Harry Bragg.

It rang and rang, and a woman answered, and I asked for Harry.

"He's not here right now," she said. "May I ask who's calling?"

"Lewis Cole," I said.

"The magazine writer?"

"That's right."

"Well, we've just had dinner and he's off to the town hall for a conservation commission meeting. He should be home in an hour or so. Can I take a message?"

I said, "No, that's fine. I'll see him there."

· · ·

THERE WAS nothing much for me back home for a meal, so I made do with a visit to Lori's Clam Shack, which squats near the border with Massachusetts down by Atlantic Avenue. I had a dinner of fried shrimp and onion rings and ate fast. I had made the mistake of not coming in with something to read, a habit I've maintained nearly all my life. Without anything to read, the meal tasted blander and went faster than usual.

About twenty minutes later I was back at the Tyler Town Hall, and what a difference from a few days ago. There was plenty of parking, only two people inside, and one of them was a woman speaking before the Conservation Commission.

It seemed like I knew the woman—who dressed and acted like the activists I had met the other night, the ones who were ready to step in and help migrants, so long as they didn't have to get their hands dirty—and she had on Birkenstocks, blue jeans, and a shapeless gray sweater.

The room still smelled of stale gunpowder and pepper spray, and there were only three town officials, all quietly sitting behind a black table. There was Harry Bragg, Sheldon Tompkins—who owned a candy store in town—and Gloria Nakamura, a realtor who was known for making cutthroat deals at the beach and donating most of her profits to local food banks. They sat and listened to the woman talk, and talk, and talk.

I didn't know her, but I gathered her name was Jane, and she spoke from the heart about the environment, the quality of the town's water and marshland, the necessity of controlling parking at the beach in the winter and the summer.

Time was still slipping away. Across the room from me an older male resident sat slumped, his arms folded, his head leaning down. He was gently snoring. I watched him for a while, because he had black-rimmed glasses that were threatening to slide off his big nose.

I wondered what would happen first: Jane would stop talking, or the man's glasses would fall off his face.

Jane took a breath and Sheldon said, "Excuse me, Jane, I appreciate you coming out here tonight, but what are you exactly asking us to do?"

Her lips were thin and pursed. "Your jobs. All of you!"

Sheldon said, "I think we know our jobs, thank you, Jane."

She shook her head. "No, you don't."

Gloria said, "Jane, look, what you're telling us tonight...are you asking us to sponsor a warrant for next year's town meeting? Is that it? I mean, you've mentioned some interesting proposals in your remarks, but there's a lot there to go into one article. You should break them up."

Jane shook her head again. "You really don't understand, do you. I'm not here to propose a warrant article. I'm here to educate you."

Now it was time for the third commission member to jump in. "You mean what you've been talking to us about for the last—" and looked up at the room's clock "—for the past forty-five minutes has been an education session on your part?" Harry asked.

"That's right," she said, her voice having a tone of satisfaction, of at last finding someone who could finally understand her motives.

But Gloria was having none of it.

"Mister Chairman?" she asked Sheldon.

"Gloria, go ahead."

"We've been in the public comments section of tonight's meeting for nearly an hour," she said. "I move that we close the public comments section at this time."

Sheldon said, "Do I have a—"

And Harry jumped in, "Second."

"All those in favor," Sheldon said.

Not surprisingly, the motion passed unanimously, and equally not surprising, Jane gathered up her stuff and stormed out.

I looked over.

The other citizen here still maintained his sleeping posture and his eyeglasses were still in place.

The meeting moved pretty quick after that, and when they were gaveled to an end, I got up and went to Harry Bragg and said, "I need your help."

He smiled, putting papers into a manila folder, and then putting them into a leather satchel. "What, you need some fish for supper next week? Be quicker to go to Hannaford's."

"No," I said. "It's about your brother. And about a migrant freighter that's due here...in less than two hours."

His hand froze in mid-air. His eyes widened.

"Jesus Christ on crutches," he said. "Are you sure?"

"Positive."

"Then let's get going," he said, and while Gloria and Sheldon were chatting and talking about going out for a post-democracy drink and appetizers, Harry headed for the door, me following, while the man in the front still dozed.

33

In the town hall parking lot, he went up to his F-150 truck, opened the door, tossed in his satchel and said to me, "What do you know?"

I said, "I know there's a freighter coming tonight, somewhere off the Isles of Shoals. At midnight, ready to drop off another load of refugees."

"Good information?"

"From someone who was working with the smugglers, and then wanted out."

"Why didn't you call—"

"I did," I said, frustrated and interrupting him. "Homeland Security, local cops, the Coast Guard...they all listened, took notes, and that was that."

He reached into his coat for his keys. "You said my brother Billy was involved? How?"

"The guy who gave up the information about tonight's drop-off said your brother was a guide to help bring in the rafts and other boats."

Harry wiped at his face, softly swore, and I said, "I went to his trailer earlier today. He wasn't there. Neither was his truck. The woman managing the campground said his place had been visited twice earlier, once from Fish & Game."

"Damn it, Billy," his brother said. "And who else stopped by? State Police? Marine Fisheries?"

Some conversation and laughter now came from the other committee members and the older dozing citizen, now awake, all leaving the town hall. I had a spike of jealousy, to be happy and innocent on such a night.

"Nothing that innocent," I said. "A couple of Russians, from what the campground manager said. It looks like they are involved in the smuggling operation."

"And Billy being Billy...shit."

He started to get into his truck, and I asked, "Where are you headed?"

Inside Harry started up the engine. It took three tries. "Down to the cooperative's docks. He's either there or on his boat."

I started walking to my Pilot. "Good," I said. "I'll meet you there."

Over the sound of his grumbling engine, he said, "Why?"

"Because I want to know what's going on."

"Not your problem, Lewis, honest. You don't have to come with me."

"But I do," I said.

I got to my Pilot and started it up, and I followed Harry out of the now empty town hall parking lot.

WE HEADED SOUTH, took a loop in the road that took us on Route 51/101 South, a two-lane state road heading right to Tyler Beach. Very soon we were riding along with marshes on each side, and before us, the lights of Tyler Beach and to our distant right, the squat buildings and flickering lights of the Falconer nuclear power plant.

About halfway down the highway we slowed down as we came to a set of blinking yellow lights, and I saw Harry talking to someone on his cellphone, which was against the law, but I didn't think Harry much minded. Probably calling home to say he was going to be late.

I focused on the driving, not wanting to think again of the man I had killed last night, or the thought of the scared and crowded passengers out there on some rust bucket, or even Paula and her anger with me.

I just wanted to drive, and drive.

We made a series of right-hand turns and headed past the beach fire station, the construction site that was now the police station, along with cottages and motels and a few restaurants. Harry was in a hurry and it was a challenge to keep up with him, and then another right-hand turn, past marinas and bait shops, and we were in the parking lot of the Tyler Fishermen's Cooperative.

I pulled in next to Harry and he got out, carrying a large flashlight in his right hand. "This way," he said. "I'll check to see if his boat is moored out there."

The air was colder here by the harbor, and the air smelled of salt and old fish. We walked around the co-op building and then to the dock, and Harry flicked on the strong light.

He moved the bright beam across the harbor waters until it lit upon a small, half-submerged orange and white buoy, and said, "Shit."

I stood next to him. "He's gone, then."

"Yeah."

Harry switched the light off and I blinked my eyes a few times. My night vision had just been burned out. He then started moving at a fast pace down the fixed dock, and to the ramp leading to the floating dock where a host of dinghies were moored.

"Do you know where the freighter is supposed to drop anchor?"

"A couple of words that don't make sense," I said.

"Tell me," he said, as he got into his dinghy, went to the rear and started the engine with three good pulls of a rope.

I got in and he said, "Whoa, whoa, there, Lewis. I said you could come with me down to the docks. I didn't say anything about you coming out on the water with me."

I started untying the bow line. "I come along, and I'll give you the location."

The dinghy's engine was burbling right along.

"You don't know what you're doing," Harry said.

I coiled up the line, pushed the dinghy away from the floating dock. "Probably, but I'm still here."

He said, "Okay. Just listen to me and stay out of the way once we get on board."

"Deal."

He flipped the engine from neutral to drive and then we went out into the harbor. It was an uneasy trip. Being out on the harbor in daylight was usually filled with fun and cheer, of windsurfers practicing their skills, folks walking along the rocks and sand of the harbor, and fishing boats either coming in or going out.

At night it was an eerie place, like some horror tale coming true. The empty fishing trawlers with their nets rolled up and the smaller lobster boats moved in the swells, like invisible spirits were aboard, guiding them. I tilted my head up and got a great blazing view of the night sky, and a splash of saltwater hit my face, bringing me back to where I was and what I was doing tonight.

Harry got us up to the *Elayne D*'s bow, flicked on a smaller flashlight, asked me to tie us off to the bright orange buoy that was the size of a large ottoman. He helped me climb up and over the side of the boat and then quickly jumped up beside me. Into the open wheelhouse he went, and he switched on soft red lights—to help preserve our night vision—and he went to the bow and reached down with a long boat hook, picked up the buoy, did some knot untying, and set us free.

I sat on a long, padded cushion near a life jacket and a round lifesaving ring fastened to the gunwale.

Back in the wheelhouse, he started up the engine, switched on the navigation lights, and then he spun the *Elayne D* around and directed us out of the harbor, heading to the bridge spanning the narrow channel and marking the border between Tyler Beach and Falconer.

I jumped as he gave the boat's horn three sharp blasts, and then I went into the wheelhouse and he said, "The horns get the bridge operator's attention that we're heading out."

Up ahead, beyond the streetlights, I saw flashing red lights appear, wooden barriers drop down, and after a few minutes of waiting and listening to the brief wail of a siren, the drawbridge opened up and we slipped out past the breakwaters and into the wide and wild waters of the North Atlantic.

. . .

OUT IN THE OPEN WATERS, as we moved up and down in the swells, Harry stood at the wheel. A padded chair on a stand—almost like a barber's chair —was behind him but he was standing for this part of the trip, hands on the wheel and throttle. An overhead marine radio was bursting out static and half-bits of conversation, and I sat on a padded seat on the other side of the narrow wheelhouse.

"Going to tell me now where we're going?" he asked, the red illumination from the instrumentation giving his skin a faint scarlet glow.

"I hope it makes sense to you, because it doesn't make sense to me," I said, my arms stretched out behind me on the cushions, holding me still as the swells grew higher and the boat moved heavier, up and down, up and down.

I said, "It's some place out beyond the shoals called Smooth Dome."

He grinned. "Smooth Dome. Yeah, okay then. I know where that's located."

"But I looked it up online, and I didn't see any references to it."

"Because you won't," Harry said. "It's a nickname that most of us fishermen use out here. Smooth Dome is a round shoal, but it used to be called Baldy Brian. Don't ask me why, but that was the name. But before I became head of the fishermen's association, Brian Bolton was in charge...and his skull was like a cue ball. Not a whisper of hair. And he hated that place, hated that name, and when he got the cancer and knew he wasn't going to make it, we all told him that we'd never call it by that name, ever again. Like an honor or something."

"That's something," I said.

"Sure is."

I got up and walked stiff-legged over to the console. There was a square screen that was dark, and a round one that I recognized was a radar screen. The view was muddy and blotched, with speckles here and there.

I said, "Can you actually make this out?"

"Sure," Harry said, touching the screen with his finger. "There's the Isles of Shoals. That's the buoy marking the start of the channel. Down there... that's the tip of Cape Ann. Everything else is boats. Freighters going in and out of Porter Harbor, fishing boats getting an early start heading out farther to the Northern Banks. And probably the freighter hauling those migrants."

The chop was getting heavier and instead of my stomach starting to turn around, my mouth was dry, like my saliva glands had decided to take the evening off. I tried chewing on my tongue, but it didn't work.

"Can you tell which one is the freighter?"

He goosed the throttles some and the diesel engine noise grew louder.

"Hell, no," he said. "This isn't like some air traffic control radar that lights up the plane's ID so you can see it on the screen. More sophisticated military radar, yeah, they can track it better, but only because most ships out there are transmitting their GPS position."

"I get it," I said. "Doubtful the freighter wants to call attention to itself. So no GPS signal."

Hurtling now through the darkness of the Atlantic and seeing the receding lights of the coast behind me, I recalled that possible apocryphal phrase from General Patton, that in all his life, all he wanted to do was lead a lot of men in a desperate battle. Well, where we were going was desperate enough, and I wasn't leading the charge, but at least I was taking part in it.

I said, "You got any idea of what we're going to do when we get to Smooth Dome?"

Harry shook his head. "First, find my brother and tell him to get his ass home. And if the freighter's there...probably call the Coast Guard on Channel 16 and tell them what we see."

I said, "It might have to take more than just that. You know how spread thin they are."

"Shit," Harry said. "Then I'll lie to 'em. Tell them that we spotted a freighter sinking. That'll get them going."

A few more minutes passed, and I was still struck with admiration of how Harry was handling his trawler, how he kept his eyes on the radar screen and the illuminated bubble compass, and how he made quick little corrective movements on the throttles and the steering wheel.

My mouth was now even more dry.

"Harry?"

"Yeah," he said, not looking up from the radar screen.

"I'm terribly thirsty," I said. "Do you have any water aboard?"

"Sure," he said, pointing down and to the left. "Go down there, we got a little galley. Should be some bottled water in the mini fridge. Bring me one up, too, okay?"

"Sure," I said.

I made my way down the steep and narrow stairway, holding on to each side of the doorframe, and then stood there for a moment, head bowed. There were small cabinets to the left and to the right, two burner stove, counter, and mini fridge. I opened the fridge just as the boat hit a particularly large swell, and I bounced around in the little area like one of those ping-pong balls you see in those lottery commercials. A door under the sink had popped open, dumping trash from a small container, and when our ride smoothed out, I opened the mini-fridge door to get the two water bottles, and used the little light inside to help me clean up.

In some way, cleaning up only took a few seconds or so.

But in another way, it seemed to take a couple of hours.

There were two crushed plastic drinking glasses, and it didn't take that much light to see the manufacturer's name stamped on the bottom.

RITZENHOFF

I didn't know what to do next.

I just ran my right thumb across the raised letters.

RITZENHOFF

The same kind of plastic glass I had found on the beach after I had pulled in the drowned woman and her child.

The same kind of glass the refugee family had brought ashore.

RITZENHOFF

"Hey, Lewis," Harry called down from the wheelhouse. "You okay down there, or did those last swells make you hurl?"

"Everything's okay," I called back. "That last swell just knocked me off my feet. I'll be right up."

I put the trash container back into the small cabinet, fastened the door, and went back up to the wheelhouse, still trying to maintain my balance and composure. It seemed like everything was swaying, bouncing, knocking me around and making my mind spin.

I stood next to Harry, opened up his water bottle for him, passed it over. I opened mine as well and took a nice long swig.

"Thanks," he said. "Not as refreshing as a Sam Adams, but it'll do for now."

"Absolutely," I said, taking another cold swallow.

I looked up at the bulkhead, past the marine radio and some more switches, to framed certificates and licenses, the same ones I had noted on my first visit to the *Elayne D.* But now I paid them closer attention.

The same name was printed in bold black capital letters, and in reading them, I suddenly felt like I had swallowed a good chunk of alcohol.

WILFRED HAROLD BRAGG

Harry saw what I was looking at.

"You okay?"

I had to answer.

"I thought your name was Harry," I said.

"It is," he said, his voice bland. "You want to go through life being called Wilfred, or Harold? Officially, I'm Wilfred... to everyone else, I'm Harry."

W. Bragg.

"And Billy?"

"My brother?" he asked. "He got it worse. Mom was really into naming us after famous relatives. He's Elihu Williams...hey, what is this? Genealogy Hour on PBS?"

"No...I was just...curious."

W. Bragg.

I took another sip of water just for something to do.

I was alone on a trawler in the middle of the night, with nearest land being that tiny strip of lights in the distance.

Bluff it through, I thought.

Bluff it.

Because there's nothing else you can do.

Harry—or Wilfred—suddenly drew back on his throttles and as the diesels quieted, he moved to face me and said, "Too much curiosity, Lewis."

"Yeah, that's been my curse, most of my life."

He said, "I told you at least a couple of times not to come with me. I warned you off. You didn't listen."

"I listened," I said. "I just had other ideas."

"Like now," he said. "What's your idea now?"

My mouth was getting dry again, despite the water I had just drunk. "Well...I'm hoping I can convince you to turn us around, head us back to harbor. Maybe we can catch an early breakfast at that all-night trucker's stop up in Porter, talk things through."

He shook his head. "Nothing to talk about."

"But Harry..."

"Why?" he asked. "Is that the next question? You're a smart guy, Lewis, you've been places. Most of us have been places, seen things. And it's changed. Corporations bribed the politicians to make the laws that let foreign factory ships come in and suck the ocean clean out here...and leaving us with no way to make a living. And other corporations are bribing politicians to bomb the shit out of countries to get their resources. And in the meantime, the innocents are fleeing. And the innocents here struggle to survive, to keep their families alive, to put enough in the bank so their kids can get to college and get off the ocean. An ocean that's going to be a wet desert once they get older."

"Harry, there's—"

A heavy sigh. "You think I have time to debate? To philosophize?"

And then, I was surprised to see what he did next.

He brushed past me, went to the other side of the boat where a small hose was curled up, and he turned a handle, bringing the hose to pressure.

Why?

He walked three steps back to me. The *Elayne D* was gently rocking in the swells, the engines still grumbling in neutral.

A small pistol was in his hand.

"You should have stayed home, Lewis," he said.

Then I knew.

The hose was prepped to wash down my blood after he shot me.

I lifted my water bottle up and gave it a good hard squeeze, shooting out a jet of water that hit him in the face, shocking him, as the pistol went off.

And I turned and grabbed something and jumped into the ocean.

34

I clenched my jaw tight so the shock of hitting the cold water wouldn't make me open my mouth and take a hard swallow that I didn't need, and I was able to keep my mouth shut as my body screamed *cold cold cold*. I thrashed around and took the life jacket I had ripped from the *Elayne D*'s gunwale and put it on.

I worked quick with the snaps and the ties, because in a very few minutes, my fingers would grow numb and useless, and I didn't have much time, not at all.

There.

Life jacket fastened.

The roar of diesel engines caught my attention.

I saw the *Elayne D* with its red and green navigation lights, moving around and then speeding up, and I had a sharp flare of fear, that Harry was going to run me down with his multi-ton fishing craft but no, the trawler was heading away from me, going to its rendezvous, out there by Smooth Dome.

A series of big swells lifted me up and dropped me as the backwash from the *Elayne D* spread over me, and as I watched the fishing craft recede, in an instant, the navigation lights blinked out.

I was absolutely and one hundred percent alone, floating in the water, my legs quaking from the brutal cold.

No wonder Harry had abandoned me. About ready to murder me with his handgun, he was going to let the ocean take care of me. And provide a better story if and when my body eventually drifted ashore.

Sure, he would say, *that magazine writer was with me. Wanted to do some dumb story about the fishing community and the refugees coming in. He was some nervous though, insisted on wearing a life jacket, and we hit a big swell, and the poor guy fell overboard. Tried to find him but I couldn't. And wouldn't you know it, my VHF radio wasn't working...*

A good story.

But I was hoping to write another one.

I SHIVERED and pushed a rapidly freezing hand into the sodden mess of my jacket, and with a hard and fast grip, grabbed my iPhone in its protective plastic case and brought it up to the surface. I was near to chattering my teeth, and I knew the precious minutes of consciousness were running away from me. My fingers felt like swollen fat cold sausages, and God bless the descendants of Steve Jobs, I was able to switch on my phone, but whom could I dial? Who would answer? Even if I dialed nine-one-one, by the time I told the dispatcher where I was, I would be drifting, passed out from the cold. And forget tracing a nine-one-one call out here in the water. It would just tell police that my call had originated from a cell tower somewhere on the beach.

There were other lights out there on the water.

I had to join them.

I held the iPhone in both hands, flipped through, found the app I was looking for.

Flashlight.

The light swept out, nice and bright, and I worked hard to keep my arms up as high and straight as possible.

Then I took my other hand, started moving it across the light, making it blink.

Over and over again.

Dot, dot, dot.

Dash, dash, dash.

Dot, dot, dot.

Over and over again.

Maybe Harry Bragg will see it.

Maybe he won't.

I was hoping and figuring he'd be on his way to Smooth Dome, to do his guide work in the next hour.

And that some other craft out here would see my desperate SOS signal.

Dot, dot, dot.

Dash, dash, dash.

Dot, dot, dot.

Over and over again.

My arms burned with pain and fatigue.

My feet, legs, and lower torso were growing more numb.

I kept at it, kept at it.

Moving light.

Over there.

The chop was getting heavier.

Salt water was in my eyes and mouth.

I coughed, choked.

Kept my arms up, shivering and freezing.

Did I hear an engine?

Did I?

I kept waving, back and forth.

Another wave hit me, harder, and I dropped my iPhone.

The darkness clamped me and I started shouting, splashing, and—

A spotlight flared out, sweeping across the water.

"Hey," I yelled. "Over here, over here!"

I splashed the water some more, harder.

The light caught me.

Never was I so happy to be blinded by a bright light.

The light grew stronger, as did the rumbling sound of a diesel engine.

A swell came to me, and the dark shape of a boat came into view.

"Hey!"

A voice came back to me. "Hey you, I'll be right there! Hold on!"

The hull swept closer, and the engine's pitch turned as it reversed for a moment, slowing. More lights came on and something hit me on the head, causing me to cry out.

"Sorry," the man said. "Was trying to get you with a gaff. Can you grab it?"

I lifted my cold and deadweight arms, felt my swollen hands slide across the pole.

"No, I can't."

"No worries...let me gaff your life jacket. Hold on."

The gaff poked and probed at me, and it was the sweetest feeling, to have a connection now holding me fast to a floating structure. I was no longer alone. I was no longer adrift.

Something else slapped at me.

A coil of rope.

I moved my leaden arms and got the length of rope underneath my arms, and the man said, "Hold on. Here we go."

I gasped as the rope cut into me and the man dragged me up and over the gunwale. I did my best to grab the side of the boat, but I was flailing around like a newborn, when I fell onto the deck, knocking my breath out.

Over me was the shape of a man and he laughed, "You are one damn lucky son of a bitch...aren't you."

I just nodded, recognizing his voice.

Billy Bragg.

I GAVE HIM CREDIT, because he didn't bring up our recent disagreements and arguments, but he went right to work, getting the sodden life jacket off me and tossing it to the deck. Then he stripped me of my jacket, sweater and shirt, rubbed me down with a towel, and then put on two dry gray sweatshirts. I was shivering and shivering, and he put a wool blanket over me, then said, "Can you get your boots off?"

"My fingers...they still don't work."

"No worries."

Billy bent over, started working on the sodden laces of my boots, and then one and the other got tugged off. This started another bout of shivering, and my pants came off, and he wrapped a quilt around me and said, "Be right back. Got some coffee in a Thermos bottle."

I kept on shivering.

I was alive.

Shivering but alive.

Billy came back, knelt down next to me. With the lights the deck of his fishing vessel was dirty with grime, grease, dried bits of fish guts and dried blood. There was rust and old oil on the equipment, and it was nothing like his brother's clean and tidy boat.

And I didn't care.

He offered me a coffee in a wide bowl, and I managed to cup it, and take a long swallow. It was heavy with sweet and cream, too much for my taste, but I wasn't complaining.

It tasted wonderful.

He said, "How In God's name did you get out here?"

"You wouldn't believe me if I told you."

Billy was wearing a filthy dungaree jacket and heavy khaki work pants, and then he reached over, grabbed the life jacket I had been wearing.

He flipped it over.

Stenciled on the back was ELAYNE D TYLER N.H.

"I guess I do now," he said.

WITHIN A FEW MINUTES I was able to stand, and I limped into his cluttered and dirty wheelhouse, leaning against the back of his chair, seemingly held together with gray duct tape.

Occasionally a bout of shivering would make me shake, but I felt so exhilarated and energetic and so damn good to be alive, and I knew it was the chemicals racing through me after my freezing ocean dunk, and that a crash was coming, but I was going to ride it as long as I could.

Billy said, "Why were you out with my brother?"

"He was taking me to where the smuggling freighter is going to drop anchor."

"Guess he wanted to be alone, hunh?

I said, "And what are you up to?"

He said, "Minding my own goddamn business, that's what."

"Does that include helping your brother?"

He shook his head, clenching his jaw. "That's a goddamn lie."

"You sure?"

"I've never worked for him, ever since we was kids. Back then we was struggling that month, and we were hauling lobster traps, and I wanted to bring in some shorts, but he said no, that wouldn't be right. Mister Goodie Two Shoes, he was. Always following the rules."

"But Billy...he's not following the rules now, is he."

"Sure he is," Billy said. "Him, he likes following rules, likes following orders. If it's the selectmen, yep. The government, yep. And some big ass folks with lots of money that he thinks is running things, oh yeah, he'll follow the rules. That's for him, not for me. Not ever."

"And why are you out here tonight?"

"Working, why else," he said. "Fewer folks around to bother me...or see me."

"What kind of work? Helping guide those migrants in?"

"Nope."

I said, "There were a couple of Russians over at your place, looking for you earlier today. You still sure you're not working for them?"

"Russians? I've never worked for Russians, nope."

"But they were there."

He laughed. "Poles? Yeah, if a couple of Polish folks were there, I'd understand that."

I was starting to crash, because things were getting fuzzy, getting confusing.

"Polish men? Is that what you're saying?"

"Sure," he said. "Couple of cousins. Opened up a new restaurant in Salisbury. Hope to open one up in Falmouth, maybe Rockport. They paid me, I promised them some cod...guess I've been late in getting back to them. Now, that's exactly what I'm going to do over the next few hours..."

"But cod fishing is illegal in the Gulf of Maine," I said. "They're trying to let the stocks rebound."

"Won't make much of a difference if I catch some, though, am I right?

This is gonna be a good start for me. You won't believe what I'm charging these poor bastards...but I'm late and I gotta get to work."

A memory came to me. "You told Fran, back at the campground, you told her that something big was going on, something to change your life. That's it, right. The deal with the Polish cousins."

"That's right, a really good deal. Even tried to bring Harry into it, but he wouldn't have any of it."

The argument I had seen between them, back dockside.

I took a long look through his windscreen.

"The freighter's out there."

"I don't care."

"Your brother's out there."

"Double that," he said.

I felt like I was an ice skater on a frozen river, doing my very best to move along, not hitting any small snowdrifts or soft spots.

Being careful, being cautious, not wanting to fall in or fall down.

"The Fish & Game were at your place, looking for you, too."

Billy snorted. "Fish & Game are always looking out for me."

"Might be nice to get them off your back."

"How?"

"You can figure it out," I said. "Do something big, something good, something that gets lots of positive press. Fish & Game and all the others, they wouldn't dare come after you."

He tapped an instrument on the control panel. "Hunh. You think making a fuss about that freighter, that might do something like that?"

"Sure," I said. "Especially if I helped make the story."

"Whaddya mean, help the story?"

"I'm a magazine writer, Billy. I can talk to the press, get the story out. You know, independent fisherman, rough sort of guy, heart of gold. Maybe breaks a few rules, but when push comes to shove, he'll help those innocents out there, being dumped out in the ocean in the middle of the night."

He thought about that. "Not sure if the Coast Guard will listen to me if I call out, tell 'em about the freighter."

Remembering what his brother had mentioned earlier, I said, "You could say that the freighter was sinking. That would do the trick, wouldn't it."

He kept quiet. Tapped a dial again on the panel. I sipped the coffee, and it was now cold.

"And there'd be a bonus."

"What kind of bonus?"

"Getting your perfect brother jammed up. Getting him in trouble, getting him arrested."

Skating, I thought, skating faster and faster, keeping a sharp eye, looking for hazards.

"Where's this freighter supposed to drop anchor?"

"Smooth Dome," I said.

Billy said, "Ballsy move, coming in that close."

I kept my mouth shut.

"Smooth Dome?"

"That's right," I said.

He laughed. "Okay, writer-man. Sounds like fun."

He spun the wheel and pushed forward the throttle, and I was again off into the night.

35

Billy kept us on a course through the night, and he flipped two switches, and the boat's navigation lights flicked off, and he leaned forward, peering through the windscreen.

I said, "Can't you pick up what's out there by radar?"

"If my radar was working, yeah, I guess I could," he said. "One of these days I should get it fixed."

One of these days. Sure.

Then he slowed the diesels, maneuvered his fishing boat some to port, and said, "There it is."

"Where?"

"Right there, damn it," he said, sounding cross. "We're practically running into the damn thing."

I put the coffee cup down on a shelf and ducked out of the wheelhouse. I felt like a fool in more ways than one, dressed in smelly used clothing and a scratchy wool blanket over me, but Billy was right. We were near the freighter and the only way I could spot it in the moonless night was seeing how it blocked out the stars and ambient light from the Isles of Shoals. Billy slowed the engine, and I could hear the whine of machinery over there, other engines rumbling, and voices.

Lots of voices.

I went back into the wheelhouse and Billy grabbed the microphone of his VHF Marine Radio and said, "Coast Guard Porter, Coast Guard Porter, this is fishing vessel Anna Marie, Anna Marie...Coast Guard Porter, this is fishing vessel Anna Marie."

A young woman's voice burst out. "Fishing vessel Anna Marie, this is Coast Guard Porter."

Billy said, "Coast Guard Porter, we have a seventy-five-foot freighter out by Smooth Dome ledge, southwest of Star Island, taking on water. She's sinking by the stern. Many souls in the water, repeat, many souls in the water."

"Coast Guard Porter to fishing vessel Anna Marie, repeat please."

Billy winked at me. "Coast Guard Porter, we've got people in the water. Am proceeding to assist. Repeat, freighter sinking by stern at Smooth Dome ledge, southwest of Star Island."

He reached up, changed the channel from 16 to 9, and he said, "Time for fun. Hey, Harry, fishing vessel *Elayne D*, you out there? Where are you big bro?"

There was static and some broken chatter, but nothing audible. Billy shook his head, "Aw, c'mon big bro. I know you're out here. You ready to take your passengers ashore?"

A sharp toned male voice: "Billy, shut up and go away. Now."

Billy wouldn't give up. "Aw, c'mon big bro, don't you want to talk no more? Don't you?"

He made a quick circle of the wheel and we doubled back, so the dark form of the freighter was now on our port. There were a few shaded lights up there. More voices. Somebody shouted.

Billy replaced the microphone to a slot on the marine radio.

"Sad when brothers fight, don't you think?" he asked.

"Wouldn't know," I said. "I was an only child."

"Lucky you," he said, going forward to duck through the door leading below. "Take the wheel. My boat's yours. Don't hit anything, okay? You'll piss me off and the First National Bank of Porter."

I held the wheel tight and hoped he wouldn't take too long, and Billy didn't. He came up with two cardboard boxes in his arms and said, "Time for some fun, shed some light on the situation. Hold tight, this won't take long."

I was going to ask him what the hell he was up to, and decided I would find out in a couple of minutes, and I wasn't disappointed.

Billy yelled at me, "Avert your eyes!"

But I didn't do it in time, seeing him take a cylindrical object out of the first box, slam the bottom of it against the gunwale, and quickly repeat the process with the second cylinder. There was a brief and bright *whoosh!* and two rockets sped up into the night sky, trailing white and yellow sparks, and then both exploded up about five hundred feet or so.

I blinked my eyes hard, and Billy came in, nudged me aside. "Take a look at the circus, why don't you."

He maneuvered us away from the freighter and the two parachute flares seemed motionless for a moment, and yes, as Billy said, there was a circus out there, and it was quickly revealed in the sharp and unforgiving white light.

The freighter leapt into view, a craft with a raised bow and stern, and a low railing in between. People were clustered along the side of the craft, leaning over, and others were scrambling down cargo nets, some with children on their backs, like some horrible D-Day invasion alternative history.

The *Elayne D* was at the stern of the freighter, two overloaded black inflatable Zodiac-like craft secured by long towlines. With the sputtering light from the descending flares, it looked like Harry Bragg was done for the night, and he accelerated his diesel engines.

One more black inflatable craft with an engine at the stern was moored at the bottom of the cargo net, and I saw two men fight to climb back up the cargo netting. More shouts, screams, and Billy said, "Looks like two crewmembers from that freighter are trying to get back in."

That's exactly what they were doing, as they fought and struggled to get to the top, climbing over and around the refugees still dangling from the net. Bells clanged on the freighter—riding low to the water, its sides streaked and pockmarked with rust and broken pieces of metal plating—and the flares swung back and forth, back and forth, as they slowly descended, but the lights stayed up long enough to show Billy and me the horror that happened next.

Once the two crew members were up on top of the deck, they disappeared and then emerged with fire axes in hand, and with three good swipes, the netting was cut and the people hanging on for their proverbial dear life fell into the ocean, overturning the black rubber raft and dumping them all into the cold deep.

Billy swore, "The fuckers!" and then moved the *Anna Marie* around, and pushed a flashlight into my hands and said, "It's gonna be panic city over there, so you be careful! We'll bring in as many as we can, but fight back if you have to! Those ain't people over there no more, those are drowning animals!"

I switched on the flashlight as Billy moved his boat closer to the screaming and splashing. Voices were yelling at me, and I didn't understand a single word, but I didn't have to. The screams were the same in any language. Billy came next to me and tossed out four life jackets and a life ring, and then I reached over and was nearly pulled into the water by the desperate hands clutching at me.

"Hold on!" Billy yelled. "Hold on, we'll get you!"

The first one aboard was a screaming boy, maybe eight or nine, who had been pushed up by his father, a tall, bearded man, who managed to get a leg over the side as I pulled him up. The father got aboard, and then joined Billy and me in trying to get the cold and frightened families aboard.

A young girl. A baby wrapped in a checked blanket. Another young man who started working with a rope, hauling in a crying, shrieking woman, and as I helped her, she punched me in the face.

I staggered back, and she collapsed on the deck, wailing.

There seemed no end to the crying, shouting, shifting mass of people who were struggling to get on the boat. Billy came back, yelled to me, "Lewis! We're gonna swamp! Move some of 'em up forward! We've got to shift the weight."

The stern of Billy's boat was settling, and I saw with deep cold fear that just less than a foot of the gunwale was between us and the hull. I started pulling, shoving, and pushing the crowd forward, yelling, "Move! Move! Move!" while pointing to the stern. One dripping wet older man with a child's light orange life jacket around his burly shoulders saw what I was doing, shouted out something in his language, and the people near the wheelhouse went through the small door to the hold up forward, and others climbed up to the narrow bow.

Billy pushed by me, flashlight in his right hand, and then with his free hand, brought up a sobbing young girl, and then he leaned over, fanned the light back and forth. The beam was powerful enough to catch the stern of the departing freighter, the churning water at its stern, and its name—MYKOS—and its supposed homeport of NICOSIA.

"Lewis, c'mon over here, give me a hand."

I stood next to him as he dropped the flashlight to the deck, and there was one heavy man, gurgling, kicking with his feet, waving his hands, and Billy took one arm and I took the other.

God, he was heavy, and it took us three good heaves before we were able to drag him over the side of the boat. He fell and coughed and vomited, and a woman knelt down next to him, stroking his wet hair, sobbing.

Billy picked up his flashlight, scanned the area one more time. The water was moving in gentle swells, and debris was floating in the water, from shoes to jackets to newspapers and two empty life jackets.

I said, "Looks like we've got them all."

"Yeah," Billy said.

There was a low roar, and I spotted the lights of an approaching helicopter, coming from the north. "Might be time to get out of here."

"You think?" he asked, sarcasm in his voice. "I was gonna ask these wet folks if they want to help me catch some cod. I got those Polish cousins still after my ass."

"Maybe they can wait a day."

"They're gonna have to."

Billy moved through the crowded stern, past the A-frame holding the rolled up net, and got to the wheelhouse and put the engine into drive, and we slowly maneuvered away from the sodden trash and the departing MYKOS.

He headed us to the west, to the thin strip of lights marking the southern end of the New Hampshire seacoast, and the helicopter roared overhead and kept on going to the freighter.

The rear of the boat now had the scent of wet clothes, unwashed bodies, and the sharp deep scent of fear.

But these folks were alive.

They looked at me like I was some sort of savior, and some sat, arms around each other, talking amongst themselves. Two of the men and one older woman smiled up at me.

I didn't feel very heroic or savior-like.

Out in the ocean, the lights of the helicopter stopped, and a spotlight shot out, catching the MYKOS as it was trying to escape out into the Gulf of Maine. A loudspeaker on the helicopter shouted out orders, and I watched for another few seconds, and then went to the wheelhouse.

Three of the refugee men were in the corner of the wheelhouse, shouting among each other, and I went to Billy, gave his shoulder a healthy squeeze and said, "Back to Tyler Harbor?"

"Best place," he said. "I'm just wondering what kind of reception I'm gonna get."

I said, "One you won't forget."

WITH SO MANY people crowded aboard the *Anna Marie*, Billy moved us slow and steady to the west, back to blessed land, and I was sitting on the edge of the port gunwale, cold and wet and bone tired. I rearranged the wool blanket around my shoulders and pressed my legs together, trying to stay as warm as possible. The people around me—Turks, Syrians, Kurds, who knew—talked low among themselves, and I wish I could have given them more, from water or hot soup or blankets, but there was nothing I had.

Just me, sitting with them.

That's all.

BACK TO TYLER HARBOR, in a boat owned by one of the Braggs brothers, and I wondered where the supposed good Bragg brother had gone with his two rafts being towed behind the *Elayne D*.

Billy approached the drawbridge, honked the horn like his brother had done earlier, and the siren let off, and the bridge started lifting itself in two. The folks around me were all standing, looking at the approaching land,

and they started talking louder, and for a change, there was some nice laughter.

A good sound.

After the bridge lowered Billy slowed the engine and steered us to the right, to the fixed dock of the Tyler Fishing Cooperative, and I was with Billy in the wheelhouse when we both saw what was waiting for us.

"Ah, shit," he whispered. "What a reception committee. And at this hour of the morning...damn it."

The paved lot next to the fixed dock and in front of the co-op building was crowded with vehicles and lots of people. As we came closer to the dock it looked like a third of the crowd were police and fire personnel, the other third were news media, and the last third were just local fishermen ready to head out for the day, wanting to stick around to see what was going on. There were police cruisers and ambulances with flashing lights, and two black passenger vans with extended seating, with men in gray jumpsuits looking on.

Television camera lights lit off and I said, "Billy, got a statement for the press?"

"Yeah," he said, voice grumpy. "Anybody want to set up a fund drive to bail out my ass?"

"For what?" I asked. "Lots of people are going to see you as a hero."

"Screw 'em," he said. "Okay, toss out the fenders, then you want to go up forward, toss out the bow line, see if anybody over there has enough sense to grab it. I'll do the same with the stern line."

I got out of the wheelhouse, pushed my way through the refugees, some of them smiling widely, others just looking solemn and quiet, probably thinking that their journey through the Mediterranean and across the Atlantic had ended, and a new one was about to begin.

Well, at least they weren't in any danger of being drowned.

I tossed out three dirty white plastic fenders, the size of small cylindrical drink coolers, and then I carefully walked up the narrow stretch to the bow. I got to the coiled line and there was a burst of diesel engine noise as Billy got us in closer to the dock. I held the bowline and three guys in uniform—Fish & Game, it looked like—held their hands out. I tossed the line, and it was expertly caught and fastened, and then Billy did the same at the stern.

We were fastened.

I stepped out and then I was surrounded, with voice yelling, hands grabbing at me.

"Where did you come from?"

"What ship brought these illegals in?"

"Migrant lover, go back."

"What country are these people from?"

A bright light enveloped me, and a heavyset camera man pushed his way forward, and in front of me was a very smiling and confident Alice Hackett, impeccably dressed in a red coat, hair done and face made-up.

"So," she called out in a loud voice. "Mister Lewis Cole, beach resident here in Tyler, how many others belong to your smuggling group?"

Just behind her was another smiling individual, looking very satisfied with himself, and he had his hands in the pockets of a dark gray topcoat, and he rocked slightly back and forth on his heels, like he was so happy with himself and the world around him.

Brady Hill, Alice's assistant, gofer, and doer of odd jobs.

I pushed past Alice and got up to Brady and punched him right in the mouth.

He fell back and as a Tyler cop came over, I yelled out, "That man has a gun! That man has a gun!"

I was grabbed by another Tyler cop, and I looked over to Alice Hackett, her cameraman still filming me, and I said, "No group, Alice. I'm more of a lone wolf."

36

A number of confusing minutes passed and, in a while, I was in a small office within the Tyler Fishermen's Cooperative building, with crowded shelves, two filing cabinets, desk, chairs, and one tired looking yet amused Detective Sergeant Diane Woods sitting next to me.

She yawned and I said, "Is this the point where you tell me I'm not under arrest, just being detained?"

That caused her to laugh. "Yeah, I sometimes see that on those reality cop TV shows. Nice sneaky way of getting someone into handcuffs without the perp getting all wound up. I mean, nobody wants to be arrested. But detained? Sounds like high school detention."

I said, "So far, no cuffs. Guess my day is improving."

Diane had a clipboard and notepad in her lap and said, "No offense, friend, you look like the proverbial nearly drowned dog. How did you get so wet?"

"I jumped off a boat."

"Billy Bragg's boat?"

"No, his brother Harry," I said. "He had a pistol on me. I thought he was a few seconds away from shooting me, so I decided I had a better chance of ending up in the Atlantic."

"You could have drowned," she said.

"Or died from hypothermia," I said. "Either choice is better than a 9-millimeter slug in my gut."

She ran a hand across the top of her notebook. "Sorry."

"For not doing anything when I told you about the freighter coming in? They were out by Star Island. Not your jurisdiction."

"Still..."

"Diane," I said, "no worries."

She nodded, bit her lower lip, and I said, "How's Brady Hill doing?"

"His jaw is sore, and he's currently under arrest for a number of violations," she said. "He was carrying a .38 Smith & Wesson in his pocket. How did you know?"

"I thought I saw him carrying it earlier, tossing it under a car seat," I said. "At another time, we shook hands, and I was pretty sure he had gun oil on his fingers. And it always seemed like one side of his coat hung lower than the other, like it was carrying something heavy. And...it made sense."

"How?"

I said, "You told me, didn't you? Alice Hackett's cable television ratings are tumbling. I guess the American people are getting tired of being lectured by a shrill character who just wants to hate."

"So the shooting was a set-up."

"Probably," I said. "Give her a ratings boost. But I bet you'll find out Brady is lousy with a revolver, or anything else tool based. He was supposed to fire close enough to make people think Alice was in danger. Not some magazine writer."

"Hunh," Diane said. "Some magazine writer."

"How's Billy?"

"Being interviewed by Fish & Game, Homeland Security, and the Coast Guard. Not my problem."

"How about his brother Harry?"

"His boat was intercepted by the Coast Guard and Maine Marine Patrol, approaching Kittery, with about fifty refugees with him. Not my problem."

"And the freighter?"

"Anchored under gunpoint by Homeland Security, Coast Guard, and ICE."

"Still not your problem."

"You got it."

I nodded. "All right. Anything else you'd like to know?"

Diane shook her head. "Nope. I wanted to pretend to do an in-depth interview concerning your assault on Brady Hill. Officially, the matter is under investigation. Unofficially, you're in the clear, my friend. And unofficially squared, Brady Hill is going to be in lots more trouble once we match the recovered slug to his revolver. Discharging a firearm so close to a building and a crowd of people, even if it's an attempt to help your boss, is against several New Hampshire laws."

"Good," I said, starting to get up as she stood up from her chair, and Diane said, "Sorry. There's someone else who wants to talk to you."

I settled back in my chair. "Okay, send him in."

"How do you know it's a him?" she asked with a smile.

"I'll be happy to be proven wrong."

"Then prepare to be disappointed."

DIANE WENT OUT and Agent Mark Stockman from Homeland Security came in, dressed like the first time I had met him, in a dark gray jumpsuit, black boots, and holstered pistol at his side. There was stubble on the top of his head. I guess he didn't have time to shave up there before rushing out to work.

He looked angry and tired.

Poor fellow.

He sat down heavily in the chair left by Diane Woods and said, "You've had one hell of a night, am I right?"

"Probably as busy as yours," I said. "What's up with all those refugees that were brought in?"

Stockman folded his arms. "Being fed, clothed, medically examined and then sent to a facility in Massachusetts for processing."

"Good for them. Where were they from?"

"Kurdistan. Not sure if it was the Turkish, Syrian, or Iraqi side... not that it matters that much."

"And the freighter?" I asked.

"Being examined, top to bottom. A number of Russians and Serbs are in custody. Unfortunately, they dumped a number of documents and computer drives over the side before we got there. And to make it more fun, two news choppers from Boston nearly took out one of our Blackhawks."

"Hard to do things in secret with all this attention, right?"

He stared hard at me. "Hard to do your job with all the attention, yeah. Especially the backbiting, second-guessing, and protests. Writers and reporters and anyone else saying they're looking for the truth. They do get in the way."

"Poor you."

He said, "Don't start with me, Lewis. I'm doing my job, and my men and women are doing their jobs, and that's life. And it's a messy process when it comes to immigration and what the hell we do with the tens of thousands who are leaving dangerous places and who want to live here. The President wants one thing, the Congress wants another, and you've got fifty governors and probably another fifty or so big city mayors who have other ideas. Some cities say they're sanctuary cities, and my folks get booed and have bottles thrown at them when they go to work. Other cities are so cooperative that they send their own cops to round up illegals and drop them in our laps."

I didn't know what to say about this mini confession, so I just kept quiet.

Stockman paused, rubbed his hands together. "So that's my tale of woe."

"Hell of a tale."

"Now it's your turn."

"Me?" I said. "It's my turn to go home, that's all."

"Afraid not," he said. "How did you know the freighter was going to be out there at that time?"

"Somebody told me."

"Who?"

Poor Nico. Why add to his troubles? And I certainly wasn't going to toss Felix Tinios into this mess.

"I forget."

"Knock it off, Lewis. This is serious, and I want your cooperation. I want you to tell me how you knew the freighter was there, how you got Billy

Bragg involved, and what you know about his brother Harry. And what his involvement was. The whole story. Give it. I've got plenty of time."

He did look like he had plenty of time. He looked patient indeed.

And then I was done.

Just like that.

I was still wet, I was chilled, and I wanted to go home. I was so tired of all of it, from start to finish, and I didn't want to argue, debate, or answer questions. I just wanted to leave.

That strong desire just came right to me.

I wanted to get out, go to my safe place, and not deal with this anymore.

I was done.

"Nope."

"Excuse me?" he asked.

"No, I'm leaving, and I don't want to talk to you, or cooperate, or do anything else. I just want to go home."

"I'm afraid you can't."

"I'm afraid you can't stop me."

"Lewis, I need your cooperation."

"I have nothing to say."

"All right, let's make it clearer. I'm going to get your cooperation, one way or another."

"Not going to happen."

His eyes seemed to turn into hard flint. "Try me."

And that was that.

I said, "All right, try this. I get to leave now, and then I won't tell anyone that I know you're having an affair with Alice Hackett. Besides the embarrassment factor, I'm sure you'd hate to be brought up to Capitol Hill to be grilled by all the Senators and Representatives that she's called nasty names over the years. Imagine the fun they'd have, grilling you and questioning you, all hoping to get some revenge in the process."

That seemed to quiet him right down.

"Do you still want to try me, Agent Stockman?"

His hard flint eyes softened, grew wary.

"Care to tell me more?"

"Here's this for a start," I said. "You and Alice Hackett meeting in Room 9, at the Worldwide Inn on Atlantic Avenue the other night. Ring a bell?"

Stockman chewed on his lower lip. "Lewis, I—"

I held up a chilled hand.

"Please," I said. "No more. I don't want to know the details, how it started, where it started, all that stuff some folks are so eager to talk about. I have no interest. But as you can tell, I'm in a grumpy mood. All right? Besides getting up and walking out of here in the next thirty seconds, you're also going to do something for me, and quickly."

He was quiet and was on the spot. A feeling I'm sure he didn't like.

"Okay, what's that?" he asked.

I told him.

He nodded.

"Just to be clear, my relationship with—"

"Never mentioned to anyone, anywhere, in public or private. I won't even mention her flunky Brady. Let me guess. You both used him as a courier, to set up your meeting places, so there were no phone or text records. Correct?"

He looked pitiful as he nodded.

"So we have a deal?"

Stockman slapped his hands on his legs in apparent disgust or anger. "A deal, then." He stood up and said, "I'd like to ask you a favor, then."

"Ask away," I said. I stood up and rearranged the smelly wool blanket over my shoulders. I needed to get it back to Billy Bragg, one of these days.

He said, "There's a lot of press out there."

"I'm sure."

"Please don't talk to them," he said. "It's hard enough to keep on top of what's happening out there, from the freighter to the refugees to finding out which local fishermen were cooperating. We don't need any more hassle."

I said, "I hear you."

"Great."

He left and I gave him a minute's head start, and then I followed him outside.

. . .

THE SUN WAS STARTING to come up over the ocean, and another helicopter was roaring out there, to where the MYKOS was anchored, still being poked, prodded, and examined.

An ambulance was still parked, the extended passenger vans were gone, and there were cruisers and pickup trucks from various law enforcement agencies, and then I was spotted by a woman with a trench coat and gorgeous make-up and thick blonde hair, and she said, "Gordon! This way!"

And like that, the news media came at me, four television crews, two photographers, and five young men and women with notepads or iPads in their hands, and this demanding crowd nearly pushed me back against the wall of the co-op building.

"Sir, who are you?"

"Were you part of the rescue effort?"

"How many were rescued?"

"Are you under investigation?"

The faces were asking, questioning, and there was a familiar one, right in the front.

Paula Quinn.

I held up both hands, and said, "Please, please...hold on..."

They quieted down.

I said, "My name is Lewis Cole. I'm a resident of Tyler."

The cameras were focused on me, notes were being scribbled and typed.

I pointed to Paula.

"And I'm only going to talk to a reporter from my local newspaper."

Groans and more questions and I opened the door back into the fisherman's co-op building, and shoved it shut, and leaned my back against it, so nobody else could follow us in.

Paula said, "Are you okay?" She had on dark tan slacks and a thick red and blue sweater, and her usually carefully combed blonde hair was messy. I guessed she had probably been in deep sleep while I was in the Atlantic and trying not to drown or die of hypothermia.

"Doing all right."

"Why are you doing this?"

"A variety of reasons," I said. "You want the story?"

"Yes," she said. "Please, very much."

Somebody was thumping against the door. I pushed back.

"Then ask away," I said.

"For real?" she asked.

"For real," I said. "Nothing to hide, everything's on the record Paula. It's your exclusive...go for it."

"Okay," she said.

37

Three days later I was standing still in a small Greek-Orthodox cemetery in Porter, watching as a silver casket was about to be lowered into a freshly dug grave. Besides me, the mourners included Felix Tinios, who was standing to my left. At the head of the grave, Father Bob Zankos of St. Gregory the Theologian was giving one last blessing, and Felix and I stayed still. The wind was coming off Porter Harbor at a stiff clip, and Felix and I had on heavy coats. Father Bob had the standard formal priestly wear of black slacks, coat, and white collar, with vestments draped over his neck and down the front of his coat.

Father Bob nodded, closed his prayer book and walked around the head of the opening, came to me, looking friendly but worn, like he was bearing the weight of the world this afternoon.

He offered his hand, and I gave it a shake, and so did Felix, though I got the feeling Felix was concerned he might burst into flame by touching a man of prayer.

"Thank you for arranging this, Mister Cole," he said.

"Glad to do it."

Then he looked to Felix and said, "See you next Sunday, Felix?"

"Do my best," Felix said.

"That's all I ask for," he said. He looked over to the casket, where the refugee woman and child that had drowned in front of my house were about to be lowered into the cold earth, sharing one final slumber together.

Father Bob shook his head and said, "Such days we live in. Such days."

He walked away and in the distance was a cemetery worker, waiting for us to leave so he could finish the job, but he stood there in khaki work clothes, shovel leaning against a shoulder, looking at his iPhone, thumbs flailing around.

"How are you doing?" Felix said.

"Moderate," I said. I put my hands in my coat, took in the rows of head-stones and said, "Lots of dead out here."

"Aren't we getting philosophical," he said.

"Trying not to," I said.

Felix said, "Don't worry."

"Who says I'm worrying?"

"I can tell," he said, "and I'll let you know that the Porter police don't know a thing. Officially and finally, there was no shooting at that ware-house, and no killing, and no body. Like it never happened."

"But it did happen," I said. "Don't try to take that away from me."

"I'm not," Felix said. "And somewhere that man who wanted to kill you, me, and Nico, is at his final rest. Better him than you or me, friend."

"And what about Nico?"

"If he's a smart boy, he's in another time zone, on the run, and will never, ever try to come to his Uncle Felix for help."

A dark blue Ford Escort came to a halt, two rows away. A young woman stepped out, closed the door, and started walking in our direction, slowly walking past the gray and dull white headstones.

"Paula Quinn," Felix said.

"Wonder how she knew I was here," I said.

"Maybe somebody told her. Maybe she made a phone call."

That caught me by surprise. "Ah…"

He gently elbowed me. "I know she despises me, but when it comes to matters of the heart, she'll do what it takes."

"What do you mean by that?" I asked.

"If you're a lucky man, you'll find out," he said, tapping me on my shoulder. "Time for me to head out. I'm sure you can get a ride home with Paula."

"Glad you're so sure."

"Later."

He headed over to his parked Mercedes, and he and Paula exchanged crisp nods as they passed each other, like professional border guards working back in the day at the Berlin Wall.

She came to me and said, "Hi."

"Hi."

Paula stood next to me and the air felt brittle, like something could break around us, and I didn't like the feeling. I also didn't like the feeling that we had shifted our relationship into something else, at a point where we were about to either rescue or discard it.

"I tried calling you," she said, "but then I remembered your iPhone is resting on the ocean floor, somewhere near Star Island. But I left some messages on your landline."

"I've been busy," I said. "Making these arrangements."

Paula said, "What did you find out?"

I said, "Her name was Elene Floros. Her one-year-old daughter was Amarantha. They lived on a remote island in Greece. There was an old hotel there that supplied jobs for the locals, including her. Then the wildfires last year destroyed the hotel, pretty much destroyed the island. And she remembered she had a cousin here in America, living and working in Manchester. Maybe she should have tried to come over legally. She probably made some bad decisions. But she did what she thought was right for her and her daughter."

Paula nodded. "How did you find this out?"

"Agent Stockman from Homeland Security told me."

"Why would he do that?"

"I guess I appealed to his better nature." I looked to her and added, "Hey. You're not taking any notes."

"I didn't want to take any notes. I hate this story, and I hate what it's done to all of us."

The wind swept through some more. The cemetery worker was now staring over at us. Maybe his game was over.

"Me, too."

She rubbed her hands together. "Just to let you know, the Wentworth County Free Militia has disbanded. Seems there was a relatively intelligent group that thought they were really protecting their neighbors, and there was another, larger, group that thought they should march around with tiki torches and raise hell. The groups fought and argued and now it's gone."

"And here we are," I said.

"Yes, here we are."

I slipped my hand into hers, squeezed, and she squeezed back.

We stood there, next to the open grave, holding hands.

I said, "You've been working very hard, these past few weeks."

"I have," she said. "And the information you gave me about the Bragg brothers, and that freighter...I had a national scoop. Beat *The Boston Globe, The New York Times, CNN* and all the rest. Pretty damn good for a small-town newspaper."

"You're pretty damn good for a small-town newspaper," I said.

She smiled. I liked what I saw.

I said, "You hard working woman you, can I convince you to take the afternoon off and come back to my place?"

Her smile widened. "Do I get to spend the night?"

"Yes," I said. "And the night afterwards. As long as you'd like."

"Good," she said. "Because I'd like that a lot."

We turned and started walking to her car, still hand in hand, and I glanced back and saw the cemetery worker finally striding over to put a named mother and daughter to rest, like I had promised.

The Exclusive
Book #1 of the Booker Johnson Thrillers

A gruesome discovery leads to a deadly conspiracy.

Booker Johnson, an Emmy-winning TV reporter on the brink of losing everything, stumbles upon a horrific crime scene in South Florida. Teaming up with no-nonsense police detective Brielle Jensen, they dive into the case, unraveling a web of deception, manipulation, and murder that reaches the highest echelons of power.

As Booker uncovers the sinister truth behind a mysterious group pulling the strings, he finds his own life in jeopardy. With personal troubles brewing and powerful forces trying to silence him, he must risk it all to expose the truth. As the stakes continue to rise, can Booker bring the mastermind to justice and reveal their dark secrets to the world?

Will the truth set him free, or will it be his final broadcast?

Embark on a thrilling journey in this crime fiction novel by Emmy Award-winning reporter Mel Taylor and Wall Street Journal bestselling author Brian Shea. Packed with authentic detail and exhilarating suspense, *The Exclusive* is an explosive read that's perfect for fans of Michael Connelly and Harlan Coben.

Get your copy today at
severnriverbooks.com

ABOUT THE AUTHOR

Brendan DuBois is the award-winning New York Times bestselling author of twenty-six novels, including the Lewis Cole series. He has also written *The First Lady* and *The Cornwalls Are Gone* (March 2019), coauthored with James Patterson, *The Summer House* (June 2020), and *Blowback*, September 2022. His next coauthored novel with Patterson, *Countdown*, will be released in March 2023. He has also published nearly two hundred short stories.

His stories have won three Shamus Awards from the Private Eye Writers of America, two Barry Awards, two Derringer Awards, and the Ellery Queen Readers Award. He has also been nominated for three Edgar Allan Poe awards from the Mystery Writers of America.

In 2021 he received the Edward D. Hoch Memorial Golden Derringer for Lifetime Achievement from the Short Mystery Fiction Society.

He is also a "Jeopardy!" gameshow champion.

Sign up for Brendan's reader list at
severnriverbooks.com